A PLACE TO PAUSE

Books in the Lowestoft Chronicle Anthology Series

Lowestoft Chronicle 2011 Anthology
Far-Flung and Foreign
Intrepid Travelers
Somewhere, Sometime
Other Places
Grand Departures
Invigorating Passages
Steadfast Trekkers
The Vicarious Traveler
An Adventurous Spirit
A Place to Pause

"Full of great talent and exceptionally well written pieces. An entertaining read." —Tara Smith, *The Review Review* (5-Star Review)

"*Lowestoft Chronicle* is a wonderful new addition to the world of creative writing." —Tony Perrottet, acclaimed author of *The Naked Olympics*

"Reading *Lowestoft Chronicle* is like jostling through a sprawling bazaar in Tashkent or Ulaanbaatar, with eyes wide open and wits on high alert." —Victor Robert Lee, author of *Performance Anomalies*

"A standout among a growing universe of online journals. Every issue delivers a cornucopia of entertaining and thought-provoking stories and articles." —Michael C. Keith, acclaimed author of *The Next Better Place*

"A brilliant, savory, sharp, amusing and varied taste of my favorite magazine, *Lowestoft Chronicle*. I'm delighted that a place exists for this kind of travel writing. Nicholas Litchfield has put together something very special, something to celebrate, enjoy, savor." —Jay Parini, bestselling author of *The Last Station* and *The Passages of H.M.*

"The *Lowestoft Chronicle* is both classy and fun to read. A work accomplished by careful attention to detail and quality." —Sheldon Russell, Spur Award-winning author of *A Forgotten Evil*

"Terrific anthology. The writing here is fresh, surprising, and alive. If you aren't familiar with *Lowestoft Chronicle*, head on over there. They publish, on a consistent basis, excellent fiction, poetry, and non-fiction." —Nicholas Rombes, author of *A Cultural Dictionary of Punk: 1974-1982*

"*Lowestoft Chronicle* publishes some of the finest work of travel writing on the Internet today." —Krystal Sierra, *The Review Review* (5-Star Review)

"This is the only literary magazine I read these days, and it's always enjoyable. It takes the reader to a wide variety of literary destinations, and makes even a confirmed hermit like me want to get up and go somewhere. Highly recommended." —James Reasoner, *New York Times* bestselling author

"Charm, a love of travel, often sly humor, and a clear reverence of story make up the backbone of *Lowestoft Chronicle*." —Keith Rosson, acclaimed author of *Fever House* and *Smoke City*

"Editor Nicholas Litchfield has once again done admirable work in selecting and presenting a memorable miscellany of fiction, nonfiction, and verse that beckons to literary travelers and leads them onward from one entertaining stop to another." —Timothy J. Lockhart, author of *Smith* and *Pirates*

"Nicholas Litchfield's selection of stories, poems, memoirs and interviews is a treasure for readers who enjoy a good dose of humor with their armchair travel." —Mary Donaldson-Evans, author of *Behind the Lines*

"The much-admired *Lowestoft Chronicle* [is] an eclectic and innovative online journal. Packed into the pages are stories to entice, enthral, and entertain…incisive and enlightening interviews…[and] a tasty blend of pleasing and deftly prepared poems." —Pam Norfolk, *Lancashire Post*

"How did I not know about the *Lowestoft Chronicle*? If you're late to this travel and literary parade as well, check out Nicholas Litchfield's superb online journal specializing in all things to do with travel, literature, and the overlap between these life-nourishing activities." —James R. Benn, acclaimed author of the Billy Boyle mystery series

"A refreshingly original collection of sharp tales. Overall, it's entertaining, varied, and clever writing." —*Kirkus Reviews*

"A fun read." —*New York Journal of Books*

In this quarterly, you'll find creative nonfiction, short stories, and a few poems, with a welcome dose of humor in many. Wander around the site and you'll find intriguing stories." —Pat Tompkins, Afar.com

"A fantastic online literary magazine that mixes humour and travel. There's lots of good fiction there." —Allister Timms, author of *The Killing Moon*

"The literary equivalent of Rick's Café in *Casablanca*, where travelers of all stripes pull up a stool and swap stories at the bar. Handsomely designed and expertly curated, *Lowestoft Chronicle* drives us into the arms of experience."
—Scott Dominic Carpenter, author of *Theory of Remainders*

"*Lowestoft Chronicle* is contemporary and worldly but with a sepia charm. It's a Baedeker for the vicarious traveler in the age of globalization."
—Ivy Goodman, acclaimed author of *Heart Failure*

"A solid collection of funny and fine travel-themed stories, poetry, essays and interviews that easily fits in a back pocket or carry-on bag."
— Frank Mundo, Examiner.com

"Three attributes of a good literary journal are variety, quality, and the unexpected. *Lowestoft Chronicle* supplies all three."
—Robert Wexelblatt, award-winning author of *Zublinka Among Women*

"A wonderful collection from a fine literary journal. Fine writing that stirs the imagination, often amuses and always entertains."
—Dietrich Kalteis, award-winning author of *Under an Outlaw Moon*

"*An Adventurous Spirit* moves deftly, displays a remarkable range, and reminds us why we crave travel literature. Read and enjoy!"
—Charles Holdefer, author of *The Contractor*

"It's unique and the quality of the writing is amazingly high. Highest praise: it made me want to write short stories again."
—Luke Rhinehart, bestselling author of *The Dice Man*

"I'm always impressed with the quarterly online literary magazine, *Lowestoft Chronicle*." —Matthew P. Mayo, Spur Award-winning author of *Tucker's Reckoning* and *Stranded*

"This cornucopia of riveting tales and vivid poetry...abounds with amazing language, arresting insight, and sharply drawn landscapes."
—Linda Boroff, screenwriter of *Murder in Fashion*

A PLACE TO PAUSE

EDITED BY NICHOLAS LITCHFIELD

FOREWORD BY MARY DONALDSON-EVANS

 Lowestoft
Chronicle
Press

A PLACE TO PAUSE

SUBMISSIONS

The editors welcome submissions of poetry and prose. For submission information please visit our website at www.lowestoftchronicle.com or email: submissions@lowestoftchronicle.com

Published by Lowestoft Chronicle Press, Cambridge, Massachusetts
www.lowestoftchronicle.com

First edition: March 2024

Cover and book design by Nicholas Litchfield

ISBN 13: 978-1-7323328-3-6
ISBN 10: 1-7323328-3-5

Library of Congress Control Number: 2023949421

Printed in the United States of America

CONTENTS

Foreword / Mary Donaldson-Evans   11
Introduction / "The Norman Rockwell Effect" by Nicholas Litchfield   13

FICTION

"Singapura" by Ken Wetherington   21
"After the Meltdown, On the Hunt" by Mark Jacobs   30
"The First American Explorers to Canyon de Chelly" by David Hagerty   64
"The Aeronautical Lawn Chair" by Don Noel   75
"A Businessman in Kilimantuk" by Michael Robinson Morris   88
"Jerusalem Architect" by Andrew Edwards   105
"Una Terra del Miracoloso" by Robin Michel   124
"Arrivederci" by Louise Turan   128
"Bulkhead Seat" by Mary Donaldson-Evans   139
"International Arrival" by Jennifer Swallow   157
"Even at a Distance" by J.L.Austin   171
"Lost City" by Robert Wexelblatt   198

POETRY

"Your Intersections with Nature" and   60
"Seniors on the Move" by William Doreski   62
"Death By Elephant" and   80
"Riding the Midnight Express to Tangiers" by Roger Camp   81
"Waxing Nautical" and   120
"The Piazza Senza Banco, Long After" by James B. Nicola   122
"Paul Explains Home" and   137
"Landscaping at the Phoenix Airport" by Ann Howells   138
"Idlewild" and "I Circle Back" by Joan Mazza   155, 156

INTERVIEW

"A Conversation with Mark Jacobs" and   43

"A Conversation with Mary Donaldson-Evans" and   145

"A Conversation with Robert Wexelblatt" by Nicholas Litchfield   211

CREATIVE NONFICTION

"Clandestine" by Lorraine Caputo   55

"The Roof is on Fire" by Ben von Jagow   83

"Bad Trip? What I Learned from Meeting Paul Theroux" by William Fleeson   97

"Irrational" by David Shawn Klein   165

"Round the Bend" by Warren Merkel   177

"Point A to Point B" by Melissent Zumwalt   187

"Something Different" by Laurel DiGangi   219

"Family Circus" by Jeff Alphin   225

CONTRIBUTORS | 235
COPYRIGHT NOTES | 241

Foreword
Mary Donaldson-Evans

Ten years after my retirement as a French professor at the University of Delaware, I remain in touch with about a dozen students. I've attended their weddings, bought gifts for their babies, listened to their conference papers, written countless letters of recommendation. But the student who has contributed most helpfully to the advancement of my own post-retirement avocation as a creative writer—and to this student, I'll give a name, Lynn Palermo—is the one who introduced me to the *Lowestoft Chronicle*. Having published her own creative non-fiction piece, "Chasing Linda," in the journal's eleventh issue (2012), she thought the *Lowestoft Chronicle* might be an appropriate outlet for my work. It was just three years later that I found a home in the pages of Nicholas Litchfield's journal for my first story, and I am delighted to report that since that time, six more of my pieces have been included in this wonderful quarterly journal. Whether nestled among poems, creative non-fiction pieces, or fiction, they're always in good company.

The pieces published in *A Place to Pause*, the latest in a series of "best of…" anthologies, demonstrate the same sterling qualities that critics have identified in previous anthologies: fluid writing, engaging narrative, thought-provoking evocations of foreign cultures, and in many cases, a keen sense of the ridiculous. The editor's preference for "humorous writing with an emphasis on travel" is apparent throughout this collection. How not to "laugh out loud" when the first-person narrator of "Singapura," an opium addict living in once exotic Singapore, meets a woman he describes as "a dumpy unappealing woman with crooked teeth" and then, after having completed a mission that pays well enough to support his habit, takes up with her: "God she was beautiful. How lucky I was!" How not to be amused by the image of a man in a lawn chair being lifted into the big sky of Montana by helium balloons ("The Aeronautical Lawn Chair") in fulfillment of a student's extra credit assignment for a physics course? Readers chuckle wryly when the wife in an American couple prepares oh-so-carefully for a trip to Italy, memorizing common phrases and requests, even translating a poem from Italian into English, but then finds that she lacks the vocabulary to book a taxi on the phone for the return trip to the airport ("Una Terra del Miracoloso"). We smile in self-recognition at the situation evoked in the poem "Idlewild," that of a stranded traveler, normally "productivity-oriented," who must accept that he's stuck in an airport lounge where he is forced to be indolent. And we snicker sympathetically when an aspiring travel writer fails to attract the interest of the acclaimed Paul Theroux ("Bad Trip? What I learned from Paul Theroux") but uses Theroux's own words to persuade himself that he "got the last word." Even such cringe-worthy pieces as "Family Circus," while not comic in the conventional sense, provoke laughter by the wit of their prose ("And then, just like in the joke, a clown walked into the bar.")

If it's true that laughter is the best medicine, *A Place to Pause* is eminently therapeutic, an excellent antidote to the dysphoria provoked by the steady flow of disturbing news items that assault us every day. And better still, the humor is supplied in manageable doses so that readers need only pause briefly to benefit from this healthy distraction. Here, as in previous anthologies, Nicholas Litchfield's "scribblers" invite us to step back from the preoccupations of our daily life, to travel to exotic places, to laugh, and to enjoy (with apologies to Coca-Cola) the pause that refreshes.

The Norman Rockwell Effect

Nicholas Litchfield

"Filled with equal parts charm, nostalgia, and a longing for the way we once were and could be again, this is a wonderful journal. Reading the Lowestoft Chronicle is like looking at a Norman Rockwell painting."

— Christopher Cosmos, author of Once We Were Here

Around the time of the publication of his debut historical novel *Once We Were Here*, author and screenwriter Christopher Cosmos gave this sage, flattering appraisal of our evolving yet old-timey magazine: "Filled with equal parts charm, nostalgia, and a longing for the way we once were and could be again, this is a wonderful journal in the great and important American tradition of chronicling both where we're going, where we've been, and everything else in-between. Reading the *Lowestoft Chronicle* is like looking at a Norman Rockwell painting."

The perceptive Cosmos admirably postulated the strength and spirit of the magazine and its habit of presenting works that evoke a strong emotional response. Poetry that elicits fond remembrances, lingering regrets, and ruefulness over the passing of time. Memoirs that linger in the memory and lead one to reminisce about friends and foes, family and childhood, summer vacations, and half-forgotten romances. Fiction that transports the reader to long-forgotten places, uncharted territory, and futuristic times that test one's mettle. Essentially, pieces that color our senses and give us pause for thought. The Norman Rockwell effect, if you will.

Years earlier, our proofreader mumbled something vaguely similar to Cosmos's interpretation of the magazine. Though far less coherent—mystifying at times, in point of fact—I remember his rambling speech and the ostentatious way he gestured to the Cassius Marcellus Coolidge print on our office wall of dogs repairing a motor car on a country lane, titled "Ten Miles to a Garage." Though he diluted the potency of his words by falling over drunk, his sentiments, together with his theatrics, left a lasting impression.

It's been days, months—possibly years—since the proofreader departed. I remember his ruddy, bloated face and the brand names of his favorite cognacs, but his name escapes me. Yet, his antics live on.

I like to think that's the way it is with many of the pieces in this eleventh volume in our annual mixed-form anthology series. Unlike the overpriced high-rise hotel that sends you home with sores on your skin and bed bugs in your luggage, this horde of evocative verses and stimulating narrative accounts scuttle around in your head, distracting you, plaguing you, sometimes panicking you. Ultimately, they leave behind a mark.

A Place to Pause lures the reader to less familiar territory and waylays them just long enough to reflect on their journey and their choices. Case in point: Michael Robinson Morris' thrilling "A Businessman in Kilimantuk," where unpleasantness on a remote island near Madagascar profoundly impacts a young nomadic couple enjoying the simple life. Faced with an unwelcome intrusion, the central characters must either confront or endure a visitor's atrocious acts of exploitation and base savagery.

In Robert Wexelblatt's beguiling "Lost City," intrepid college friends destabilize their mental balance while excavating the skeleton past of an uncharted region of the Silk Road. And while David Hagerty's fabulous historical drama, "The First American Explorers to Canyon de Chelly," charts the beginnings of tourism on Navajo tribal land in northeastern Arizona and the price of intrusion, Mark Jacobs' provocative dystopic yarn, "After the Meltdown, On the Hunt," considers a brave new world lusting for grisly, big-game sport.

Interestingly, unlike in Jacobs' thrill-ride, where the career-driven journalist becomes repulsed by his assignment and feels compelled to subvert the system for the greater good, in "Singapura," Ken Wetherington's suave noir, the decadent, down-at-heel journalist turns to crime as a means to survive. Though ambitious, with aspirations to deliver a superlative debut novel, opium addiction thwarts his creativity, and there's the distinct possibility he might actually be more accomplished as a smuggler than a writer. Something most newshounds contemplate, I'm sure.

In Andrew Edwards' humorous, futuristic adventure, "Jerusalem Architect," we encounter another enterprising writer looking to improve his situation but never quite managing to distance himself from dangerous encounters. The screenwriter, whose current TV show is on the verge of being canceled, travels to a parallel dimension, but instead of finding a new narrative, he's targeted by an angry mob.

In "Bad Trip? What I Learned from Meeting Paul

Theroux," the budding travel writer succeeds in finding a new narrative. In this assured travel memoir, William Fleeson, seeking approbation, pursues his idol at an author lecture in DC, armed with a portfolio of his first drafts. Mercifully, Theroux escapes danger and misadventure on this occasion.

Elsewhere in this collection, you can find plenty of menace and mishaps of the type to make most men resolve to become hermits. The terror begins with the daily commute to work. American highways—hunting grounds for hoary, white-haired sociopaths—are full of inexplicable horror. Statistics might not entirely back up my claim, but it's my understanding that rather than the rickety bridges and cavernous potholes, deathwish geriatrics weaving along your local artery routes are the most common nuisance. They will cut you up at every intersection and try to rip apart your tin can convertible on the most picturesque coastal roads.

Oddly, essays about centenarian savages are few and far between, and though there are none here, various stories and nonfiction pieces focus on road-related pitfalls and motoring challenges. In J.L. Austin's tense, sultry drama, "Even at a Distance," traffic hazards on the California highway cause a driver hot bother as he attempts to leave his city for good. In Jennifer Swallow's ironic crime yarn, "International Arrival," set in Moscow, flight delays, bad weather, and a pesky thug cause a busy chauffeur's plans to go horribly awry. In his essay "Irrational," David Klein drolly confesses how dreadful Uber ratings have impacted his daily commute around New York City. And while Warren Merkel's entertaining memoir, "Round the Bend," explores the mechanics behind the rigorous Norwegian driving test, Melissent Zumwalt's charming "Point A to Point B" maps the highs and lows of her beloved first clunker.

The rickety mode of transport demonstrated in "The Aeronautical Lawn Chair" takes aviation to a new, crude level in Don Noel's exhilarating tale of a man's spirited science project. For the acrophobe, this wicker chair adventure is the stuff of nightmares. Speaking of which, Mary Donaldson-Evans' hallucinatory "Bulkhead Seat," in which a passenger is discombobulated by the strange disappearance of a man with an eerily familiar face onboard an international flight, feels like a masterly fit for *The Twilight Zone.* Wit, worry, and just plain weird can also be found in "Family Circus," Jeff Alphin's recollections of filming in Old Tucson, Arizona. Having lampooned spaghetti Westerns for a commercial, a shudder of clowns ropes him into attending a wacky Halloween gathering at a range house hideaway.

Clever examinations of sounds, language, conversation, and standpoints on the cultural divide can be found in the Italian-themed "Una Terra del Miracoloso." In Robin Michel's comic story, a Communications Specialist uses half-remembered phrases and a book of poetry to overcome poor planning and language barriers while traveling through Rome. In Louise Turan's breezy "Arrivederci," a plumbing disaster introduces the sumptuous sounds and culinary delights of Italy to a woman starved of romance. Meanwhile, James B. Nicola offers lyrical reflections on ocean life and witty contemplations on erroneous sounds and the embarrassing tone of a false step.

In other poetic contemplations, William Doreski considers one's deep-rooted penchant to explore and the obstacles carved by the aging process. Ann Howells provides observations of time and evolution from the airport shuttle and an affirming tribute to the lure of home. Roger Camp explores the gateway between Africa and Europe by railroad and finds his life in jeopardy attempting to capture death on film on a highway in southern India. And Joan Mazza explores self-assurance and prevailing when one's patience is thoroughly tested.

The limits of tolerance are examined further in

"Clandestine," Lorraine Caputo's eye-opening railroad reminiscences. Here, the adventurous hitchhiker, detained in a remote mountain village, parlays with railroad workers and sneaky passengers on a cramped cargo train bound for Mexico City.

Likewise, having been starved of entertainment for months, a bored couple gets suckered into shelling out big bucks for a wearying pop-up drive-in theater experience in Laurel DiGangi's witty essay, "Something Different." In contrast, in the entertaining travel piece "The Roof is on Fire," sociable camper Ben von Jagow trades lethargy for hard work as he finds himself working as a roofer in Texas in exchange for a ride to the nearest highway.

This volume also includes in-depth interviews with *Lowestoft Chronicle* regulars Robert Wexelblatt, Mary Donaldson-Evans, and Mark Jacobs. Wexelblatt's cherished tales featuring the nomadic poet Hsi-wei grace numerous editions of the magazine, and here he discusses, among other things, his interest in the Sui Dynasty and the roots of some of his stories.

Though best known for her popular academic works, Mary Donaldson-Evans's amusing travel narratives consistently earn appreciative comments from fellow writers. This interview focuses on her fascination with Guy de Maupassant, nineteenth-century French literature, and her father's deployment in Italy during WW2.

Critically acclaimed novelist Mark Jacobs, whose exceptional stories now number about 200, must rank as one of America's most prolific storytellers. In this interview, which was subsequently reprinted by Peace Corps Worldwide, he discusses literary magazines, mentors, and the extraordinary Latin American media attack on his famous short story.

Regrettably, Norman Rockwell never staggered into our offices and smeared paint over a hefty canvas in the magnanimous pursuit of capturing the quintessence of the *Lowestoft Chronicle*. If he had, undoubtedly, his rich, heartwarming depiction of life-nourishing pilgrimages would have brought everyone together, huddled in the hallway in quiet reflection, intoxicated by more than wine. The long, delightful break from chatter would have been stuffed with heavy, pulsating curiosity and a maddening yearning to excavate the bones of the masterwork. A momentous, restorative pause to commemorate.

Instead of the painting, savor this Rockwell-worthy rest stop—the perfect way to take a breather.

Singapura
Ken Wetherington

I first met him in the Black Russian, a tawdry excuse of a bar tucked away in the narrow backstreets of Singapore. The opium had kicked in, and the slowly rotating disco ball fought for my attention with a couple of pelacurs who stretched languorously, hoping to appeal to my fantasies while the jukebox poured out the incongruous rockabilly stylings of Conway Twitty. The beer on the table in front of me represented the last of my fiscal reserves, and I didn't care.

Into that scene, he glazed, looking like a Hollywood movie star in a brilliant white Bogart suit and Panama hat. On his arm hung the most beautiful woman I had ever seen. He spoke a few words to Hashim, then approached my table, leaving his woman at the bar.

Without waiting for an invitation, he sat down across from me. "Mr. Johnson? Wesley Johnson?"

"Don't know him. Can't help you."

He produced an envelope and placed it on the table between us. I paid no attention and refocused on the spinning globe.

"Take it," he urged. "I'll be in touch."

My eyes didn't drift from the ball. "Might forget," I murmured.

He picked up the envelope and stuffed it into my shirt pocket. "I won't."

When I looked down, he had vanished. I ran my finger along the edge of the envelope to confirm his existence, then sank into a sublime appreciation of Conway Twitty. I don't remember returning to my room at Zarina's house that night.

I arose from bed in the late afternoon of the following day. At least, I supposed it was the following day. Devising a scheme to avoid Zarina's demands for the overdue rent claimed my attention until I recalled the envelope. It took a few minutes to locate it wedged between the bed and the wall. Nine crisp one hundred Singaporean-dollar bills spilled out. I searched the crevice and found another. Not as good as American dollars or euros, but I couldn't be choosy.

Downstairs, I shoved one of the bills into Zarina's hands and hustled off to meet Faisal. The humid air and darkening sky portended rain. Dryness in my throat called for hydration, but my psyche demanded immediate gratification.

Faisal operated a café of sorts. He did the cooking under an awning out front. Behind him, his narrow business stood, sandwiched between two similar establishments.

"Six grams," I said across the steaming grill.

He casually poked at the fried meats. "Show the money." Faisal's English had been perfected by decades of providing contraband for Western ex-pats.

I flashed a handful of cash. "How much?"

He glanced thoughtfully at the awning and adjusted his turban. "Um…three hundred."

I winced but quickly agreed. He accepted the cash and motioned to his fat wife, who led me inside, past a tiny dining area, and through a curtain to the back room. She measured out my allotment and handed me the packet.

"Feels a little light," I said.

She shrugged and turned away.

The rain had begun to fall. Lacking an umbrella, I turned up the collar of my coat and made the best of it. When I returned, Zarina's soulful singing filled the house. The money had cheered her. The hundred I pressed upon her would discharge my debts and provide advance payment for a while. She had a good heart, and I was happy for her. She often apologized for the spareness of the room, furnished only with a single bed, a small desk with a wooden chair, and a dresser far too large for my limited wardrobe. That was okay. I didn't need an extravagant living space, and it kept the rent reasonable. I stripped off my wet clothes, lit the pipe, and quickly drifted into bliss, lying naked on the bed.

When I came down, my stomach reminded me I had not eaten since the previous day. Out in the streets, food stalls beckoned, their myriad aromas hanging heavily in the damp evening air. I settled on a bowl of laksa at a popular lunch spot. The vendor examined the hundred, rubbing his fingers over its surface. Finally, he put it away and doled out my change.

Back in my room, I pulled out the fifty pages of my unfinished novel and pondered the next scenes. My former colleagues at the International News Bureau would be jealous when it got published. Mackenzie had called me a washed-up journalist. I'd show him.

The old-fashioned typewriter sat inert on my desk. I fingered the keys, but sustained concentration eluded me. My protagonist had traveled to Angkor Wat in search of spiritual enlightenment but discovered the site overrun with tourists. Disillusioned, he lacked direction. The plot had stalled, and inspiration failed me. With a sigh, I pushed it aside, took a hit from my pipe, and made my way to the Black Russian.

I considered paying one of the pelacurs for a quick servicing, but the last encounter left me unsatisfied. Once the opium took effect, I had no other needs. I bought a beer so Hashim wouldn't kick me out. The ball spun, the jukebox played, and the night evaporated.

───── ✦ ─────

I awoke to find them standing in my room. With the clarity of sobriety, I saw them as they were—he, a short, swarthy man in a soiled white suit, and she, a dumpy, unappealing woman with crooked teeth. I dragged myself out of bed, still dressed in yesterday's clothes.

"Been spending your advance, Mr. Johnson? May I call you Wesley?"

"Whatever pleases you." I blinked and rubbed my eyes. "What shall I call you?"

"Um…Gomez will do." Obviously, no Hispanic blood ran through his veins, but I accepted his choice. He indicated his woman. "Mia."

I made a slight bow, and she seated herself at my desk.

"I've instructions for you, Wesley."

"I might refuse."

"Not an option. I dare say you've exhausted a considerable percentage of your advance."

"It was given without obligation."

"Come, sir, you don't really believe no conditions were attached, do you?" His tone remained unemotional yet direct. "It's not as if you won the lottery."

Damn him. He was right. Spending the money confirmed a tacit agreement—as ironclad as a fine-print contract. How evil of him to wait until I had blown through a big chunk of it. "Okay, okay. What's the deal…Gomez?" I tried to bend his name into a slur.

He ignored my intent. "A trip. A kind of vacation. How long's it been since you had a vacation?"

"Go to hell. Just tell me what you want." I ached to flee into a pain-free world.

"I'll send a plane ticket tomorrow. On Friday, you'll fly to Canberra. A room is reserved for you

at the Hyatt. That's all. Oh, and don't take any luggage. It's a ten-hour flight. And you'll have to keep off the ah-pen-yen."

"Ten hours? No luggage? Just me?" I stroked my chin to give an appearance of thought and glanced at Mia, who surveyed my living conditions with bored eyes. "I can do it. It was an advance, you said. When do I get the rest?"

"Set your mind at ease, Wesley. You won't be cheated. You will receive an item at the airport to carry."

"Drugs?"

He snorted. "Nothing quite so obvious."

"A bomb? State secrets?"

He shook his head. "Trust me. It's best for you not to ask."

I agreed to his terms, pretending I had a choice, and hustled the two of them out. Within minutes I lay on my bed, drifting into pleasant, carefree dreams to the sweet sounds of Zarina's singing.

━━━✦━━━

I stared at the typewriter. Got to get a computer. Then it would be easier to write. Had to save up for that sort of thing. Shouldn't have spent so much at Faisal's. Maybe Mackenzie would consider rehiring me. Tomorrow…tomorrow, I might drop by and see him. If I could just get the next chapter going, I wouldn't need anyone. Perhaps a hit from my pipe would stimulate my creativity. Just a little one.

As I reached for the pipe, a knock on the door froze me. A big bruiser of a man with a jagged scar carved into his left cheek stood there, an envelope in his hand. He waited silently while I unfastened the clasp. In addition to the plane ticket, it contained a hundred Australian dollars in small bills. I gave a nod and dismissed the courier. He departed, treading heavily on the stairs. He probably frightened Zarina. I hoped the recent flurry of unsavory traffic wouldn't prompt her to evict me.

On Friday, I showered, shaved, and took a taxi to the airport while fighting the urge to stay home and indulge in my vices. I mopped the sweat from my brow and paid off the cabbie with a generous tip. Taking slow, deep breaths, I entered the terminal and showed my ticket. The TSA agent examined it closely, and for a moment, I feared he might bar me from boarding. But he waved me through the metal detector.

On the other side, a security officer put his hand on my shoulder. "Your bag, sir." He held a small leather briefcase.

"No, it's not mine. Oh…I'm sorry. You're right. Uh, thank you."

What an idiot I was. How clever of my…uh, sponsors to give me the item after passing the security checkpoint.

I clung to the briefcase and fidgeted throughout the flight, drawing an annoying series of sighs from the middle-aged woman in the seat beside me. She tried to sleep, and so did I. Neither succeeded. By the time we landed, a mix of desperation and relief clashed within me. The taxi to the hotel slogged through heavy traffic. I kept looking out the back window. Was I being followed?

My hand trembled as I checked in at the Hyatt. The clerk eyed me with suspicion but handed over the room key. Stopping by the necessities kiosk, I purchased a tiny, overpriced packet containing two sleeping pills. At the register, the young female cashier recoiled. I may have frightened her. The elevator made its painstaking ascent to my floor. Finally, in my room, I swallowed the pills, stashed the briefcase in the closet, and spread gratefully on the bed.

As drowsiness began to ease my anxiety, a knock on the door drew me back to the real world. I forced myself to rise. A uniformed steward stood there with a package. I accepted it and handed over a tip with no idea of the value of the bill I surrendered. Then sleep, blissful sleep, came.

The phone awoke me. I fumbled in the dark to answer it. Through the window, the nighttime lights of Canberra blinked like stars.

"Mr. Johnson?"

I cleared my throat. "Yeah."

"I've been trying to reach you. Did you receive the package?"

"I think so. I mean, yeah. It's here somewhere. Oh, I see it now."

"I hope it meets your approval."

"Yeah, sure."

"I have some instructions. Meet me at the bar downstairs in a half-hour with the...um...commodity."

"How will I know you?"

"I'll know you, Mr. Johnson."

After hanging up, I tore open the package and found a small amount of opium and a pipe, along with an airline ticket for a flight to Singapore the next day. They, whoever they were, did not believe in wasting time. Summoning a herculean effort, I set the drug aside and counted on a few rounds of stiff drinks to get me through the evening.

At the bar, I knocked down a couple of whiskeys and motioned for a third. I perched one foot on the briefcase, which sat on the floor beneath my barstool. Would my connection be able to find me among the chattering tourists?

A heavyset man on the next stool leaned toward me. "Got a wife, mister?"

"Uh...no."

"Lucky son of a bitch. Nothing but trouble, they are."

I considered moving to a table, but the bar offered better visibility. Only five minutes until the appointed time. I decided to humor the drunken man. "Yeah, I know what you mean."

"How the hell do you know if you don't have one."

Oh, God. How could I escape? "Well, I had one about a decade ago."

"Good riddance, huh?"

"Right." I signaled for another whiskey. Where was my connection? He should appear any moment. I scanned the barroom for a possible candidate. They all looked like tourists to me.

The drunk grabbed my arm. "Hey, buddy, I'm talking to you."

Damn. Was he spoiling for a fight? I pulled free of his grasp. All I could think about was the pipe in my room. I hurriedly drained my third whiskey and decided to give up on the meeting.

A sharp, sudden pop broke through the babble. Another pop. And another. Panicked screeches ricocheted across the room. A stampede of humanity rushed by. Someone's elbow knocked me from my seat. Another pushed me to the floor and stepped on my leg. I fought to rise, but a large body rammed into me. By the time I righted myself, most of the crowd had dispersed. The complaining man still occupied his stool, oblivious to the chaos, but my briefcase had vanished.

"Hey, man, did you see my briefcase?"

"I don't give a good goddamn about your briefcase. Keep track of your own shit."

I scrambled under nearby tables, searching for it, even checking behind the bar, which had been abandoned. No trace of it. It was as if it had never existed. The cops began to arrive. I beat a path to the elevators and up to my room, where paradise awaited.

The room phone rang the following morning, providing a wake-up call I did not request. Hanging around Canberra, waiting for something unpleasant to happen, seemed a bad idea. Besides, I had a plane ticket in hand. At the front desk, the clerk said my bill had been paid.

I endured the flight in a state of anxiety. The beefy man beside me slept soundly despite my agitated restlessness. The commodity, as the voice on the phone called it, had been lost. Though I saw myself as blameless, someone, somewhere, would likely cast doubt on my story. Might they come after me? Could I explain my way out of it?

I had no plan, so I returned to Zarina's and discovered an envelope had been slipped under my door. I felt it to be a bad omen, announcing a threat or a summons, but it contained a bank book in my name. The balance astounded me. What the hell? Was the shooting at the hotel bar a ruse to pass the commodity on to the next link in the chain, so I couldn't identify the connection? Had I been simply a pawn? Of course, I had, but did the scheme work as planned? Could I be in the clear? Surely the answer would come soon, or not at all.

———— ✦ ————

I resumed work on my novel, but the plot had become confused. One afternoon while returning from Faisal's, I spotted Mackenzie getting out of a taxi in front of the International News Bureau. I waved to him, but he didn't see me. I was the best writer he had. He would jump at the chance to rehire me. I should give him a little more time. He'd soon realize that he needed me.

A week or so after getting back, Gomez's picture appeared in the newspapers, now identified as Ibrahim. He had been arrested, though the charges were vague. A few days later, the word went around that he had been found dead in his cell. When I asked Hashim about it, he just shrugged.

Mia materialized on a dreary evening, flashing her crooked teeth and projecting a desperate hopefulness in her weary eyes. She latched onto me and became my constant companion. We spent our days together and our nights sleeping separately in the same bed, much to Zarina's displeasure. She had not bargained for two tenants. Mia spoke little English but seemed comfortable in my company. We squandered our evenings at the Black Russian, where Conway Twitty's greatest hits played endlessly. I watched the disco ball spin and the pelacurs strut, occasionally glancing at Mia through an opiated haze. God, she was beautiful. How lucky I was.

After the Meltdown, On the Hunt
Mark Jacobs

Only after we got separated from the rest of the hunt team did I tell Vanilla Marie I loved her. Melodramatic, yep, and poorly timed. The sun was going down, and our way back to the ship was blocked by angry people waving weapons. To make things worse, I had a lousy sense of direction.

The day's wet heat was hanging on. We were standing in an alley alongside a high mud wall catching our breath. V had high frizzy hair and the roundest dark eyes I ever saw. When I told her I loved her, she said, "Fulton, you are a mindless idiot."

We heard drums.

Probably none of this makes sense. Let me go back to the beginning.

After a long spell of lemons, my luck changed, and I scored a sweet assignment. All I had to do was cruise to Africa on the Burthen, go out on the hunt, and write a puff piece with embedded 3-D art for Adventure International. Submit piece, get paid, cruise home in the sun.

Before your outrage meter shoots up to 11, think about what I knew at the time: All participants—those who ran and those who ran after—signed a consent form. If something happened, AI compensated the victim's family. In the promo holographs, the alumni raved about the opportunities the hunt gave them and their families. They were grateful to AI. What would you have done?

I am an average individual. Before the trip, I never gave much thought to the cruises, the hunts, or what used to be called, back before the meltdown, international relations.

I'm tired of people saying the meltdown changed

everything forever. As a planet, we blew it. Agreed. We let hate win and technology get the better of us. We underestimated the killing capacity of robots and drones and the multiplier effect. We crawled into our shells and told scary stories about people in other places.

Africa took more than its fair share of the destruction when the drone war spiraled out of control. And then, of course, the robots made everything worse. One of the casualties of the meltdown was curiosity. Safer not to have any. Hardly anybody wanted to travel. If you saw pictures of misery, you closed your eyes. If AI said they were doing a good thing with the hunts, you believed them.

Go ahead and hate on me.

On board the Burthen, I was surprised by the diversity of the travelers. Young and old, male and female, there were examples of every American kind and color. Right off the bat, I started interviewing people, building a file for my piece. I figured I'd profile a few of them and have the background ready to stick in when I needed it. Not all of them were of equal interest, journalistically speaking.

And then there was Vanilla Marie.

Our second night out, she was standing at the rail on seven deck drinking a Tropical Storm. It came in a tall glass in which miniature lightning bolts shot continuously through cloudy blue liquid; a gimmick, but a cool one. She was staring out over the Atlantic, looking as if her puppy had just washed overboard. I really liked her spike-heeled flip-flops. When I asked her if I could profile her, she turned me down.

"Not interested, Journo-Boy."

"They say there's no such thing as bad publicity."

"You obviously don't get it."

"Get what?"

"What's going on."

"Then tell me."

"This whole thing…we've been here before."

"Not me," I said. "This is my first time out."

Shaking her head in disgust, she walked away. I was strongly drawn to the tall, self-possessed woman and wasn't going to let rejection stand in my way. So I stuck with it. Whenever she thought she had escaped, up popped Fulton. Across the ocean and the days, she got sort of used to me. Two or three times, she let me buy her a drink. The drinks didn't cost me; they were part of my deal with AI.

Once, I stood her a Tropical Storm in the bar on the top deck, which was done up in a jungle theme and included colorful parrots with clipped wings in the branches of real trees.

"I know you think I'm stupid," I said.

She sucked on her Storm as mini-lightning jags crashed around the liquid blue. "Not stupid, just ignorant."

"Enlighten me."

"The sins of the fathers," she said. "We're committing them all over again."

It made me uneasy, not knowing what she was talking about. And as we approached the west coast of Africa, the atmosphere on board changed. People tensed up. It had to do with the hunt. The handful of veterans developed cult-like followings of first-timers. I recorded a few of the stories they were tossing off, but that got old. I knew my craft. I didn't have to hear every last self-serving anecdote to put together my piece, which I was calling *All Aboard: The Burthen Africa Hunt Cruise*.

I managed to sit next to Vanilla Marie at the final orientation session, which they held in a conference room amidships on the same level as the pool. To set a serious tone, they served no alcoholic drinks. I was struck by the ferocity of her note-taking.

In the vid they showed us, a lissome man in his twenties

named Moussa was filmed having the locator chip implanted in his chest. He smiled and chatted with the technicians. There were symmetric chevron scars on his cheeks, markers of tribal affiliation that stretched back into the fathomless past. In a later clip, we watched him disappear into a surging city crowd, taking advantage of the head start he was allowed.

The evening before we docked, we were divided into teams of five. Each team had a tracking device keyed to the locator chip of the individual we were hunting. Competition was ruthless; there was a prize for the first team to score. We wore armbands with our team color. We were the green team.

Sounded simple enough. You disembarked into the chaos of the port. You kept in touch via wrist radios. You followed the signal emitted by the implant in your guy's chest.

He had some advantages. One, he knew the city. Two, the population of the city was on his side. (AI had learned the goodwill value of spreading swag around. There was an active gray market in trinkets, especially the electronic stuff. Of course, I could not include that in my piece.) Three, as the day went on, the signal strength from the chip decreased. If they hadn't designed it that way, there would be no sport involved, and your kill inevitable. This way, it was a real hunt.

I told the organizers a lie. I was featuring Vanilla Marie in my article, so I needed to be on her team. It worked.

"I should have known," she muttered as the green team congealed by the gangway. She was dressed in khaki with lots of pockets, some of them big. In the morning sun, she looked graceful and slightly sweaty.

"Mind if I call you V?"

Rounding out our team was a professor of communication sciences from Vanderbilt, an introverted woman of forty who constantly brushed her hair off her forehead; a rancher from Montana with the steely glint and steady nerves you expected of a man who dealt in livestock; and a guy with no discernible personality who ran some kind of import-export business. We'd had dinner together the previous evening, a bonding exercise that tanked. The rancher talked firearms. The professor talked about her feelings. The business guy picked at his ear. V radiated her disapproval, and I tried to express some silent solidarity with her. Go Team Green.

"You notice we don't know his name," whispered V the moment we touched solid ground.

She was a head taller than I and had to lean down to catch my ear.

"Whose name?"

"The man we're hunting. It's part of the desensitization process."

"What desensitization process?"

If I had tried, I could not have said anything better calculated to irk her. But I knew something was not quite right. Adventure International patrons did not start off after their target fretting about the desensitization process. Vanilla Marie had reasons of her own to be on the hunt.

You've seen scenes like this in a hundred action vids. A mass of poor people, elbow to elbow in a dusty space, buckets and bundles, children in slings on the backs of traditional mothers. A rising tide of foreign sound fills your ears with strangeness. A mélange of smells: animal, vegetable, and mineral. Bicycles and overladen handcarts are on the verge of constant collision. Eyes you can't avoid. Misery you can't escape. Crumbling buildings. Donkeys, goats, and emaciated cattle with visible ribs.

"Let's stick together," the rancher said. "No freelancing. Everybody got that?"

We got it. With no discernible effort, he had become the head of our team. I had thought he would stand out like a sore thumb in his ten-gallon hat and alligator boots, but once we were in the crowd, I realized how outlandish all of us were.

The Vanderbilt woman said, "I'm getting a signal."

Okay, in retrospect, I knew more than I admitted to myself. I knew Vanilla Marie was opposed to the hunt. And I knew—a small unruined part of me did, anyway—that we intended to commit murder and call it entertainment.

The locals knew the drill. As we formed a pack, they parted to let us through. A little kid grabbed my pant leg and howled. I shook him off. Never mind what I knew about our dark purpose, the sense of excitement was heady. I had chosen a pistol because it was easy to carry. Anyway, my job was to observe and report, not to kill. The AI logo was embossed on the grips, which somehow made it look harmless.

The signal led west into the congested heart of the city.

I tried not to look at Vanilla Marie. She, too, had selected a pistol.

Our guy was good. Any time we thought we were gaining on him, the signal dipped and shifted, and suddenly he was moving in a different direction. Even the export-import guy was impressed.

"I got to hand it to the son of a bitch. He knows what he's doing."

"We'll get him," the rancher said.

We had stopped to reconnoiter. He lifted his hat, ran a meaty hand through wavy gray hair. He was fit and tough, an experienced hunter. He had persuaded us not to hire an AI guide. *It's not because of the money, folks. It's because we want a clean hunt.*

"Do you really think we're going to get him?" asked Vanilla Marie.

He settled the hat back onto his head. "Sure do."

Her smile was bright and hard as she told him, "We'll see, won't we?"

They didn't like each other.

We set off again at a pretty good clip. The day's heat was

upon us. We had been warned about water consumption but went through a lot of it. Despite my intake of fluid, after a while, I felt light-headed.

We fell into a pattern. Pick up a signal. Trot. Draw stares as clusters of citizens made way. Watch the signal fade. Stop. Pick it up again. Trot.

The morning was consumed, and then the afternoon.

"Now's the time to make our push," said the rancher at another rest stop, inflating his leather cheeks and puffing. "Mark my words, that damned signal is going sideways on us any minute now."

We scarfed down some energy bars, knocked back an energy drink full of electrolytes. *Make sure you talk about the hunt-day rations. Your reader needs to know that we take meticulous care of our guests. We are attentive to their every need. Adventure International is not just a company, it's a way of life.*

Because I am a journalist, sentences formed in my mind as we jogged along, and I observed unusual new things. Clauses, dependent and independent. Bon mots and telling adjectives. You can't change who you are.

Or can you?

The moment arrived. We came to a small square surrounded by shacks of mud brick. Strips of burlap hung limp in the doorways. The roofs were mismatched sheets of battered aluminum held down by stones. People sat in doorways and along the outer walls of houses in latticed shade. Babies played in the dirt. Boys kicked a lopsided soccer ball. A blind man with a grizzled beard leaned on a stick, head cocked to one side, smelling us or hearing us. Then, out of the door of one of the smaller houses stepped our man. The tracking device was going crazy.

"Got him," said the import-export guy, his satisfaction huge.

Seeing us, the man with the locator chip in his chest pulled up short. He smiled.

He was young. They were always young, perfect specimens of healthy humanity. He wore red sneakers, a blue T-shirt, yellow running shorts with a military stripe. He was a handsome man who had accepted his fate, doing his best to keep the benefits package he was bequeathing his family uppermost in his mind. His wife's welfare was assured. His children would eat nourishing food. They would remember him as a hero. His smile, full of grace, did not erase the fear from his face.

The rancher was keen to take aim, tense as a pointer downwind. To my surprise, he offered the kill shot to the rest of the team.

"Anybody want to do this?" he said. "I'll be the fallback, in case you miss."

The Vanderbilt woman and the import-export man both wanted to shoot. Skill development. Experience. Bragging rights. A story with a long shelf-life. Their money's worth. All those reasons were part of it, but they were pretexts. Really what they wanted was to pull a trigger. They wanted to kill a man. He had made them sweat. His blithe flight through an alien landscape had mocked them.

"This one is mine," said Vanderbilt.

She raised the AI rifle she had been lugging, but before she could shoulder it, Vanilla Marie made her move. She ran to the side of the square where the victim was waiting to be cut down and put an arm around him. Suddenly, she was shouting in French. From one of her big pockets, she pulled a head cam. Fastened it on. Whatever went down, she was capturing it. With luck, the recording would be posted on a site that mattered.

For a moment, nothing. The square quickly filled up with people flabbergasted to see a tall white woman with a camera on her head. Then they began paying attention to what she was saying. My French was not good, but I followed it. Wake up. Save this man, find your freedom. Like that.

It worked. For one sickening moment, I thought the rancher would shoot Vanilla Marie. She had gone over to the enemy. But people were rushing us, and we were overwhelmed. They took away our weapons. I was never so happy in my life as I was to get rid of the damn pistol. I was laughing.

In a different world, Vanilla Marie would have been hailed as a liberator. They would have made speeches. In this world, after the meltdown, on the hunt, she was subject to the same fury as the rest of us.

It was going badly for her. I pushed through the crowd to the side of the square where she was making a noble but stupid effort to film the melee. Someone knocked the camera from her head. It went flying.

I grabbed her by her slender arm. "Let's get out of here."

"Wait, Fulton."

"Do you want to die?"

She shook her head. She couldn't get past the idea that they hated her as much as they hated me. I yanked her along, and because the rancher had become the focus of people's anger, we were able to skate.

We escaped the square but not the city. The fire that Vanilla Marie lit was doing its work, spreading fast. Across the capital, I was betting, residents who had only pretended to be indifferent were turning on the hunt teams.

There was a smell of burning, the sound of women ululating. Our wrist radios were gone. That meant we couldn't talk to the ship. We needed a plan.

We kept going. Every time we reached a turning, we chose the direction that felt safer. We were quickly lost. That was when the drums began.

After I told Vanilla Marie I loved her, and she told me I was an idiot, I felt entitled to make a comment.

"Well, you got what you wanted."

"What?"

"Now we know how it feels to be hunted."

She glared at me, and I asked her, "Will you answer a question?"

"What?"

"Are you in some sort of resistance group?"

"I wanted to be."

"But this, it was all on your own."

She nodded. Her lower lip turned out. She was proud of what she had done.

"I thought if I did something that mattered, people would take me seriously."

So there was an organization. At least, she thought there was. Now was not the time to dig into it. Any moment someone would happen past the intersection and notice us.

We followed the alley in the darkness back to where the wall ended. Across the way, next to a field, we could just make out a small house squatting alongside a big tree. There were no lights. It was quiet, and the place had a deserted feel. We took a chance. It seemed safer to stay in one place than to wander around until somebody caught us. We went into the house, which was empty. When Vanilla Marie shined a flashlight, the beam fixed on a low door in the back wall. We went through it into the yard, which seemed to be an open-air kitchen. The ashes were cold in the brick fireplace.

The ground was lumpy. I bent over and picked up a lump. It was a mango from the big tree. I peeled a couple of them with a pocket knife, and we ate.

There were chairs in the backyard. We sat in them, hoping whoever lived in the house would not come back.

"Did you plan on spending the rest of your life here?"

"I thought people would be grateful."

"Never mind. We have to get back to the ship."

She shook her head. "If I go back, they'll arrest me."

"Only if people from our team make it back alive. Which I'm pretty sure is not going to happen."

"So, what, I'm supposed to slink back and pretend nothing ever happened?"

My brain quit working. I was tired of everything, including Vanilla Marie. You wouldn't think a person could sleep under such circumstances, but sleep we did, on the ground under the mango tree. There were constant cats, and a hen flew up to a low branch of the mango and roosted. Gradually the drums stopped, the shouting stopped, and the city went quiet, although smoke drifted in long low clouds.

I did not want to wake up. Waking meant thinking. But something kept drilling into my brain, and I sat up in confusion. Vanilla Marie was already awake. There was a smear of ash on her cheek, and her eyes were red and swollen from catastrophe smoke.

"It's the ship," she said.

They were blasting the horn. That was what woke me.

"They're telling us how to get back," I said. "Now's the time, V. We have to make a run for it. They won't wait forever."

"You go. I don't want to be arrested."

"Now who's the idiot?"

She turned away, trying to make defection easy on me.

"Get out of here."

"Vanilla Marie."

"Go."

As mentioned above, I am an average person. I went cautiously through the house. Back down the long alley, staying close to the wall. It was late night or early morning, and I was grateful for the smoky half-dark and the horn bursts from the ship. To get back, all I needed was a little luck.

So why did I stop? Why did I turn around? I wish I had an answer that didn't make me seem better than I am. I went back.

The sky was beginning to lighten. The city was still. Vanilla Marie was eating a mango, a gray kitten playing at her feet. Out of all the things that could happen to a person to change his life, this was what changed mine. We ate more mangos. We went out into the street. We walked.

At the corner that decided our destiny, a black goat grazed on weeds sprouting in thick clumps in an empty lot, and an old woman walked toward us, balancing a basket of onions on her head with her good arm, the other swinging uselessly at her side. She did not seem surprised by the sight of us.

Nor was she taken aback when Vanilla Marie spoke to her. Everything seemed normal. Everything was fine, or that was what I got from the reassuring sounds coming from the old woman. We followed her home. The house was full of kids. They fed us rice with chunks of goat meat. I felt my strength coming back. Somehow it seemed normal when the man we had been hunting came through the front door.

He looked amazingly good for a person who had been through the ordeal he had been through. He had changed into a pale blue robe. He was calm and seemed rested. He spoke first to the woman of the house and then to Vanilla Marie.

It sounded, to me, like a story. When he stopped for breath, I asked V what he was saying. She looked at him for permission to translate. He nodded.

"His name is Abdulaziz," she told me. "He has two wives and seven children. They are the sun and the moon and all the stars of Heaven to him."

My sense of shame was beyond acute.

"Will you tell him I am sorry?"

She looked at me with the contempt I deserved.

"Just tell him."

She did. He listened but did not respond. They talked again for a while as the woman's children fluttered around the yard playing hide and seek. I listened until I couldn't stand it anymore and asked Vanilla Marie to translate again.

"Abdulaziz thinks I must be some sort of powerful person. If I go back home and tell people about the hunts, they will stop. I'm trying to explain that I have no power, but he doesn't believe me."

At that moment, I did not want to be an average person. That was exactly what I was, though, the last in a long line stretching back to the original horror. Maybe the thing to do was cut off my hand, the one whose fingers might have pulled a trigger. Better yet, cut off the head whose eyes had failed to see. That was what I was thinking, but what I did was stand up. I went to the pot of rice and meat on the wood fire. The woman of the house understood what I was about and handed me a clean plate. I filled it. I carried it over to Abdulaziz. Everything that mattered in the world was riding on whether he would accept the plate of food from me. After an interval of centuries, he did.

A Conversation with Mark Jacobs
Lowestoft Chronicle

Mark Jacobs
(Photography: Anne Jacobs)

In spite of a lengthy government career requiring extensive travel and prolonged stays overseas, ever since the 1980s, Mark Jacobs has managed to forge a successful dual occupation as a writer of fiction. His enviable body of work includes critically-acclaimed novels and story collections lauded by illustrious authors and editors like Robert Olen Butler and C. Michael Curtis. For decades, his stories have appeared regularly in dozens of commercial and literary magazines, sometimes featured in leading newspapers like *The Washington Post* and *The New York Times*.

In this exclusive interview with *Lowestoft Chronicle*, Jacobs discusses his publication history, from significant mentors and literary influences to early writing accomplishments and the media frenzy that accompanied one of his short stories.

Lowestoft Chronicle (LC): Over a span of 40+ years, you've had well over 180 stories published in literary journals and commercial magazines. Much of your work appears in prestigious venues such as *The Hudson Review*, *The Atlantic*, *Alaska Quarterly Review*, *The Iowa Review*, *The Kenyon*

Review, *The Idaho Review*, *Southwest Review*, and *The Southern Review*. Your stories continue to appear in abundance, affirming your view that writer's block is "a literary conceit." But when did your desire to be a writer actually begin? Did storytelling always come naturally and fluidly? Is that desire to tell a story and see it appear in a periodical the same as it was in, say, the 1980s?

Mark Jacobs (MJ): I wanted to be a writer from as far back as I can remember. When I was a kid of ten or thereabouts, I went into the kitchen in the apartment on East Falls Street in Niagara Falls, where my father was stirring a pot of spaghetti sauce, and told him that was what I wanted to do. He told me a writer needed three things. If I could remember those three things today, I'd be farther along than I am.

In our junior high school, once a year, we had something called 'Career Day.' It consisted, for the most part, of going to filing cabinets in the back of the classroom and reading pamphlets available there on various jobs one could hope to get. I read the pamphlets for diplomats and for a writer. I saw then no contradiction between the two vocations and saw none later when I was doing both jobs at the same time.

LC: I read that your first story, "Spring Cleaning," a tale told from the perspective of an American missionary nun in Peru, appeared in the college literary magazine *Webster Review* (now defunct) in 1980, and but for more enthusiastic effort in pursuing journals, you might have placed more. What inspired you to write that story and seek a literary market for it?

MJ: I wrote "Spring Cleaning" just after returning from two years in Paraguay as a Peace Corps volunteer. I was at Drew University in a doctoral program. The English department at Drew invited the novelist Mary Lee Settle to come to campus and arranged to have her read, ahead of time, the draft of a novel I was working on. When I went into the office they assigned her to talk it over, the first thing she said was, "You're a writer. You know that, don't you? I can see it in your eyes."

Settle set up a meeting for me with an editor in New York. The editor was affable and interested but did not buy my book. She told me to get myself a box of manila envelopes and start sending out my stories. I did. I think I found the *Webster Review* in one of those writer's guides that used to come out annually. I sent "Spring Cleaning" to them and was blown away to get their acceptance letter back in the mail. I remember opening the envelope and reading it in a kind of stupor. The pleasure of seeing a story in print, either online or on paper, never goes away for me. It's a way of saying goodbye.

But the most useful advice that Mary Lee Settle gave me was to be arrogant. She knew I was in for heart-crushing rejection. A writer needed a certain amount of arrogance to get through the ordeal. None of the people who were going to tell me 'no,' she said, could do what I was doing, and don't forget it. I stand by that advice. Mix your arrogance with some stubbornness, shake well, and put it somewhere you won't lose it. You're going to need it.

LC: In terms of sheer volume and story placement, you are perhaps more prolific and globally read now than ever. Who were the authors who most influenced your early writing? What are some of the lessons you've learned about writing fiction, approaching periodicals, and finding an audience for your work? Are there magazines you would have liked to have been part of but, for whatever reason, never placed work with them? Would I be correct in thinking that "Famous People" was explicitly intended for *The Saturday Evening Post*, the oldest magazine in the U.S.?

MJ: Three writers shaped my sense of what fiction was or could be, early on: Thomas Hardy, Joseph Conrad, and Graham Greene. I read them uncritically. I was not trying to learn anything specific from them, really, or to figure out how to write, and probably not to extract anything of practical value from their books. I read them, rather, for the sheer pleasure of the story, along with the sense of a world opening up that I had not been able, until I opened the book, to imagine. I read in the possibly naïve faith that they were translating reality, getting at what mattered. I was hungry.

As for lessons learned, I don't know for sure that I have learned any. When I sit down in the morning to write, I often have the sense that I am starting all over again. Nothing matters, in the moment, except the next sentence. (The unexpectedness, the unpredictability of certain writers' next sentences, such as Kafka's, is a source of joy.) The drive to get that proximate sentence right is all-consuming. That said, it seems to me that you have to be ruthless with your own stuff. Cast a deeply critical eye. Frequently. Throw things away: whole stories, a whole novel if you have to. Expand the boundaries of your natural affinities when it comes to what you read. Turn off your phone; forget you have one. Close your email. Write in the space and the time your circumstances give you; I wrote *A Handful of Kings* by hand, on a commuter train, in hard-backed notebooks. In fact, I still write mostly by hand. Transferring a day's work to the computer amounts to the first edit.

Mary Lee Settle gave me one more piece of advice. Find one or at most two people to read your stuff, she said, and tune out everybody else. That notion runs somewhat counter to the way that many writers do it, sharing what they are working on in groups of other people who care about writing or are themselves writers. That seemed to work for them but was never going to be right for me. Of course, I was exceptionally fortunate to have as mentor Robert Ready, whom I would describe as one of America's finest readers. He has worked with numerous writers through the years. There is an imbalance inherent in the relationship between a writer and her primary or first reader. It's exploitative. You ask a lot of that person, and the next time you finish something, there you are again knocking at his door. There may be nothing you can do to change that, but it's good to be aware, at a minimum, of what it requires of that person to give you his best take on your work, time and again.

"Famous People" was not written with *The Saturday Evening Post* in mind. In fact, it was first published in a literary magazine, the *Delmarva Review*. The *Post* editor reached out to me and asked to republish it. It's a comic story. I take a deep delight in writing stuff that is, one hopes, funny. When the *Post* republished the story, I immediately sat down and wrote a follow-up called "Restless People." I'm particularly keen on a comic story forthcoming in *The Hudson Review* called "Stiff," which has to do with an illegal effort to dispose of a dead body.

When it comes to tailoring a story to a specific magazine or a specific editor, I have had absolutely no luck. I've tried, a handful of times. On no occasion was the story or novel I produced taken by the intended target. So I pretty much quit trying.

The question has to do with the one you asked about finding an audience. I can't generalize. Other writers probably have the knack for identifying and pleasing a specifically defined group of readers. Not in my skill set. In fact, I have to go at it in the opposite way. Every story or novel I write establishes its own demands. It wants to be about something, to be something, though perhaps the 'something' is resistant to paraphrase. Just as importantly, it has its own inner logic, which has to be teased out. Part of this is connected with the conventional things one takes into account: plot and pacing and characterization. But it's more than that. I continue to be convinced that a story has a kind of sui generis integrity, without which it will flop. Often it hides or otherwise eludes you. Sometimes you find it, sometimes you don't. When you don't, the story careens off into permanent irrelevance.

For the record, I'd still like to place a story in *The New Yorker*. To date, no dice.

LC: Of all your publishing credits, *Playboy*, in particular, catches the eye. Did you make a conscious effort to appear in that magazine? Was "The Bull You See, The Bull You Don't" written with *Playboy* in mind?

MJ: No, I wasn't thinking at all about *Playboy*. The story idea came to me while I was at a bullfight at Las Ventas in Madrid. (I went with a couple of other Americans who were curious, but they wound up being turned off by the violence involved, no matter how stylish the killing of the bull was meant to be and, in fact, was.) I had lived and worked in Spain previously and went back as part of a State Department team inspecting the American mission there. Certain places seem to goad me into stories; Madrid is one of them. Paraguay and Turkey exercise the same power over me.

LC: As a longtime reader of Kinky Friedman's novels, I was intrigued to come across his glowing recommendation of your books: "if John le Carré were an American, his name would be Mark Jacobs." Other luminaries like Pulitzer Prize winner Robert Olen Butler described you as one of the most exciting new writers he's read, comparing your talents to that of Graham Greene. How does it feel to hear these impressive endorsements? In the course of your travels, literary relationships, and work with the Peace Corps, did you ever meet Friedman or Olen Butler?

MJ: I never met Kinky Friedman, unfortunately. I did meet Robert Olen Butler. This, too, was in Madrid. He was riding high, having won the Pulitzer for a fine collection of short stories, *A Good Scent from a Strange Mountain*. He was generous and enthusiastic, and I'm still grateful for his support. I've run into a handful of well-known writers at different times and in different places, under different circumstances. Bob Butler stands out for his magnanimity. No point naming those who were less than that.

I met the great American poet Robert Creeley in Izmir, Turkey, when he went there on an embassy-sponsored speaking tour. One of the finest nights of my life happened with him in that city. Izmir is on the Aegean. We sat drinking Turkishrakı, until reaching satiety, at a café on the promenade that runs along the Bay. The weather was mild, the night breeze was beneficent. When the time came, I walked him back to his hotel room. On the way, he stopped next to a statue of Kemal Atatürk, took my arm, held a finger in the air, and pronounced in an oracular fashion, "This." Yep. It was this all right, around us everywhere. We were practically swimming in it.

Bob Creeley remained a good friend, bucking me up when my writerly spirits were low. At my request, he came to Asunción, Paraguay, to headline a conference on American studies. I was driving in Fairfax, Virginia, in 2005 when I heard on the radio that Robert Creeley had died. I pulled over to the side of the road and cried.

LC: Your work as a Peace Corps volunteer and employment with the State Department allowed you to experience Turkey, Bolivia, Paraguay, Honduras, and Spain. Obviously, these cultural experiences have enriched your writing. Did your work take you to other continents? Were there parts of the world you would rather have been stationed? I read in a 2016 article that you spend five months a year abroad inspecting American embassies. Did you continue to work overseas until the COVID-19 pandemic?

MJ: I've worked in Africa, the Middle East, and a number of countries in Asia as well. I tend to be drawn to places that are not tourist havens. I particularly liked Cambodia, Tajikistan, and Mali. I no longer work for the State Department's Office of Inspector General, which took me to embassies around the world. I stopped doing that about the time that Covid hit.

LC: The nonfiction project you proposed, *Writers on America*, proved universally popular. Were you involved in deciding which writers took part?

MJ: The idea for *Writers on America* came to me in the wake of the September 11th attacks. It seemed like all anybody was talking about had to do, in one way or another, with terrorism. I thought there were other things to say, other things to hear, other ways of engaging with foreign publics. I proposed the project at the State Department, and a publications team headed by a genuinely literate man, George Clack, took it from there. I had no say in the choice of writers from whom an essay was solicited about what it meant to be an American. The writers George contacted were responsive and enthusiastic and represented a worthy cross-section of American letters.

LC: You once said that "all writing is a kind of failure. The story you write displaces the stories you did not write from the universe of possibilities. The question one keeps asking is this: in the story I chose to write, did I get it right?" Are there previously published stories you find yourself drawn back to, looking over them with a desire to rework or recreate from a new perspective?

MJ: Once a story is published, I take my leave from it. I seldom think of it again. A few times, many years after a story is in print, I've picked one up and read it again. Each time I do, I am surprised by how much I have forgotten. I can't remember where the story is going. It's like the old dementia joke: you keep meeting the nicest people.

LC: Would you mind elucidating the backstory to the novel *Stone Cowboy*? I believe it started out as a short story for *The Atlantic* ("Stone Cowboy on the High Plains"), later morphing into a novel. The aftermath of that short story feels like a strange and sensational fictional movie: protest marches, boycotts, political cartoons, and broad media condemnation, including columns in *The Los Angeles Times* and *The Washington Post*. Were you really burned in effigy?

MJ: The story began in Europe a long time ago, when I traveled for a month with a guy who was the prototype stone cowboy. (His name, in fact, was Roger, and he told me a story that stuck with me about standing on the beach in Spain, holding a harmonica up to the wind and hearing it play.) The controversy began when the Council on Hemispheric Affairs asserted that I identified with the anti-Bolivian sentiments of Roger, the stone cowboy in the story. There was a short-lived media frenzy, mostly in Latin America, but the contretemps was echoed in some of the American media as well. I found it painful to be condemned as I was, but one grits his teeth and keeps going. I was gone from La Paz by the time the story appeared and the issue blew up, but I was told that yes, I was burned in effigy. Quite possibly, no one took pictures.

Shortly thereafter, a book editor in New York suggested

I make the *Atlantic Monthly* story into a novel. It went through several versions. The writing was complicated by the demands of my job. I was in the U.S. embassy in Asunción, doing my own public affairs and spokesman job, acting for long stretches as the ambassador's deputy, and presiding over a school board that was melting down into dysfunction due mostly to personality conflicts. My time to write was severely restricted. I finished the novel by the time I transferred to the Madrid embassy, but by then, the New York editor who made the original suggestion had disappeared from my horizon.

LC: Conversely, in terms of critical reception for the novel, you couldn't have asked for better. *Kirkus Reviews* described it as "an impressive debut from a writer with a generous imagination and a daring, if deeply weird, sense of character and fate." *Publishers Weekly* applauded the "lucid, sinewy prose" and your "intimate knowledge of the Bolivian people and landscape," and *Library Journal* called it "essential reading for anyone attempting to understand the human side of our drug policies." Did the controversy surrounding your short story make you want to distance yourself from it? Did unanimous support for your novel vindicate the writing?

MJ: I never had the slightest inclination to distance myself from the story. The stubbornness I mentioned above kicked in. I knew there was nothing offensive in "Stone Cowboy on the High Plains." The controversy over Rushdie's *The Satanic Verses* was still fresh. I was heartened by an op-ed in one of the La Paz newspapers entitled "The Satanic Verses of Mark Jacobs," which not only defended my intentions but made a strong case for the necessary independence of fiction and fiction writers.

As for vindication, it involves an emotion that is a luxury I can't afford if I'm going to get the work done.

LC: I've long been an admirer of Soho Press, so I'm curious about your experiences with them. How did you get involved with the publisher? Did the experience differ greatly regarding your subsequent novel, *A Handful of Kings*, published with Simon & Schuster?

MJ: Juris Jurjevics was the editor-in-chief of Soho at the time. He liked the novel but thought the ending was weak. I was in Madrid. I stayed up most of one night thinking about his criticism, then quickly rewrote the ending in a way that seemed consonant with his recommendations but also true to my sense of Roger. I was pleased that Juris also published a book of short stories, *The Liberation of Little Heaven*, now out of print.

LC: It's been more than ten years since the publication of your last novel, *Forty Wolves*. Are you working on a new novel, pursuing a suitable publisher for completed projects, or focusing on short story collections?

MJ: I have stories, I have novels. We'll see what happens.

LC: Concerning the impetus for a story, you once said they develop in different ways. "Sometimes it starts with a character. Other times it's a situation, or the flavor of a memory. Once in a while, it's just a phrase." Your latest story, "After the Meltdown, On the Hunt," is an interesting variation on the big game hunt tales and the various Connell derivatives. What motivated you to write this story?

MJ: I've always been drawn to dystopic fiction, dystopic movies. *1984* and *Brave New World* are perfect complementary halves of a nightmarish future. Whether humankind will be undone by coercion or diversion, or some canny combination of the two, is a question worth posing. "After the Meltdown" came to me as a way of thinking about how people allow themselves to become accustomed to brutality, gradually and insensibly, until it becomes the gruesome new normal. The story's narrator is not a highly principled individual. His rejection of the hunt and the hunters takes time—the length of the story—to come to fruition.

Clandestine
Lorraine Caputo

That cargo train that arrives every other day will be my, and anyone else's, ticket out of these mountains. There's no other way to reach this village now.

When that *tren carguero* (cargo train) comes into town and stops at the old station, I pop down to talk with the crew. We sit on the platform's wooden benches in the fading colored light of another dying day. Moths flit around the bulbs lit as night arrives. They tell me how, since the railroad was privatized, passenger services have been dropping like proverbial flies. Sometimes a line with be canceled the night before, news arriving to the *jefe de patio* (station chief) by telegram.

And thus it was with my planned route to the capital. My itinerary has had to be scrapped, as the train no longer arrives at the transfer point. On the concrete platform, the rail workers and I study the maps, looking for an alternative route. The first leg will be hitching a ride with them.

Almost a month ago, I had ridden the last passenger train to this village deep in the sierra and took a room in the village's only inn near the depot. I have spent the time talking with locals about their lives and how life will go on (or not) now that there's no train (officially).

In a small, hole-in-the-wall eatery, I met a woman who was surprised there was no longer a train. She had heard nothing about it—how would she get to her aunt's birthday party in a few weeks' time?

The middle-aged daughter of the inn's owner will be emigrating to the great north in search of work; a young couple will be her centenary mother's caretakers. I have spent evenings sitting in a kitchen lit only by an oil lamp, eating cookies and milk while listening to that *anciana's* memories of the Revolution.

I have spent many hours, too, writing, recording these memories, these stories, and images…

When the day comes for me to move on, I wait until first light and the crow song to leave. As I walk down to the locomotive shed, heavy mists rise from streams and rivers. The *sierra* is bathed in clouds.

The engineer pushes his cap back and greets me. "Would you like to ride in the second locomotive or the caboose?"

What a choice! For a train aficionada like me, it's like being a kid in a candy shop. Ay, but riding in the caboose will be riding with the people, conversations, eating, learning. I shift my Rocinante (that is, my faithful travel companion, my knapsack) on my back. "With permission, sir, the caboose," I respond.

I walk by eight cars loaded with timber. Aside from the ninth and last one, the yellow caboose, five other clandestine passengers await. A mother and a grandmother watch their two young boys kicking rocks that clang against the metal rails. The conductor's girlfriend clasps her hands in front of herself, an overnight bag at her feet.

I climb the grate-steps into the caboose. I drop Rocinante in a cubbyhole before climbing the narrow steps into the cupola and taking a seat there. My neighbor is the *carretero* (brakeman). The conductor joins our conversation about the changes the new rail owners have brought (and wrought).

I sink into the beauty of a train ride. It is much different from traveling through a country by bus because the rails wend into deep countryside and landscapes, and trains pass only once a day or only several times a week. Wildlife is more abundant. It is like signing up for a safari! And the local human life one gets to observe, from children playing in front of adobe homes, mothers hanging flapping laundry on a line, farmers in a small plot of land. The small villages of whitewashed houses and a lone parish church—now to be endangered species.

I watch the thick clouds drift around and over the crag-faced mountains. The countryside is greener after last night's rain. A yellow tree brightens in the early morning sun of this agéd autumn. Other *árboles* are turning burnt orange. The undergrowth is browned by the cooler weather. In a field of harvest-gold corn, two campesinos tie the stalks into standing bundles.

Our train speeds along, horn-blowing and slowing for villages, not stopping. No longer does this train have an obligation to stop to pick up passengers—officially, there are none. And like the village from where we departed, those people, too, will have no way out. There are many villages like this that are now isolated. We roll on, rattling, clicking, swaying southward—but many of those townsfolk will be heading northward, migrating in search of work. In the distance rises a blue steeple bell tower.

At the outskirts of a village, more clandestine passengers—two women, four children—slip on. A man at trackside asks the conductor when they will pass again. May he ride then? The conductor gives him a thumbs up before we roll on, ever southward.

The kilometers click by. From out of the small windows of this cupola, I watch the countryside. A blue heron soars upstream just inches above the river's surface. Far from its *pueblo*, a cemetery gleams bright white in the sun breaking through yesterday's nebulous sky. A hawk atop a tree peers across the cold, damp morning.

We stop at the most important town between where we were and where we are going. Those newer stowaways go only as far as here. The train is growing in length. More open freighters, heavy with raw logs, are added. Before we reach our journey's end, we will haul nineteen cars.

A dog and his young boy run down the dirt path along the tracks. The dog races us, falling behind one car after another until this yellow caboose clacks past him. The boy waves and yells adios.

In one corner of this caboose, the workers cook their lunch on the diesel stove. The aroma drifts through this small railcar, wafting into nooks and up to this cramped cupola. The smell touches my stomach. The railroaders invite their passengers to join them in a feast of beans, tortillas, and stewed beef. One *carretero* pours steaming, syrupy coffee into metal cups. For our dessert, I add a jar of peaches the family at that village's inn had gifted me.

We climb high and deep into the *sierra*, winding along rough-rock walls. Thin waterfalls snag on the splintered stone like stray threads. Gullies fall off steeply into unseeable depths. The heavily forested mountains crumble into one another. Clouds drift through their valleys.

We pass by scattered farm fields deadened by the coming winter. Grasses bow under the weight of dew. The sun sears the thick, sullen blanket of clouds. Bright blue sky seeps through.

At a field of shriveled vines in the middle of nowhere, the engineers stop the train—the diesel motors hum like out-of-season cicadas. The *maquinistas* run out, hauling squash after squash into the locomotive cabs. The clandestine boys aboard this caboose also dash out. They carry one squash after another into this car. When we leave, six large *calabazas* roll about the floor with the rhythm of our journey.

Later, down the line, we suddenly brake mysteriously. Beneath our wheels lie two cows. The *zopilote* buzzards begin circling near us. As the caboose rides over the beasts, the sour smell of their flesh fills the swelling heat of the afternoon. A rabbit hops down into an *arroyo seco*, fleeing our rumbling train.

Up in this cupola, I fall asleep. The warmth of that star soothes my face, my tired body. In the hazes of my dreams, I hear the girlfriend reading off numbers to the conductor as he fills out his paperwork. Their knees touch and depart, like dancers moving in time with this train's syncopated melody.

In my dreams, dense smoke suffocates me, burning my closed eyes. I claw the darkness to escape this nightmare. I awaken.

The inside of this caboose blackens with the stove belching fumes, licking up flames. I stumble, half-falling out of my seat in the cupola. We all—railroad workers and clandestine passengers—move away to the far end, coughing, rubbing eyes. One of the *carretero's* dampens the fire. It recedes into the belly of the stove.

(Uff! If this car had gone up in flames and exploded, how would all the extra bodies within the burnt, splintered remains be explained? How much more illegal can this ride get—clandestine passengers, stealing from farm fields, killing some *campesino's* cattle. Next …?)

A roadrunner (a trickster, old-timers say they are) crosses the desert. A golden horse runs wild, its black mane streaming in the sun. And we run wild, clacking, swaying southward, ever southward.

At dusk, we roll steadily through the railyards of our destination. But we clandestine passengers cannot be seen by the *jefe de patio* or any railroad exec that might be around.

To hide our reality, our presence (and this train's crew's blatant disregard for the dictates of the new owners), the caboose stops at the far end of the platform. We clandestine passengers slip along the tracks to a distant gate, blending into the growing shadows of the coming night. The conductor waves a quick, silent goodbye to us and walks off to the station, embracing his girlfriend.

Your Intersections with Nature
William Doreski

The slump of autumn invokes
bone-white sticks and mossy rocks
too stubborn to crack in frost.

You like walking in the woods
where rabid animals congregate
and spit up their little lives.

You like to see the ponds freeze
like the cataracts you someday
will have to surgically excise.

I don't want to disparage
your intersections with nature
but you might avoid the snakes

flirting from bedrock ledges
and the spiders mapping places
too dark for the human soul.

Every year crumbles like cake.
Every summer generosity
fades like an old watercolor.

You agree that every temper
is seasonal, that the incline
to Christmas is always too steep

for us to maintain a foothold.
Yet you persist by embracing
the dying parts of the planet

and weeping over their vacancies.
Today the equinoctial storms
arrive with hail and pearly gusts.

We must stand up to them but
I wonder if you're still committed
to the angular fate of our race.

Seniors on the Move
William Doreski

Worry lines divide the sky.
Lightning could cancel our hike,
even cancel us. Our little group
shelters in a lean-to built
by Boy Scouts after school
almost half a century ago.

The smell of rot doesn't stop you
from crowding a sleeping bag
with your lover, whose gestures
suggest millstones grinding wheat.
I look away, into the distance
pouring over hazy peaks.

The storm breaks with a roar of rain
alloyed with antimony and zinc.
Trees toss their mane, and boulders
open their pores. A hawk circles
with royal disregard for the wind.
I can't watch your sleeping bag writhe

so with the rest of our group
I stare at collapsing horizons
until my eyes hurt. The shame
of such overstated weather
reminds me that childhood guilt
encapsulates to tease old age.

Our clutch of hikers suffers
not only from age but apologies
for age, our compromised sight
and sorry muscles rebuking us,
and you and your lover chuckling
like bullfrogs mating in puddles.

The First American Explorers to Canyon de Chelly
David Hagerty

The motorcar rattled to a stop at the head of the canyon, and a family of pale Americans stepped out. They dressed wildly—a father in white trousers and skunk-striped shoes, a mother in a flour sack dress and bell-shaped hat covering her short hair, and a red-headed boy in pants that reached only his knees—looking as out of place on the reservation as a parrot. Despite their flamboyance, they advanced toward the Indian as they would an unfamiliar dog they feared might be aggressive. Once they stood close enough for him to smell the woman's scent—of some foreign flower—she said, "Can you help us? We're visitors."

Rather than acknowledge the obvious, Aditsan waited for her to continue, the image of the strong, silent Indian. His name meant listener, and he'd always found it safest to adhere to the moniker around the bilagáana

"Do you speak English?" the woman said slowly, enunciating each word.

He nodded but said nothing.

"Thank goodness. You're just about the only person here that does. Where is the road to the bottom?"

Aditsan looked toward the mouth of the canyon, which followed the Chinle wash through porous sand, then back at their Model T, its black metal gleaming in the sun like the railroads that pushed onto Dinétah many years before, bringing the first Americans. "There is none," he said.

"How do you get through?"

He inclined his chin toward his horse and wagon.

The woman glanced back at her husband, who was wiping

the red dust from his white shoes with a handkerchief. "I suppose we could see most of it from the rim?"

Aditsan nodded and turned away, only to hear the boy whine, "But you said we could go in."

"Wait!" said the woman. "Can you take us?"

Not long before, Corky O'Bannon, owner of the local trading post, predicted that Canyon de Chelly would soon draw tourists to Dinétah. "Everyone wants to meet you Navvies," he said.

Most tribesmen scoffed. Why would Americans travel for days over rough wagon ruts to see Navajo grazing lands? Still, the entrepreneur talked of national parks and tours led by Fred Harvey.

Aditsan shared the skepticism of his kin, though for other reasons. For years, he'd traded and worked with Americans, enduring enough of their exploitative commerce to know their disdain for traditional ways. Besides, when had the nation ever shown interest in Indian country?

"I'll pay you a sawbuck," said the husband.

Aditsan knew how to price rugs and jewelry, but tours were a new commodity. He calculated how much food he could purchase with ten dollars, then nodded.

The trail descended gently, following the stream past clusters of yucca and cottonwood, into the red rock of the canyon. Both mother and son looked comfortable on the buckboard, rolling with the dips and divots of the river wash, but her husband struggled to sit upright in the bed, gripping the rails as though he feared falling off. Several times he groaned in pain when the wagon ran over a ditch.

"Go faster!" said the boy.

"This is fast enough," said his father.

Around them, the canyon's walls drew closer, amplifying the trickle of water. A dry wind carried yellow leaves from the cottonwoods and the scent of roasting piñon nuts. Aditsan enjoyed the tranquility until the woman filled the silence.

"I can see why the automobile has replaced these," she said. "Riding out in the open, you eat all the wind and dust. And this wool! It's positively primitive. We're lucky that little James is so hearty. But really, if you're going to carry people, you need a hansom. You can't expect all youngsters to adapt to such rough passage."

While the woman kept up a ceaseless sermon about the amenities expected by tourists, her husband did not speak for many minutes. When finally he did, he uttered only one word: "Stop." He said it so forcefully that the horse startled and trotted another dozen paces.

As soon as they halted, the passenger leaned sideways and vomited, eliciting gasps from his wife and giggles from his son. Aditsan looked away and waited for him to finish, yet once he'd expelled his beans and fry bread, he slid from his perch and landed in his own spittle. Even stationary, he looked unnaturally pale, with a trickle of drool hanging from his mouth. "No more riding," he said.

———— ✦ ————

The father continued on foot, trudging behind the wagon as though captive, forcing the party to halt frequently so he could catch up.

"I remember these old carriages," the wife said during one respite. "I grew up with them. My father maintained a whole stable to pull our buggy. Now, living in town, I hardly ever see them. People mostly travel by cable car."

"What's that?" Aditsan said.

"You never heard of one? I guess you wouldn't, living all

the way out here, but in San Francisco, where we're from, it's the easiest way to get around. Until the Model T, that is. Nowadays, nobody uses a hackney.

"You all should really build roads. I mean, if you want to appease visitors, you'll have to make some adjustments. You can't have people risking their lives on this trail...."

To distract himself from her prattle, Aditsan checked on the boy's father, who trailed in their backwash, his shoes and white pants stained brown by mud. For this, the guide decided to call him the Dust Man.

——◆——

The river descended so gradually that its fall was perceptible only by the rise of the canyon around, yet soon the walls reached many times taller than a tree. To an outsider, their party might appear as an alliance of settlers investigating a foreign land, except Lewis and Clark never navigated the streams of Dinétah.

As they rolled over a sand bar, the boy turned to Aditsan and studied his guide for an uncomfortable time. "You're not a real Indian."

"Face forward, James," said his mother.

The boy ignored her and continued to stare until Aditsan asked, "How's that?"

"You dress like a cowboy. Real Indians have feathers and moccasins."

Aditsan noted the brush of his jeans and the stiffness of his leather soles. "Most Navajo dress this way," he said. "The boots work better for riding."

"What about your hair?" said the boy to his guide. "How come you tie it up?"

Although it broke with tradition to do so, Aditsan removed his headband, letting his long tresses flow down his back. "Convinced?"

The boy touched Aditsan's hair as he would a horse's mane, then answered, "Nope."

———— ✦ ————

At the canyon's divide, Aditsan paused to consider where to lead his party next. Most bilagáana showed more interest in things than people, captivated by rugs and pots and jewels, even as they ignored their makers. Maybe they'd like the petroglyphs that dotted the walls with images of tribes and animals long extinct.

"Where are the ruins?" the woman said.

Of course, Aditsan knew the ones she meant, but still, he asked, "What?"

"The ones from the cliff people."

"Scattered," Aditsan said.

"I want to see," said the boy, all eagerness and greed.

"Most hide up high near the rim," Aditsan said. "You can't get close to them."

"There's none at ground level?" the woman said.

Nearby, a waxwing called to its mate as Aditsan debated his reply. "One."

"Then show us that."

———— ✦ ————

They followed the stream into the main branch of the canyon until the walls rose so high that they obscured the sun. Once they came within sight of an octagon of mud packed around a timber skeleton, the boy pointed and said, "What's that?"

"A house," said Aditsan.

"Where are the tee-pees?"

"We don't have those. We live in hogans."

"All Indians live in tee-pees."

"For those, you need hides, and buffalo are hard to catch."

"Buffalo?" said the boy's mother. "I haven't seen any. Why don't you show us those?"

Aditsan stifled a smile and led them around the dwelling. Once they'd passed out of earshot, he paused to let the boy's father catch up. Instead, he sat on a sandstone ledge and wiped his face with a handkerchief, which only spread the dust into moist swirls like a river's eddy.

As everyone waited, the woman shielded her eyes to scan the canyon. "Is there nowhere to get a drink down here?"

Aditsan nodded toward the stream that trickled through the center.

"That filthy thing?"

Aditsan refrained from commenting that the river ran purest in the dry season when the silt had settled to the bottom, and no storms disturbed it.

"I don't see how you people survive," she said, "with no bathrooms or faucets!"

Aditsan looked to the squash and cornfields by the river, which to anyone should have signaled fecundity, especially in the high desert. "This canyon has sustained people for many generations."

"Those little sprigs wouldn't feed a crow."

Overhead, the clouds passed swiftly on winds blocked by the canyon walls, reminding Aditsan of nature's potency. He decided to call her the Blind Seer.

———— ✦ ————

When they came to Kiníí' Na'ígai, the house with white streaks across it, even the Blind Seer fell silent, staring with awe. The ancient dwelling nestled in a sandstone cove, its red bricks camouflaged by the canyon walls behind it. Despite its age, it rose several stories, with dozens of rooms intact many generations after it had been abandoned.

"We call this the White House," Aditsan said.

"Who built it?" the woman said.

"Anasazi. Our enemy's ancestors."

"And you just let them live here? I wouldn't welcome my enemy to move in right next door to me."

"It was before us. Before we emerged—" Aditsan started to explain how the Diné came from the earth, then silenced himself. Missionaries laughed at the story of his people's origins—since everyone knew the first humans were Adam and Eve—and persecuted anyone who said otherwise.

After an idle moment, the boy jumped from the wagon and ran to the ruins, tracing his fingers over its rough walls.

"Is it safe?" said the woman.

Aditsan recalled his grandmother's warnings about the place—that it contained chindi, spirits of the dead, which could bring ghost sickness. "People are buried inside."

"JAMES," his mother called. "Leave that be."

From her handbag, she extracted a black box that fit in her palm and produced a click like a bird. Aditsan had seen a camera once before when the headmaster at his Indian school wanted a class photo for his office, but not such a compact one. After several moments, he asked the woman where the picture waited.

"Inside."

Aditsan still did not understand how such a small box could hide a photo the size of writing paper, but he didn't want to question her, fearing that it would provoke more derision. Instead, he debated silently where to take the family next—to another ruin or Spider Rock—until the woman asked her husband, "Where's little James?"

The Dust Man slumped on a fallen cottonwood, looking defeated by his untidiness. "He was right here."

"JAMES!" Her voice caromed off the canyon walls without reply. Aditsan scanned in all directions to where the stream wound behind the rock walls, but he saw no one.

"I'll wager he's playing inside," said the Dust Man, pointing toward the ruin. "You know how he is."

"How he is?" said Blind Seer.

"Always into something."

"Only when no one's watching. He hates being ignored. JAMES!" she shouted toward the building, but again only her own voice echoed in response.

"Go look for him," she said.

Aditsan thought she was speaking to her husband, but she stared at him instead. "He would hear you calling."

"He might be playing hide and seek. You have to check."

Aditsan scrutinized the ancient site with its crumbling walls of loose mud brick. "He's nearby," Aditsan said. "No other trails lead out." He turned his back to the one behind them, which trickled invisibly from the sandstone.

"We're paying you to guide us," said the man. "If my son gets lost, expect no money."

Money concerned Aditsan the least. He would gladly forsake the ten dollars to be rid of these trespassers, but his conscience wouldn't allow him to abandon them in the canyon. Who knew what havoc they might cause? So he strode toward the ruin and called the boy's name again.

After a long silence, filled only by the wind whistling through the rock, Aditsan turned to the parents. "He's not there."

"How do you know without checking?" the woman said.

"There's nothing to interest a child."

"I'll bet you played there plenty of times when you were young."

Aditsan resisted explaining again his ancestor's prohibitions. Even to him, they sounded superstitious, yet something about the place repelled him, like a house that recalled bad times. He moved closer so that he could peer over the low, broken walls but saw nothing. The dirt floors held a few sticks and strands of plant fibers, probably nests from some bird or animal.

"He's not here," Aditsan called back.

"Look in back," said the Dust Man. "He likes to burrow."

Aditsan circled the structure and peered into the shadows. As he leaned in, something shrieked past him, brushing his face and knocking him backward. His next sensations were confused: pain at the back of his head, a rush of blood in his ears, a struggle for breath. His eyes were still throbbing when the Dust Man called, "It was just a bird. Check the tower."

A small doorway accessed a square chamber several stories high, but to reach it, Aditsan had to scramble up the rock walls, digging in his fingers and toes until they cramped with pain. Inside, the room pressed down upon him, too low for modern man to stand, so he squatted amid the dust and the debris: a straw mat, a pottery fragment, and a denuded corncob. Tentatively, he pawed the ground until he felt something solid and leathery, then drew it back toward him—a dusty shoe of modern vintage, yet too large for the boy. Overhead, square holes led higher into the ruin, but the roof sagged already without added weight. Aditsan left the artifacts and climbed out.

"He's not there," Aditsan said.

"What about there?" said the Blind Seer. She pointed to a second tier of buildings embedded in a cove, but it lay several times higher than a man, with only narrow handholds cut into the rock.

"There's no way in," Aditsan said.

"There must be," said the woman.

"Not for a boy."

"You must find him."

To show her determination, she sat on the log next to her

husband and rocked herself as she would a baby, mumbling reminders of her cherished offspring. The Dust Man stood and walked toward Aditsan, looking forceful. "I thought all you Indians were expert trackers."

Face to face, Aditsan measured several inches taller and broader, yet the father looked so determined he nodded and scanned the sand for clues. Overtop their own tracks ran another set heading back the way they'd come. After a hundred paces, the prints split, with one pair heading to the wash. He followed this spur until it ended at the water's edge, with the couple following just behind.

"My God, he's drowned! Has he drowned?" cried the Blind Seer.

The Dust Man stepped so close that Aditsan could smell the vomit on his breath. "My wife is very delicate. If she's upset, it could take days for her to recover."

Since the dry season had depleted the stream, the boy would have to lie face down to gag. Still, the trail eluded him until he saw a large bank of sandstone across the water with a broken tree limb at the boy's height. Past it, the prints resumed.

Behind, the woman cried, "He's lost! Is he lost? He must be lost."

Her husband said, "He's just wandered off."

The parents followed Aditsan's every step, second-guessing him each time he paused. At the top of a rise, prints led to the hogan, but a dense weaving covered its doorway, so Aditsan stopped several paces away and called inside, "Yá'át'ééh."

"What are you waiting for? Just knock," said the Blind Seer.

"That's not our way."

Shortly an old woman pulled back the curtain. She wore a traditional wrap banded in blue, white, and red: a chief's blanket from a prior era. This elder would expect a formal greeting, so in their own language, Aditsan introduced himself as being of the Salt Clan and the Bitter Water Clan. After a polite pause, the woman explained her own family connections until the Blind Seer interrupted, crying, "Has she seen our James?"

"We're looking for a little boy," Aditsan said, still using his native language, "a bilagáana, with red hair and no manners."

"He's here," the old woman said. She lifted the blanket to reveal James sitting quietly by a fire. Before Aditsan could say more, his mother pushed past both Diné to clasp her child.

"Are you hurt?" she said.

While she assessed his scratches, the old woman explained that she'd discovered the boy stroking a sheep. "He acted as though he'd never touched one before."

———— ✦ ————

Within minutes, all of them sat inside the hogan, inhaling the wood smoke of the fire while eating the woman's mutton stew. Custom required that she share her meal with guests—even intruders. While Aditsan enjoyed the tenderness of the meat, the bilagáana only picked at it.

"How long have you lived here?" said the Blind Seer.

In her own language, the woman explained that her family emerged from the third world to inhabit Canyon de Chelly during the time of Monster Slayer, that her great-grandparents died at Massacre Cave, and that during the raids by Kit Carson, her mother hid on Fortress Rock.

"A long time," Aditsan translated.

"Surely she said more than that," said the Blind Seer.

But Aditsan would no longer explain things she could not comprehend.

The Aeronautical Lawn Chair
Don Noel

To my astonishment, Dad welcomed the idea like an old friend. He'd heard a story years ago about someone doing the same thing.

"Jean Shepherd," he told the four of us. "Greatest storyteller of my time." Apparently, on WOR, a radio station in New York where he'd lived back in the 50s and 60s. "Never knew whether the stories were true or not," he added.

We would soon find out. We were east of Helena, on a stretch of pastureland off Highway 287 below Louisville. We'd seen a few joggers, but the area was otherwise deserted. Dad sat comfortably in a big wicker lawn chair with comfortable cushions. Four clusters of balloons were tied to the arms and back corners.

What balloons! They were orbs the size of medicine balls, drab gray weather balloons designed to carry instruments up into storm clouds to send back data. The whole thing was my pal Jerry's idea; his community college physics professor had helped him find the balloons. Later in the day, when they became hard to spot against gathering clouds, we would wish they were more colorful, but early in the morning, we had no reason to anticipate that.

And we had no idea what the lift would be; the professor was offering Jerry extra credit to find out. How high off the ground could $120 worth of helium—two 12-pound tanks, thirty cubic feet, evenly distributed in balloons—lift a 200-pound man?

We'd aimed at four or five balloons at each corner, but the tanks gave out after only three. Just as well, as it turned out. "The professor says solar heating makes air expand, and helium too," Jerry said, "so, once the sun comes up, there should be plenty of lift." In case his optimism proved warranted, we'd bought 100 feet of clothesline and had four 25-foot guy lines tied to the legs of the chair to keep Dad from getting away.

When we tethered him at 25 feet up, he should be able to see back to Helena and have a view of the Missouri River, where it bellies out into a wide lake.

The sun edged over the horizon, bright in a blue sky. "How about a seat belt?" Dad said. For the first time, he sounded a bit nervous. "This contraption just may rock around, and I don't want to be shaken out." At his age, he added, "I could break a leg from six feet off the ground."

Howie found a multi-colored silk scarf his wife had left in the pickup, long enough to wrap around Dad's hips and knot behind the chair. He protested but then decided that being securely trussed into his lawn chair was a good idea.

The sun was well up by now. We'd unknowingly held him down while strapping him in; the moment we stepped back, the chair surged six feet over our heads. We each grabbed a guy line. Dad bobbed around a bit, but we soon had him stabilized and back down to maybe four feet off the ground.

"I think," Dad said, sounding calmer than I would have, "I should have a sharp knife with me to puncture a few balloons if need be."

That proved the decisive moment. In unison, Jerry and Howie each said they had sheath knives in the truck and ran to get them. Bill and I still had the front lines, which we held down as the back of the chair rose dramatically, tilting Dad forward. He would have been pitched out had he not been strapped in with that silk scarf.

"Let go!" he shouted.

We did.

"No!" he said in the next breath. "I mean, grab the other ropes too!"

Too late. He went up like an elevator, the guy lines whipping in the air. The other two guys came running back, but the ropes were well beyond our reach. Dad and his aeronautical lawn chair reached equilibrium with gravity, maybe forty feet up.

"Make a note," said Jerry, mindful of his extra credit. "Two 12-pound tanks of helium lift a 200-pound man to 40 feet off the ground at . . ."—he checked his watch—". . . 8 a.m., an hour after sunrise." He looked up. "Now, how do we get him down?"

The morning was still warming; Dad and the chair were gently ascending again.

Howie proved the coolest: "Call him on his cell phone!"

I did. It rang for a while. We could see Dad fishing through the silk scarf to dig it out of his pocket. He finally answered, and I handed the phone to Howie.

"Mr. Armstrong," he said, "try to reach down and untie those guy ropes. Pull them up into your lap and tie them together. Then we'll have one long rope that will reach the ground."

"OK," Dad said. "I wish I had a knife."

We could see him stowing the phone again, then reaching gingerly down for the ropes. He got the front two loose but couldn't reach the knots on the back legs. Finally, he pulled up one of those back ropes, tied on both lengths from the front, and lowered away. Too late; he was now well past 75 feet up.

Just then, a KXLH news van and a police cruiser appeared. One of the joggers had seen what was happening and called both the station and the police, sending photos when Dad was only 40 feet or so off the ground.

"What's going on?" asked the cop.

"Does he have a phone?" asked the reporter.

I let Jerry explain to the police; I started to dial Dad again on my phone.

"No, give me the number," the reporter said. "I need to get him on a live line." In a moment, he was dialing, and we could see Dad squirming in the chair to get his phone out again. "What's his name?" the reporter asked. I told him.

"Mr. Armstrong," he said into his phone, "hold on a moment." He turned to face his cameraman. "This is Tom Dennis," he intoned, "live here, within a mile or two of the Missouri River. A local man, Arnold Armstrong, is in the air above me in a lawn chair suspended by balloons. We're going to pan up now to give you a look. I have Mr. Armstrong on the line. How are you doing, sir?"

"Doing just great, thank you."

I knew my father: I could tell from his voice that a moment's television fame had eradicated any fear.

"How's the view?" Tom Dennis prompted.

"Great! I can see planes landing and taking off at Helena Airport."

"I expect so, sir. My producer back at the studio tells me pilots are being warned to stay clear of you. Am I imagining, or are you drifting east?"

"You're right," Dad said. "I am. But it's a gentle breeze. I'll be out over the Canyon Ferry Lake in a while."

"And how will you come down, sir?"

"Damned if I know."

I won't belabor it; you can imagine what the rest of the morning was like. Another TV station arrived with a drone camera, so they had terrific close-up pictures of Dad as he answered telephone questions. He had a series of radio and TV interviews until almost noon, when he discovered that his phone had less than 20 percent power left. He declined any more broadcast stuff and turned it off, saving it for emergency use wherever and whenever he landed.

He was, by now, halfway across the Missouri River, which was more than a mile wide at that point. Prompted by police, a man had phoned from the Goose Bay Marina to say he had a cabin cruiser and volunteered to come over to ferry us and track Dad's progress. Several TV crews had lined up boats, too.

Dad neared the eastern shore in mid-afternoon, but then a wind shift began pushing him southward toward the area where the Missouri and lake got to be two miles wide. I began to worry about a water landing. A state trooper had hurried up to the bridge at Canyon Ferry and was on his way down toward Goose Bay, trying to anticipate where the breeze would steer Dad. He was joined by a fleet of TV vans. Some network and cable guys had shown up.

Meantime, Amazon had reached us, offering to deliver Dad a hamburger and milkshake by their still-experimental package delivery drone. With his phone turned off, I couldn't reach him to explain. Lest he panicked and thought he was under attack, I turned that idea down. Besides, it occurred to me that the less he ate and drank while in the air, far from any men's room, the better he would be.

Thickening clouds as he drifted to the south made it harder to see him but also cooled the helium, so he started coming down. He finally lucked into a soft landing on the Old Baldy Golf Course at about 5:45; a squad of troopers promptly punctured the balloons so he wouldn't be dragged.

With equally remarkable collaboration, a gaggle of television teams arranged a mass live interview, the lawn chair behind him, a forest of microphones in front, that led the 6 p.m. news on every broadcast and cable station.

"Mr. Armstrong," one of the reporters asked, "could you ever have imagined a day like the one you've had?"

"Oh, sure," said Dad. "Heard a story just like mine six decades ago, on radio. A guy named Jean Shepherd, on station WOR. One of the great raconteurs of that era.

"I'd thought maybe Shep made it up," he added. "But I guess it was real after all. We just proved it, didn't we?"

Death by Elephant
Roger Camp

Straddling the Kerala highway
our Ambassador's beetle green roof pales
against the chlorophyll jungle
across the road, firecrackers explode
blessings for *Vishnu*.

Our trembling rearview mirrors a pachyderm
fast approaching, confirming things are closer
than they appear.
Resigned to a trampling, I turn to photograph
death by elephant.

An elephantine shuffle sidesteps the car
a trunkful of fronds sweeping the roof
as I release the shutter.

Editing the images
I see a shaken frame within a frame
a blurred rear window smeared palm green.

Riding the Midnight Express to Tangier
Roger Camp

for William Wertz

We boarded the train in Rabat
    a classic 1st class compartment
with wooden seats
                plush to ourselves.

My fevered body no match
    for the burning North African desert
on a desperate run
              to Spain,

seeking medicine for dysentery.
    Tremulous with chills, brain fogged,
our unscheduled stop
             in the sandy void

birthing a hallucination.
    The moonlit white robes,
a shimmering mirage of Bedouins
                  flooding the train

streaming to our seats. My disordered mind
    invented a headline, *Two Travelers Murdered*.
Waving his woven Peruvian bag
              that held camera and film

Bill weaved a web of brilliant threads
    swathing the cabin in swirls of color
a delusional texture so dense

                                it scattered the intruders.

As the train entered Tangier
    we witnessed the conductor
collecting copper coins from the nomads,

                            the desert stop

a simple bribe
    benefiting both tribes.

The Roof Is on Fire
Ben von Jagow

On one especially hot day in July of 2016, I found myself walking through Big Spring, Texas. I had spent the previous night camping on a small patch of grass behind a department store and had fled the scene just after dawn. After a supermarket breakfast, I began heading north towards Highway 20, where, if all went according to plan, I would hitch a ride west to Odessa.

Despite being early, the sun was high in the sky, baking the pavement, cooking the streets. I had been walking for close to twenty minutes and was already drenched in sweat when I heard someone shout from across the street.

"Hey, guy."

Being the only person dim enough to stroll the Texas streets in the heart of summer, I knew the call was directed at me. I turned and saw a tattooed gentleman standing atop a roof. He was waving me over.

As I crossed the street, I took note that the man was not alone atop his roof. Four or five other shirtless individuals, no less tattooed than he, were casually hammering at nails, lugging bags, pulling shingles.

Ah, I thought, roofers.

"What are you doing?" asked the man once I was in earshot.

"Walking to the highway," I said.

This caught the attention of a few of the workers. They had stopped attending to their tasks and were evidently trying to decide if what they had just heard was worth any further attention.

"Why?" he said.

I began to think about how I was going to answer when

he interrupted me.

"You want a job?"

I blinked. Recession, my ass.

"No, thanks," I said. "I need to be getting to Odessa."

"How are you getting to Odessa?" came out as "How you gittin' ta Dessah?"

"Just going to hitch a ride somewhere near the highway," I said.

This caught the attention of the entire crew.

"What?" asked the inked man.

I scoured my brain for an explanation but found nothing. All of a sudden, I was very conscious of the five men staring down at me, literally and figuratively. "I'm not crazy," I wanted to say and probably would've done so if one of the workers, positioned on the roof's crest, hadn't spoken.

"I'll take ya," he said with the nonchalant air of someone volunteering to take out the trash.

I turned towards him. He was using a flathead to pry loose a stubborn shingle.

"Yeah," he said, not interrupting his work. "I got a meeting with my parole officer in Midland, so I'll drop you off."

Before I could comprehend the significance of what I had just been told, the first guy piped up.

"Perfect. You can work half the day, make a little money, and then ride up with Keith."

And so, just like that, I found myself atop a roof in Big Spring, Texas, pulling shingles, where, at the day's end, I would depart for Odessa with "Keith."

After agreeing to the terms, I started to contemplate if this was, in fact, an intelligent decision. I knew I'd be taking a chance with Keith, who, let me just say, was All-American in the sketchy department. But then again, I looked sketchy, and Keith would be taking a chance on me. Despite not having a mirror, I knew I looked and smelled like someone Jeffrey

84

Dahmer might associate with. Besides, hitchhiking had proved to be rather difficult in Texas; who knew if someone would pick me up. So, I thought, to hell with it, and decided to take the ride.

As it turned out, the roofers were friendly. The work was hard, and the fiberglass from the shingles was forever penetrating the skin, but it felt good to be earning some money. It was also painstakingly hot. The black tar paper appeared to crave the sun's attention, and the sun seemed more than willing to accommodate. We cooked like the contents of a stir fry until our fleshy pink backs had been seared to a nice candy-apple red.

At one point in the day, I asked about the weather in Texas, and to my surprise, the group remained silent. They looked at each other as though I had just inquired about the conditions in Honolulu. This I didn't understand because one of the guys had told me that he had never left Texas, hadn't even seen the ocean. After a couple of seconds, one of them answered.

"We don't really know. We've all been in jail for the last few years."

"Ah," I said. "Cool."

The group seemed reluctant to talk about their time behind bars, so instead, the conversation turned to me. Where was I coming from? What was I doing in Big Spring? I told them that I had spent the last six months backpacking around South America, but instead of receiving the standard "Oh cool, which countries?" response, I was greeted with a very genuine "Why?" It was the initial guy, the one who had called me over. His tone suggested that I had just confessed to voluntarily peeling my eyelids back with a can opener.

"I guess I wanted to see the world," I said.

The consensus was that this was not a viable motive, and the discussion quickly returned to something more interesting.

At three o'clock, I was offered a couple of sweaty bills and a handshake. I said my goodbyes and then hopped into the passenger seat of Keith's black pickup truck.

"All set?" he asked.

I nodded.

Keith glanced at the digital clock on the dashboard and then peeled out of the lot, leaving a cloud of gray dust in our wake.

For the first few minutes, we refrained from speaking and instead soaked up the AC's cold air. At a traffic light, Keith scanned through his radio presets.

"You like country music?" he asked.

I did, but even if I didn't, I wasn't going to tell him otherwise.

We rode in silence until Keith stopped in front of a small residential home, where we were joined by Keith's girlfriend, Misty. Suddenly, Keith wouldn't shut up. It was like he was a battery-powered toy, and Misty was his switch. He was animated, he was witty, he was everything the previous Keith wasn't, and it made me anxious.

The source of Keith's excitement, I was surprised to learn, was me. The man was more than eager to tell Misty all about his newfound friend in the front seat.

"He was just walking down Simler and decided to work with us for the day. He's from Kansas!"

"Canada," I interjected.

"Right, Canada. And he has a backpack with a tent and everything," he said.

Misty wasn't listening, and I wasn't listening, but I don't think Keith noticed, or he simply didn't care.

The ride dragged on as though lulled by the Texas heat. Keith rambled like a small engine while Misty and I sat in silence, awaiting a chance to enter the conversation, but Keith's mouth was a faucet, his dialect a steady stream, free of interlude. He also shifted between topics so rapidly that, if an opportunity did arise to contribute, your point was about three topics past its prime and was thus irrelevant. It was exhausting, and after a while, Misty and I gave up and tuned out.

After an hour, we reached Odessa, or, as Keith called it, "The Murder Capital of Texas," a point I wish he had withheld because I was planning to camp there that night. I said my goodbyes and thanked Keith for the ride. He really was a nice guy, despite what his file at the Texas State Police Department might say.

Keith didn't tell me much about his jail time or his crime. All I found out was that he had tried to smuggle a copious amount of marijuana across the US-Mexico border. He had told me that, had the border patrol officer not looked in the bed of his truck, he would be stinkin' rich.

Had Keith looked in a mirror prior to that trip, he likely would've seen a pretty shady character staring back at him. So, it didn't surprise me much that border patrol had asked him to pull over to the inspection area. Also, Keith was rather talkative. I'm sure that, after being questioned if he had anything to declare, Keith told a long and convoluted story that touched on a few topics before concluding with the fact that he was trafficking some narcotics but to keep it on the low because his goods weren't exactly "legal."

Again, I'm not certain about the logistics. All I know is that Keith ended up in a State prison, and I ended up in the front seat of his car. I also know that he didn't feel it necessary to add the first-degree murder of a Canadian hitchhiker to his sentence. And because of that, Keith is going down as an alright dude; maybe not in the books of the law, but in mine, he's top-notch.

So, on the off chance you're reading this, Keith, maybe you're doing all right for yourself, or perhaps you're back in the slammer. Either way, if you ever need someone to speak on your behalf, whether for a parole hearing or a job reference, I would be more than happy to vouch for you. Texas forever.

A Businessman in Kilimantuk
Michael Robinson Morris

Sarah and I escaped to an island southeast of Madagascar, a dot missing from most world maps. Upon this remote island was an isolated village that the locals called Kilimantuk. It took thirteen months to find a place where we didn't want to escape again in under a week. And though the villagers were unapproachable at first, for it wasn't the first time they had been intruded upon by Westerners, a growing trust among them began to settle.

Without the deceptive crutch of a common tongue, our friendship with the villagers began to emerge out of the universal language of survival. If Sarah and I began to look brown but gaunt due to living on berries and the few crabs we were able to corner, then that was the dialect they understood. Within a few weeks, they had us spearing fish in their sea cove and deriving puddings made from sour, stringy plants. It was hard to trace how they concocted an alcoholic mixture that served as an emollient for our growing friendship. Many a festive night was spent sharing a mangled gibberish across the community hut fire as we passed the drinking gourd around in circles. I caught a gleam in Sarah's eyes across the room that said: *We found it, didn't we?*

The term 'civilized' had become a farce throughout the course of our restless lives, like an expensively aged wine that fermented into bitter syrup for having been kept from the open air for too long. What were we left with now? Insurance, real estate, stocks and bonds, taxable interest, equity loans— Where does the trickling stream lead us? Who knows the secrets that lie behind the waterfall? While mankind wandered through the forest distracted by daydreams, his boot stepped into the bear trap he'd set the day before.

Sarah was always the dark-haired and pale beauty long before I'd met her several years before, a no-frills woman who showed little grief when the promises of corporate life in Los Angeles fell apart before her eyes. In a world of stimulation seekers who lived with the safety belt on, we found each other in a miracle of mutual commiseration. We struck off from the sinking ship together. I wouldn't have had the strength to do it alone.

It was after each of those festive nights in the Boyanda Gindu (community hut) that, with countless gestures, Sarah and I giddily agreed each woozy morning that we might have actually found our home away from home. I suppose we were too much in an inebriated haze to notice that the supporting beams of the Boyanda Gindu were designed, unlike the rest of the family huts, with an architectural skill not in character with these fish and berry hunters.

The second warning would be more obvious.

——— ✦ ———

One morning, when I was trying to wash my tattered and sun-faded clothes in a trickling stream, a man appeared from the bushes wearing boots, a wide-brimmed hat, and a mess of tattered khaki.

"Oya, Chief. Up to a bit a' recreation, are ya?" he said to me.

It was the first white man I'd seen in nearly six weeks. He didn't look surprised to see me at all, however. From the irreverent twang of his accent, I immediately surmised he was an Aussie. Damned Aussies always have a way of beating you to every far-off corner of the Earth. Expatriation was in their blood.

I chose to remain mute in honor of the peaceful quiet he had trod upon, squeezing a paltry smile from between my teeth.

"Don't want to spoil ya party a'nothin'. Just thawt I'd give ya a little heyds up. Beeznessman's comin'. Best you settle up with 'im. Know what I myne?"

My mouth had opened to express some kind of tangled vexation, but the Aussie was gone before I could sort it out.

———— ✦ ————

By the time I got back to our self-made hut, I just then connected the uncharacteristic hush that had fallen over the Mantuk village that morning with the Aussie's visit. After talking in circles with the only other person who knew as little as I did, I dragged Sarah toward the Mantuk chief, who merely shrugged a smile that bespoke the fathomless inevitable.

We noticed the other Mantuks preparing themselves for some mysterious ceremony in an unusually hurried fashion, either clearing the Boyanda Gindu area from dried palm leaf debris or rushing to finish up a carving or weaving they had been calmly puttering over the day before. Nobody else shared the look of disconcerted hesitation that Sarah and I now betrayed.

As the sun began to turn crimson at the end of the day, torches were lit in a configuration I hadn't seen before as if to clear a path through the dewy night air from the Gindu hut toward the beach. Villagers began to line up as if waiting to pay their respects to a sea god about to emerge from the surf. More unsettling was the appearance of the Aussie taking his place amongst the others, carrying a rugged tote bag over his shoulder. What sea god was charismatic enough to charm an Aussie? So, not having lost all sense of our conformist instinct, Sarah and I settled in the sand at the fringes of the greeting party. We couldn't quite discern why we were getting uneasy looks from everyone else. Only in retrospect might I have known why. We were empty-handed. All the villagers, including the Mantuk Chief and the Aussie, had something to present to their honored visitor.

Our piqued curiosity wasn't allowed to suffer for long, for soon came a warbled buzzing sound from the darkness beyond the lapping foam, followed by the ghostly specter of a white motorboat. When the sputtering craft finally nudged the sand, five men got out of the boat and made their way up through the walkway of standing torches carrying a large satchel. As they came closer, I could now see that one of them was a more distinguished man, garbed in a rumpled safari outfit, while the other four merely surrounded him in cloaks of a disquieting grayish-green. These four brooding courtiers with their bony, sun-leathered, rodent-like faces couldn't help but show glinting teeth, though they were far from smiling. Their captain was a man of some combination of Asian and Nordic descent. The flickering baldness of his head was tarnished by some wild gray strands blown askew by the night wind. He reminded me of a textile merchant I had met once in Jakarta. After sharing a few gestures and utterances with the Mantuk Chief, he commenced with his pending affair.

We watched each of the villagers stand one at a time before his grim countenance with an offer of something to which he would bid nothing in return but an appraising glance just short of disapproval. What they were giving him was hard to see at first until it became apparent. In some cases, there were works of craft that each of the villagers had been toiling over for weeks—a wooden carving or a necklace of dainty seashells. In other cases, the gifts were preparations of food wrapped in a handmade basket or drink bottled in an intricately painted gourd. The man impatiently accepted the fruits of their labor. Despite the slowly curdling sense of alarm creeping over me, it was the why that held my anticipation on tenterhooks.

After a countless number of inequitable exchanges made, it was my turn at the front of the line. The man looked me up and down as if I were no different from the others.

Then he asked me in his strange Indo-Nordic accent where I'd been, where I was going, where I was from, what I did. When done asking me questions and I had answered them hesitantly and vaguely—his evident disinterest increasing the feeling that my answers were meaningless to him—he turned toward his entourage of lackeys behind him and spoke in an unrecognizable tongue. The sniveling, half-native, half-urban rodents offered nothing more than hushed primal chattering in return.

After he had decided on something already made up in his own mind, he turned back to me and held out his hand:

"Thirty-two thousand dollars," he said in perfect English.

The unspoken implication was that this is what we already owed for our time spent at the village, a debt owed to him for having already used something of his. This parody of calculating a figure in his head was probably meant to mock the international stamp of the American dollar value on pleasures we had already usurped. And by his very implication, it was something irreversible. No room to go back and dispute, our time in this far-off and untainted village had already been imposed, and there was no recourse but to hand him thirty-two thousand dollars in cash right on the spot. I've been subjected to situations where a desperate porter will grab your bag, walk it over to a bus stop, and then expect a tip for a service you didn't ask for nor could refute, but this was gross exploitation of such a cagey rule.

What an incredible businessman. This 'civilized' outsider had this whole village of simple-hearted people under his thumb with his numbers and taxes and securities foisted upon them, such that they seemed grateful for his visits. Was it safety from foreign invaders he offered in return? Appeasement of some angry god he held monthly conferences with? An incredible businessman indeed!

Standing there in front of him with empty hands, I had

no choice but to laugh. It was not a hearty laugh but one of piqued exasperation. It was as if he had just asked me to bring him the fishbowl I smashed when I was eleven years old. He must have thought I was one of those escaped trust-fund refugees he could soak dry because he had me trapped in his village far away from Mom and Dad. Ridiculous! $32,000 was more than a month's stay at the Four Seasons in Tokyo. What choice did I have but to laugh?!

No one else found this funny, least of all the businessman. So sure of his rightful dominion, he refused to explain and once again turned to his lackeys behind him. One of them handed him a can of bug spray from the satchel, with which he began spraying me in spurts here and there around my body as if I had the occasional insect buzzing around my shoulders, waist, and neck. Now it was their turn to laugh uproariously. And soon, the whole village broke out in nervous laughter with the rest of them. Looking back at Sarah's mortified pallor, I realized the joke. He was spraying me like a bug! A pesky nuisance that stood in his way, no more than a mosquito on his elbow.

My blood boiled over so quickly that I was as much a spectator of my actions as I was responsible for them. Furiously stabbing a finger toward him, I yelled at the top of my lungs: "No! *You're* the laughing stock!"

A chill shot throughout the assembly that instantly suppressed all laughter. The businessman returned to his natural state of severity. He casually pulled out a revolver, shoving a staying hand toward his courtiers. Then he escorted me to a spot near the Gindu hut, away from the crowd. His face looked like an angry child's, the neighborhood bully who was momentarily thwarted in the moments before he violently lashed out.

"Is she yours?" he asked, indicating Sarah with his cocked brow. Without waiting to read the worry on my face, he called her over.

After summoning his best courtier to follow her close behind, he forced us both into the Boyanda Gindu hut, where the many festive days and nights spent within now seemed a thousand years away. As he forcefully pushed Sarah into a corner beneath the low beams that only now suggested an insidious by-product of their construction, I saw that a thick rope coiled on a peg in the upper rafters ended in a noose. And the businessman was only just beginning to concoct the temper of his retaliation: he was succumbing to the intoxication of a woman's scent. With his gun lowered toward her hips, he closed in on her. The rat-face locked my arms behind me, intending for me to watch.

When he yanked her body close to his, I saw the only split-second of salvation I would ever see. With a strength I'd never known, I shoved rat-face back into the wall behind him. There was a sickening crack as I sandwiched him to the bamboo pillar. When I stepped away from him, he hung on the wall with a puzzled expression. I had tried to show the Mantuks how to hang their garments, but I hadn't installed a blunt peg with the intention of impaling a man's skull there.

The businessman was too preoccupied with Sarah's belt buckle to hear the dying man's groan behind him. I leaped toward him, grabbed his scanty hair, and yanked his head back with everything I had—all $32,000 worth—until I heard his neck crack. His body shuddered and went limp, the gun dropping to the sand. I was sure this killed him, but my boiling adrenaline refused to comprehend that it was over so quickly. Pulling his lumbering body away from Sarah with my left hand, I grabbed his gun with my right and shot him three times in his already lifeless head. And still, that was not enough!

The thought of all the fearful people outside, afraid of this man who took them for everything they had and gave them nothing in return, continued to fuel my rage. Seizing a nearby machete, I sliced through the strained fibers of his neck! Half of it by now severed, I pulled the rest of his head free from his body, dangling tendons quivering. Sarah did not comprehend what was happening, still trembling with shock.

Holding the businessman's head by the crowning scruff of his hair, I emerged from the hut and thrust it into the air for everyone to see.

Instant panic and pandemonium broke out. Everyone scattered in aimless directions, scampering from an invisible horror as if to escape a swarm of angry bees.

As I stood like a stone statue holding Medusa's head after having glimpsed her accursed gaze for an irreversible second, I watched as the villagers and the three remaining courtiers evacuated through the trees and over the nearby mountainside.

━━◆━━

At the dawn of the following day, I was alone in what was left of the empty village and its abandoned huts. I had buried the severed businessman's head in a ditch in front of the Gindu Hut. Two bodies, one minus its head, still lay festering inside. I continued to mutter to myself that it was only because of my 'net worth' that the businessman forced me to defend my life and Sarah's, forced me to kill him and end this peaceful way of life for everyone in the village, which was now forever tainted.

I thought Sarah would have recovered from her state of shock after so many hours had passed, but instead, she continued to stare at me with a hollowness I'd never witnessed in her before. It was as if she had turned into a different person.

Leaving her in our hut by herself, I walked up the steps carved into the cliff leading out of the village. When I reached the top and looked back down to the huts, I saw a few villagers returning to sift through their scattered offerings with solemn dignity, seemingly unaware of my looming presence above them.

Was I a hero, or was I a terror? Sarah's piercing orbs had burned darkly into my soul. I dropped to my knees in overwhelming anguish.

Down below, I saw a young boy of about nine sifting through the debris half-buried in the sand. His tired but sinewy grandfather watched over him, taking little concern in what he found. The boy now tugged at the hem of his shirt, showing him something I couldn't see.

Drifting into a strange trance, I touched a set of cold beads in my pocket. I couldn't remember having received metal beads from anyone in the tribe. Uneasy, I let them be. The object the boy had found was the businessman's gun.

The old man took the gun from the boy, pulled him toward the shore, and handed it back to him. With fervent gestures, he compelled the boy to cast the weapon into the sea. The boy took the gun and stood uncertainly, poised to hurl it, until two other boys rushed up and tugged at the gun, shouting and taunting. The skinny old man could only watch helplessly as one boy ran off with the gun, leaving the other two to chase after him in a spirit of tormenting fun.

When Sarah and I left this godforsaken place, another businessman would come. He would take advantage of them the way the last one had, taking everything, all for the promise of safety. Didn't they need at least one trustworthy person to protect them? For all I knew, I had just killed the most generous tyrant possible.

As I descended the carved steps toward the sand, I took two of the metal beads out of my pocket. They were not beads at all. They were the bullets I had taken from the gun, fingers still trembling. In a flash, I saw it all happening again some other day. I knew that I would return to this island. Did I not already recognize the temptation of my own destiny? I would come back as the businessman himself.

Bad Trip? What I Learned from Meeting Paul Theroux

William Fleeson

"The benefit of a bad travel experience is you can write about it," Paul Theroux told the crowd. "If you live to tell the tale, you get the last word."

Theroux is a distinguished American of letters, and through his many books on travel and trains, a legend in the eyes of reading travelers everywhere, including me.

And if "the writer has supreme vanity," as William Faulkner once contended, Theroux distinguishes himself here as well. He is by many accounts a narcissist, misanthropic, a famous grump who has crafted and shattered relationships and myriad stories about himself. The latter pattern of subterfuge has long swirled around him, like the dust kicked up by his countless train departures, leading critics to wonder just who Theroux is, anyway.

So it was with some trepidation that I went to see the man the day he came to my hometown of Washington, DC. He would be speaking at a travel industry roadshow. He would share stories, and their morals, of his peripatetic life. A book signing would follow his remarks. Here was a chance to talk with the American emeritus of travel writing—a longtime personal hero!

I had writerly aspirations of my own and a now-or-never compulsion to make the opportunity count. I printed a few samples of my work, my name and email address stretched hopefully, vulnerably, across each first page.

The event began on a blustery morning in end-of-winter Washington, as the world-altering effects of coronavirus were only beginning to dawn on travelers (and victims) worldwide.

After a metro ride, check-in, and the obligatory sticky wristband, I descended the escalator to the conference floor.

The scene confirmed a truism about travel enthusiasts: they were not the cool kids in high school. Oddness and awkwardness reigned. A large crowd watched a demo on how to best pack toiletries. Photography nerds talked shop at the Kodak booth. A Chinese company offered package tours, its attendants' thick accents even less clear from behind anti-coronavirus masks. These were the types of characters Theroux has lampooned in his own reporting. The Switzerland booth gave out tiny packets of cheese.

Theroux's own travels began in the early 1960s, when he served in Africa in the Peace Corps, before staying on to work as a writer-teacher. He moonlit in journalism, as a stringer for *Time-Life*, and ground out Africa-based novels. Theroux later moved his family to Singapore, where he wrote Asia-based novels, and eventually to England. His 1975 breakout train chronicle, *The Great Railway Bazaar*, in which he describes a four-month odyssey from London to Japan and back, reinvigorated a moribund book genre more associated with Victorian Britain than the seventies' morality-busting experimentations. Theroux's travel-writing overhaul, by turns called "cranky" and "dyspeptic," made use of open criticism of places and people by name. It was an early sign of his unflinching readiness to air the dirty laundry of others and himself over a lifetime in print. Theroux's travel writing has helped to define, at a popular level, the globalization of the late 20th century.

And it is significant that Theroux is American. The global ascent of the United States, with the optimism of the Roosevelt-Kennedy hybrid—and in seeming lockstep with Theroux's own lifetime—incubated his mindset of wanderlust. It was opportunities such as the Peace Corps that fueled and shaped Theroux's growth as an artist. As a thenuntraveled American, the young man had no other point of reference against which to compare his later years living in Africa, Asia, and the increasingly global village called London. "I left [home] and kept going," he writes of his youth in his 2018 book *Figures in a Landscape*. The experiences he would gather, and the sense he would make of them on the written page, had a common American starting point.

Theroux's family makeup may have predisposed him to awareness and curiosity about the broader world. His salesman father, with strong French-Canadian roots, made a suburban Boston home. The Therouxs lived life somewhere near the middle of the middle class. The writer's mother, of Italian-Catholic background, was ambitious, by her son's description, in the American-immigrant vein. Simultaneously, the Theroux family was perhaps *the* source of the child Paul's itch to venture out, to break from the conformity of 1950s American life. "Ever since childhood, when I lived within earshot of the Boston and Maine, I have seldom heard a train go by and not wished I was on it," Theroux has written. The author himself draws a short, thick line between his compulsion to travel and the urge to take leave from his closest kin—a pre-viral kind of social distance. "One of the great things about travel is, it gets you away from your family," Theroux asserted back in Washington.

Before his speaking time, the conference offered its own curiosities. It was a marketplace of travel ideas, a souk crammed with inspiration for one's next journey—abroad or perhaps, given the coronavirus, closer to what and where the attendees call home. In the "Discover America" section, the Delaware state park service passed out fridge magnets from the window of an Airstream—the silver-bullet cabin on wheels, now in surging demand as a virus-beating travel alternative. A hundred feet away, the West Virginia park service handed out its own magnets from its own Airstream.

I nearly missed Theroux, who was sitting in a camp chair

among the West Virginians, alone and doing nothing an hour before his speaking time.

"Mr. Theroux!" I called. My over-eager tone surprised us both. He stood and said hello, offering a fist bump in lieu of a handshake, his own virus precaution.

I told him the books of his I'd read, several of them borrowed from my father's bookshelf (and never returned). The first was *Riding the Iron Rooster*, published in 1988 after Theroux spent a year crisscrossing China by train. I mentioned my pint-sized travel writing accomplishments. He asked me where I'd traveled recently and what I did for a living. When I disclosed my non-writerly day job, he looked at the floor, the light of interest gone from his eyes. I asked if I could give him my writing samples or if I should keep them until the book signing later. He blinked and said simply, "Later."

Theroux was, for many years, an Asianist. In addition to Singapore and China, he has written long and well about Bangladesh, Sri Lanka, Tibet, and Turkmenistan. He witnessed American fighting in Vietnam. His work on Asia makes more sense when seen as a variation on the theme of Anglophone travel narratives from the previous three centuries—a canon Theroux knows intimately, given his encyclopedic references to them throughout his own œuvre. In this way, *The Great Railway Bazaar* is a kind of grand tour in the British-aristocratic mold. But instead of canvassing Europe, Theroux turned the notion sideways. The ground he chose to cover was through India, Thailand, Japan, and eastern Russia—a concept journey both Asian and contemporary. Theroux showed his readers the possibilities of a grand tour-style trip through what the westerner calls the east. He wrote and traveled at a time when many Americans were not long familiar with the place of Vietnam, Laos or Cambodia, or the other active theaters of US combat on the world atlas. All of this preceded Asia's meteoric rise, especially that of China, to undreamt levels of social, economic, and geopolitical opportunity. If the 21st century is to be the 'Asian Century,' as the preceding one was deeply American, then Theroux—the globalist from Boston—bore witness to Asia's earliest green shoots as they strained toward the sunshine of international primacy.

When the author's time to speak finally came, I squeezed into one of the few remaining seats of about four hundred among actual and armchair travelers. Many listeners were clearly Paul Theroux disciples, their hardcover editions already out for the signing.

The author read from typed notes, but any pretense of organization vanished in the first minute. With his opening anecdote, he cast himself in the familiar role of writerly voyeur. He described his mesmerism that morning at his hotel breakfast, watching a child with a smartphone—or "smahtphown" in Theroux's old-New-England cadence.

"Can you imagine? So much information, so easily had!"

This is a drum Theroux has beaten for twenty or thirty years—since the advent of the internet, at least. In *Fresh Air Fiend*, a collection of travel stories published between 1985 and 2000, the writer makes a trademark curmudgeonly claim: "'Connected' is the triumphant cry these days. Connection has made people arrogant, impatient, hasty, and presumptuous... I found out much more about the world and myself by being unconnected." In Washington, Theroux contrasted the idea of connectedness with the years he spent in Africa. Information came at a premium there, when it came at all. Africa and other places he visited back then—Afghanistan and Iran—posed real dangers to solo travelers like him. Theroux had lived to tell and write the stories.

One tale divulged his experience as a traveler, and as a sex-tourism client, in what is now Malawi. "She likes you!" the pimp encouraged a twenty-something Theroux before the lady associate led the American to a more private place.

"And we'll draw a veil over that," Theroux said, to the packed audience, after a level of candor that tore any supposed veil to shreds. He described the paid-sex episode in detail through his story "Trespass," first published in 2003. The writer claimed the experience profoundly shaped his views on the developing world, germinating several stories and an early novel. Such behavior could hardly be called ethical—not least for a humanitarian aid worker, taking pleasure or taking advantage in a poor faraway place. The moral of "Trespass," if there is one, seems made of the cynicism and What-can-you-do? that Theroux has used in his work ever since.

"The worst thing that can happen to a traveler," Theroux said a while later, "is to be held at gunpoint." The experience had befallen him three times. (Dying, apparently, does not top his worst-travel-outcomes list.)

As his talk muddled on, Theroux expounded on his other values of travel and other putative morals of his stories. Honesty was a matter of convenience more than principle. He described his moment in Herat, Afghanistan, in the early 1970s, when a pushy pawn broker demanded a trade for the luxury watch off Theroux's wrist. The broker offered an antique rifle in exchange. He kept the gun pointed, for persuasion's sake, at Theroux's chest. The writer stalled, fighting panic, before ingenuity struck.

"But my mother gave me this watch!" Theroux protested. That was not at all true, he quickly told the audience as if to reassure us. Yet the ruse compelled the broker to let Theroux on his way. The example was supposed to show how connecting with locals over a local value—in this case, the assumed Afghan veneration of the mother—was of vital importance to the culturally engaged visitor. It did not seem to matter, at least to Theroux, that the connection was specious, the human bond built on a lie.

Theroux's other morals, shared as imperatives with a half-charmed, half-dismayed Washington crowd, included several doozies: when bribes are demanded, or simply useful, "Pay up"; when death-threatened, the impossible "Stay calm"; when wanting to meet ordinary locals, as Theroux did while in Arkansas for his 2018 book Deep South, ply them with fast food and compel them to talk to you. Theroux has written that "Travel had to do with movement and truth... [with] offering yourself to experience and then reporting it." He has also said, recalling his year on Chinese trains, that "the truth is prophetic, that if you describe precisely what you see... then what you write ought to have lasting value." Yet the author's own record testifies to a movement of truth, to a bob-and-weave approach to hard facts, even and especially about himself. Part of Theroux's challenge for travel-writing fans has been his bald assertions of what the truth was—what it had to be—on a given journey. He condescends to tell you what your truth would have been if only you had been there.

Theroux has shaped my own philosophy of travel more than I realized. Seeing and hearing the man up close brought my fixation into sharper focus. His suggestions of 'good' and 'bad' travel sensibilities ring true today, perhaps because he helped write the book—in fact, dozens of books—on contemporary travel ethics, no matter where you're from. Long before smartphones and budget flights began to explode borders, Theroux was admonishing his audiences to go it alone, to suspend connections to home, and to slow down. To rest, in other words, while still moving.

Theroux's remarks ran late. Fans amassed by the signing table. I milled around the floor a half-hour before the line dwindled, and I got in it. The man ahead of me, when he approached Theroux, made a flattering reference to a character in *The Great Railway Bazaar*—a figure the writer later admitted he made up.

My turn came. "What did you say your name was?" Theroux asked as I pushed his 2005 novel *Blinding Light* across the table. The story is about, among other things, an aging travel writer. Theroux signed a spidery 'Best wishes' and passed the book back.

"Is now a good time to give you my samples?" I asked, with more hopefulness in my voice.

"Oh," he said, remembering only vaguely, his expression as flat as his tone. "Sure."

I slid him the folder, said thanks again, and left the building. I took the metro home. My train voyage was far more modest than those Theroux has made—and those that made Theroux.

———— ✦ ————

I haven't heard from the writer, nor did I really expect to. Hope, as I am learning in the writing world, is a much different bird than probability and far more common than the concrete goodwill of someone on Publishing's Other Side. But I would welcome a surprise email or phone call, or a second meeting.

More importantly, I made my own journey and wrote about it after a pilgrimage to the high priest of the modern travel narrative. The setting could have come from a Theroux story—a lone young man on a quest, the American surrounded by foreign faces, in Washington's own travel bazaar. But if the trappings were exotic, my encounter with the writer, a globalist whose home country I shared, was a firmly American affair.

My trip was hardly dangerous, as some of Theroux's have been, though it did prove a little disappointing. No matter. I'll keep traveling. I'll keep writing. What Paul Theroux said was true, even prophetic, in his self-fulfilling way: I got the last word.

Jerusalem Architect
Andrew Edwards

Father Damien Carmody had recently taken up the position of Dimension Monitor for the Vatican Council on Universal Expansion, and on a fine, green-tinted afternoon not far from Port Shantabula, he accepted a fancy cigarette from Don Martin Prosper who had brought me to Dimension K on his transformer-driven yacht. The Don smoked Turkish Ovals, and he leaned across the wrought iron cafe table to light the cigarette for Carmody with a lighter that looked like a tiny silver pistol.

I had come to Dimension K with Prosper on his invitation. This he had offered as a way to "refresh the narrative" for my prime-time network show about ghosts and cryptids. In development, the producers had thought about calling it "Things That Go Bump in the Night," but that was too long, so we called it "A World Beyond." It was doing better than "The Screaming" but not as well as "The Twilight Zone," and the network was floating the idea of changing up the format or possibly just canceling it unless ratings improved. So far, a long weekend in Dimension K had offered a few trivial concepts for the show but nothing quite like what Carmody was about to tell us.

"You both came Friday on the del Q'annaqui," he said.

"Much as you did a couple of weeks back," said the Don. "I took it out beyond the shipping lanes this time because we are still working out some of the time-lock seals, and effective range is always a wild card. Would *not* want to boost anybody into Dimension K who didn't want to go!"

"Nor anyone who has not paid," observed Carmody. In the same hand, he had the flat fancy cigarette between the fork of his fingers and also managed a glass of whiskey on ice with his thumb, ring, and pinkie fingers in what looked to be a practiced maneuver.

"It did not cost either of you, of course," said the Don, spreading an exculpatory hand in front of the paisley ascot at this throat.

"My understanding," said Carmody, "is that you've made an arrangement with Rome on my behalf. And I'm sure your old friend Victor Princip may find a way to cut you in on development money if the show gets picked up again."

Don Martin Prosper produced a grin, almost as if he'd been caught out. He was taller than me, and I was slightly above average height. He was broader too, considerably so, and was evenly tanned as if to attest his presence at sun-soaked venues around Mallorca or Bermuda when many of us were struggling with galoshes in the snow. His hair was still thick on his well-shaped head and silvered at the temples. No doubt, he considered himself both a gentleman and an explorer, and the twinkle in his eye was mostly an indicator of personal ease and good humor.

A waiter came by wearing a service apron over his nylon mesh overall. The waiter was a smallish, mohawk-haired, hare-lipped, cat-faced cryptid called an Elomptereen with a slotted hole in his throat. The waiter asked if we wanted any more cake. We did not. He removed a plate of blue and white crumbs, and Don Martin asked him for another martini, up, dirty, and with three olives.

Reporting back with the triangular glass on a tray, the Elomptereen asked if we had come on the del Q'annaqui. The Don asked why he wanted to know.

"I was told it almost sank," said the waiter, hiding a smirk with only moderate success.

"We know how Elomptereens hate boats and enjoy their sinking," said the Don. "Now, if you don't mind, I am talking with my colleagues about subjects that do not concern you."

The waiter laid down the drink with a bowl of peanuts and backed away with an ambiguous grin. I noticed he had a shiny medallion pinned on his front pocket that reminded me of a little house.

"And as a reminder," I said to the Don, "I do have to be back on the sound stage in a couple of days. I don't think they will let me postpone again."

"It's a small matter of getting transit papers," said the Don less than reassuringly.

We were on the open top deck of the airship Queen of Agriconnaughtrie, and I expected to disembark in the morning. That, presumably, would allow me enough time to get a transit pass from Kedgers down at the Capital. That, in turn, would grant me an untroubled return to standard dimension and my day job on television. Don Martin Prosper had often been generous and forthcoming about his transdimensional boat and the "fresh perspective" I might enjoy having crossed to a Near Vibratory Present such as Dimension K. The idea was that some esoteric feature of Dimension K might provide intriguing storylines for new episodes of "A World Beyond." But the more I saw of Dimension K, the less this seemed a likely outcome. Network television would never, for instance, allow me a tale about boat-hating cryptids with slotted holes in their throats.

Elomptereens may have hated boats, but apparently, they were indifferent to airships, and many were employed thereupon. The Queen ran on a small amount of fossil fuel, but it was not a fast traveler, and its main function was to float a thousand people in comfort a mile high above the surface of Fwomptwynghe, which, for what it's worth, is the Dimension K equivalent of the United States. The serene flotation of the airship is accomplished by virtue of a device called an AGM. At an early date, the anti-gravity modules were too heavy to operate. Once Kedgers had perfected a lightweight AGM,

Dimension K humans were able to abandon their surface dwellings, typically to float in luxury airships a mile above the lab-grown Elomptereens that outnumbered them in Fwomptwynghe.

Probably I had left it too long before getting transit papers from Kedgers, and now it would be catch as catch can that I might not lose the show and much else with it. Without the show or something like it, there promised little savor in what life I might obscurely lead. Wanting not to think of my old friend as an opportunistic dissembler who had enticed me into a dangerous endeavor by partial concealment, I would concentrate on getting back to Manhattan on time and in good shape. "A World Beyond" may have needed me, but almost certainly, I needed it more.

Some of our older filmgoers may remember Victor Princip as The Terrible Ogg, a cinematic monster big on the silver screen during the silent era. Ogg was my early invention, and Ogg's gaunt visage was famous from Saginaw to Singapore for a time. He was compared favorably to the German Nosferatu character and probably was a precursor to a cinematic Dracula. But Ogg was not a blood-sucker, nor even truly a monster. Ogg was, in a way, an early vector for dimensional transformation—insofar as he could transform any being into any other type of being, real or chimerical. "Iconic" would not be an inaccurate way to describe the way Ogg, in a feature called Senator Doom, turned a corrupt judge into an owl that flew up into a corner of the courtroom and hooted at the prosecution. It might even be argued that it was my demonstration of "extra-dimensionality" that had sparked Don Prosper's interest in the subject.

But Ogg's star faded, and I was forced to scrape together a life after Ogg. Lean years and setbacks notwithstanding, recently, it had become my excellent good fortune to have been "rediscovered" by network television as an avuncular figure suitable for introducing mildly unsettling tales of premonition and untimely death. Where I had been The Terrible Ogg, now I became Doctor Dennis, at nine pm Eastern (eight Central) weekly to be seen before a crackling fire with a cup of tea and an invitation to explore the unknown.

Anyone with questions as to why humans in Dimension K might want to float in an airship above Fwomptwynghe is encouraged to reference the recent Kedgers report on Elomptereen Uprisings and how their general chaos has made all but the most private gated communities almost insufferable. As to Elomptereen misbehavior generally, one is directed to the Uprising Appendix to see how they were created in a laboratory as worker drones; and how the genetics team had not bred out sarcasm and anger quite to the extent that the designers had intended.

Not that Elomptereens were dangerous in a criminal sense, more that they were typically angry, prejudiced, intolerant, and suspicious of any and every attempt to give them access to what most of us would call a more refined type of life. To the arts, medicine, and boats (and, as will be demonstrated, birds), they were hostile and, too often, actively so.

I put all these matters aside because Carmody was talking about his church and how it operated across an array of parallel dimensions.

"If you've been in touch with Rome about my passage," said Carmody, "you probably already know about the Vatican Observatory. And that the Vatican has taken note of so-called flying saucers and such. And because we have a robust science budget, we don't pretend that the world we see is the only one we've got."

"Jesus saves little green men?" I was gazing down at an amber Islay single malt that sat before me in a sweating glass. Nominally a Catholic, I had been much a doubter since Austria.

"I will say that the personality of Jesus is dependent on

the dimension," said Carmody, with a smile that never quite got past his lips. He was slightly built, sandy-haired, and was endowed with a dusting of faint freckles across his nose. His eyes were larger than the average, and they featured a downward pull at the outer edges as if to emphasize a concern that might never be expressed. "In Dimension K, we have a fascinating history of the Jesus figure—unlike standard dimension where the story of the cross is well-known."

"Does it not involve a cross?" I said.

"In Dimension K, there is a Jesus figure. But He did not die on the cross."

"Would I come across as disrespectful if I asked why He then matters in the first place?" This was Don Martin Prosper.

The elder Prospers had attended the same Catholic church as the elder Princips in Austria many years back, and I had, as a lad, exchanged many an unrepentant, cross-pew smile with Don Martin back when we were not much more than tykes. We had lost touch but had become friends again somewhat by chance—if mutual, unplanned attendance at a flying saucer convention in Reno can be considered "chance." In any case, soon, we both would be heading back home to Manhattan but on opposite sides of the park.

The transformer that brought us to Dimension K had been developed by Don Martin Prosper over the course of years on the Continent and only recently had become viable for transport. He had brought me along to Dimension K because of a mutual interest in good stories and good money (Carmody had been accurate to suggest that the Don wanted in on development dollars if "A World Beyond" might be reconfigured), but he was charging a premium for passage generally.

"Jesus matters here because of what he said," said Carmody. "Not because he suffered."

"I'm sure I've heard more about the suffering than the insights," I said.

"Yes, in *standard*, that is all true," said Carmody. "But in Dimension K, there was no cross, no death, no resurrection. He was a philosopher, and Christians here try to follow his word. The symbol for Christ is a book with a little roof over it. Not a cross, which in Dimension K is only a meaningless distraction."

"And what did the Christ figure end up doing if he didn't get crucified?" I said.

"He went to work at his father's architectural firm in Jerusalem. He became a mid-level architect, and he managed to design several important public buildings."

"So he gave up."

"He wrote everything that we already know about. 'Suffer the children,' et cetera. It's just that when he saw the tide going against him, he figured it was no help to anyone to get nailed up with criminals, and he told the Pilate he'd just stop preaching altogether. And they let him do that. So the words come down to us here, but the crucifixion does not. There are factions in the church that wonder if this might not be a better model after all. Needless to say, it is a struggle."

"Perhaps we want more of the philosophy but less of the blood."

Father Carmody stubbed out the end of the cigarette. "We are not a well-understood nor even a hopeful faction within the church. In Dimension K, He never died for your sins. He worked as an architect for your sins instead."

"Do you think it makes the philosophy itself more effective to decouple it from suffering?"

"Yes. But let me quickly add that you would be surprised, perhaps, at how *similar* belief here is, despite there being no cross. There is no data to suggest the Christian message is any more effective *minus* the cross than it is with the cross."

The slot-throated waiter came by again, unbidden. He had a dead pigeon in hand. "We don't like birds very much."

He lifted the feathery bundle to his face and bit hard into it. Blood spurted past the Don and produced crimson paisley on the white tablecloth. The waiter tossed the flat, bitten bird onto the table. He wiped the blood from his chin. A feather floated down into my lap.

"Are you a Christian?" said the Don, indicating the little metal pin that looked like a house on the waiter's apron. Prosper's composure was remarkable, but I had come to expect this from people who knew Dimension K better than I did.

"Very much so," said the Elomptereen. "My name is Belvedere, and I believe in the architecture of faith."

"Thank you, that will be all," said Carmody.

"We don't like boats, and we don't like birds," said Belvedere. "We also don't care to be told that we need to hire out an incubator to complete our gestation period—when it's common knowledge that we are viable at five months just like the rest of you."

"Thanks for the update!" I said, feeling assaulted by disastrously incorrect assumptions. I knocked back the Islay malt. Carmody and the Don shared what seemed a less alarmist outlook.

"We struggle with our flock in every venue," said Carmody with a thin smile. He finished his whiskey and plunked the cut glass tumbler down next to the mangled bird. The Elomptereen asked if he would want another, and, of course, Carmody agreed to it. We were guests of the Don, and it would all be on his invoice. The waiter retreated.

"I had always thought the problem with Christians is their confusion," I said. "The contrast between the words of the Christ figure and the awfulness of his death have become conflated into self-sorry righteousness that destroys any positive message in the text. But here we don't have that, and still, the words are, at best, background noise to a world of prejudice and stupidity."

"In standard dimension," said Carmody. "we have a plot twist that ostensibly makes it harder to ignore the words of the crucified. But the crucifixion has no impact on the words themselves. Or at least, in my personal opinion, the resurrection is a parlor trick. And so we are left with the words alone. For instance: '*For what shall it profit a man if he gain the whole world and suffer the loss of his soul?*'"

"That is a good one," I said. "But I don't see Belvedere benefiting much."

"Would it help," said Carmody, "If we added a crucifixion? Because the teaching can be adjusted."

"Don't do anything on my account!" I said. This drew a chuckle out of Carmody. I turned to the Don, who was busy tapping out another cigarette from a white cardboard box. "You ought to have told me I would need transit papers to get back."

"It was a rule change while I was away," he said. "It's only a formality. Probably I could sneak you back on board the del Q'annaqui when I go back the day after tomorrow, but if they caught me, it could cost me the franchise. Kedgers is tightening up because they see there's demand for inter-dimensional travel."

"It does not make it any easier," said Carmody, "that the day after tomorrow is Gar Flancie Day."

"I had forgotten," said the Don. "I'll have to secure the yacht tonight. But I am sure it will work out."

I asked what they meant about Gar Flancie Day, and Carmody said it was a twin holiday of sorts, but apart from that, very much a reaction of opposites. Several years ago, an excursion boat sank off Port Shantabula, drowning as many as a hundred human children on their way to an island picnic. It is still mourned by thousands in town. Thousands of humans.

Kedgers had decreed that humans could have their somber remembrance in the morning. But the rest of the day was given over to Elomptereen demonstrations that would typically turn to a bacchanal at night. Elomptereens had already commemorated the sinking of the Gar Flancie with parades, songs, strutting performances, and general abandon. It was a celebration of the disaster for Elomptereens, and Don Martin Prosper said they had in the past tried to drill holes in boats on Gar Flancie Night.

Leaving the airship cafe with Carmody and Prosper, I asked the cryptid waiter if he had plans for Gar Flancie Day. He told me he was picking up his costume after his shift.

━━━ ✦ ━━━

The transit desk was "closed for renovation" when I got down to the Capital. After chasing down more than one uncooperative functionary, I gave up and hired a Throckmorton all the way back up to Port Shantabula. There I would present myself to the Don and let him know I expected an accommodation from him because he had brought me over, neglecting to relate at least one important detail. With no real apology, he agreed and told me to meet him at the pier the next morning.

I needed to be back at Studio Seven by 4 pm. Passage across dimensions was more or less instantaneous, but the trick was to "stick the landing," as Prosper would have it. Already it was plain I might blow the schedule, lose the show, and much else, and so far, all I was coming back with was a cockamamie story about a loser Jesus who wimped out and went *bourgeois* when it counted. That tale was never going to make it to network TV, so my trip to DK would likely prove a waste of effort at best.

On the morning of Gar Flancie Day, the homestar cast long shadows across the waterfront, already the site of two counter-demonstrations. The first one was a smallish, somber, and for me anyway, a moving ceremony where an array of flowers provided a backdrop to the recitation of the names of ninety-eight children who had drowned on the boat that day. Behind it, a row of substantial boats stood at anchor, including, several yards north, the big del Q'annaqui, a resplendent example of the shipbuilder's trade with a broad command deck and gleaming brightwork throughout the superstructure.

Carmody was there to spend a few minutes with the mourners though none of them seemed to pay him any mind. He said the ceremony had gotten smaller of late. For the first couple of years, it had seemed half the human population of Port Shantabula was in attendance. Now there were perhaps two or three hundred. The ceremony was not over-long, and soon the mourners seemed ready to make way from the watery commemoration.

Now at the base of the pier, another kind of crowd approached. I ought to have been aboard the yacht already, but I had hung back out of respect for the Gar Flancie memorial. The Don, tall, silver-haired, and robustly tanned, was visible on deck aboard the del Q'annaqui, and he waved at me as if to say (literally) the coast was clear.

It was not.

The new crowd, already shouting glad hatred of boats and all who floated upon them, stood to outnumber mourners by a considerable number, and still, it was early. Already I could see banners with the DK Christian symbol: an upright rectangle with a little triangle over it like a roof. My passage to the gangway on Prosper's yacht was, in fact, blocked by a shouting, can-banging vanguard of Elomptereen demonstrators.

Later, they would parade all the way from their warrens beyond Muddy Poo down Tomorrow Street to Shantabula Square with gaudy floats and hundreds of kazoos and flutes. They would keen and catcall into the night. By then, humans, in their grief, would have long retired back to airships high above the Elomptereen.

One of the more memorable placards read, "Jesus Walked on Water Because He Hated Boats." Half a dozen slightly built cryptids re-enacted an imaginary drowning: they gagged, they clawed the air, they fell. And glub-glub after the third time down. Drums and flutes played the background to these antics while over a hundred happy cryptids cheered them on. Together they exuded a swampy odor that pervaded the waterfront.

Carmody got up on a pair of stilts. His slim, black-clad figure towered over the cryptids in their nylon mesh uniforms, and they hailed him with a brassy cheer. Swaying on his perch, he quieted the crowd only enough to say they must back away from the memorial and allow the human mourners to vacate the waterfront. With resentment, they complied, but the human mourners, who seemed a defeated rabble, were forced to run a gauntlet of taunts and tossed vegetables. Carmody did nothing to prevent Elomptereen projectile vomiting that spattered some of the retreating human mourners with an obscene yellow ichor.

As the Elomptereens were preoccupied with mourner-taunting, I was able to gain the ramp up to the del Q'annaqui. Struggling to keep my footing on the slippery ramp, I heard what I thought were frogs calling across a pond in a burpy-sounding cadence that seemed louder than it ought. Also, frogs do not gather but at ponds; indeed, the bay of Port Shantabula was no pond. Only a few moments it took to understand the repetitive keening was out of the Elomptereens, who had lapsed, it seemed, into a sonic trance. The slotted hole in their throats allowed them to caterwaul without opening their mouths. The unified, *clud-clud* rhythm produced by their slotted throats—technically "Ingersoll's Declivity"—was loud, insistent, and demoralizing.

Halfway up the gangway, I twisted an ankle and fell. Typically, I'd have gotten up without ceremony, but the buzzy croaking had reached a pitch that seemed tuned to maximum sonic discomfort. I found myself dizzy and drained and as if needles were piercing my eardrums.

Now, I can vouch that this cryptid phenomenon, often called a "Panish Vortex," was known to produce peculiar effects on humans caught inside it. Somehow, it triggered both deep memories and a sort of vibrating paralysis that was difficult to think through and painful to feel.

In a matter of moments, I found myself reliving a fiction that allowed me to transform police officers into feral hogs and slobbering hounds into pink-eyed bunnies. But now it was as if the Terrible Ogg had turned on me. Perhaps it was a factor of having aged considerably since those first cinematic transformations, or perhaps it had never occurred to me how Ogg's power would manifest in the body. If it was not bad enough that my head throbbed with Panish vibrations, I also felt as if an electric charge were driving my limbs apart. Somehow, I managed to stand myself up on the narrow gangway, an unmoored twig, it seemed, feeling my age.

Carmody came to the edge of the pier in a black cassock. On wavering stilts above the rabble of smallish cryptids, he waved at me as if to signal some way toward the del Q'annaqui. One of my feet was numb, and I had to stand on the other while trying to balance against a swaying chain "railing" that provided much more of a guideline than a barrier. The spongy timbers were green and black with slime, and I slipped one more time. But this time, I went splat down into the water.

I choked in the freezing bay water and somehow managed to wrap my arms around a mossy timber. I did haul myself even with the surface, but a gulp of water had gone down the wrong way, and it was all I could do to see straight.

Carmody came towards me—yes, he was walking on

water, or at least it looked that way. It may have been the stilts.

The Panish Vortex was stronger, louder, and faster, and the sound of it only added to the confusion I felt, having dropped into the drink. Carmody was close enough that I clutched the dry bottom of his cassock just above the surface of the water. I searched the mild, gray, hooded eyes in Carmody's head to see if he was as disturbed as he ought to have been. But the recesses of his sad-looking eyes were distant and even officious. He had a job to do, and it involved getting me on a boat. On stilts and with me in tow, he maneuvered us both close enough to a pier that I could climb up a rudely hammered row of creosoted cross-beams, and soon I found myself back on the gangway, soaked, embarrassed, and exhausted.

The cryptid mob now deployed a novel projectile that seemed in plentiful supply from the back of a freezer truck. These were pints of hard ice cream, Kedgers brand, of course, and tasty, no doubt. But here, it seems the frosty treats—perhaps donated by the manufacturer—were half-pound projectiles hard as stones and, well-aimed, capable of delivering real damage to an intended target.

Carmody backed away, stilts in the water, and with ready cryptid help, soon was back up on the pier where he towered, again, over the badly-behaved Christians of his Dimension K flock. Pints of Kedgers ice cream flew past me and above my head, a dozen of these at a time. They bounced on the gangway and flipped up and over into the boat. Don Martin collected what fell in and set them off on a bench where a deckhand removed them, presumably to a nearby freezer.

Some of these also ricocheted off the boats and back into the crowd of Elomptereens, where the lids flew off to reveal colorful creamy solids. The little cryptids, having tossed all the pints, now retrieved of them what they could, tore them open, and fought one another with fists and teeth to scarf pints of chocolate, pistachio, or even the Dimension K "gweem" flavor, something like vanilla and fried fish and better tasting than it sounds.

The Don was quick to assist as I reached the top of the gangway, grabbing me under the arm with almost hurtful strength as I tried to secure my footing. Altogether I felt like the lamest old nuisance and that I ought to hide away until I could once again be of some use to the human experiment. What business had I to come looking for something fresh at my age! Better that I should retire quietly and let some young(er) hopeful take my place. Wet, angry, and half-numb from a combination of anger and cold, I sat on a bench next to a dented carton of vanilla fudge ice cream.

Carmody, now careering above the heads of his roistering Christers, spread his arms wide as if to imitate a cross. He maintained this curious posture even as his very stilts were lifted from the ground giving him even more height. The last image he presented was a T-shape silhouette, often jerked sideways by his bearers, against the faint-green sky over the bay of Port Shantabula. I was convinced he was play-acting with the "cross" configuration, but he was far off now, and it was difficult to tell if he wasn't somehow a captive of his co-religionists.

The ice cream attack melted away, and the cryptids and the mourners left the pier. The Don sent me to a quiet cabin where he provided a change of clothes. I slept for at least an hour before letting him know we needed to get started on the Dimensional shift if I was to get back to New York and still have a living. I was with him on the bridge when a message came through the wireless.

It was Carmody: "My friend, why have you forsaken me"?

The Don said Carmody was always quick with the one-liner and that I'd be back on the set in plenty of time.

Waxing Nautical
James B. Nicola

There's a sea to me
   miles, fathoms, mains, bays,
     and I would be free

        but am as I am
         only when I am

            chained at a bottom of The Great
             where it is
               too deep for a drop of sun to reach

                though this Prison below
                is so
                  well
                    lit.

All I can do is lie,
   removed,
     moved and unmoved,
       seduce, sip, swallow and, sadly, slay,
         add to a collection of what salt tears,
           currents, creatures, and time dissolve
           to swill,
             egest as ambergris.

Another vessel has embarked; another's lit ashore to safety.
   And I cheer for both:
     The one, wish Godspeed, clap, and pray
       for a better experienced life away
         from me

for having sailed upon salt seas
awhile;

The other, beckon,
    now that I rage, hungry,
        with my mask of stillness,
            reflective and reflecting
                on the surface
                    with an illusory, projecting
                        sheen of day and firmament
                            for anyone on board who might
                                wish to ponder,

While underneath, the darkest realm of tombs
    summons night, and never likes to lose.

My lungs, heart and stomach, rapacious, beat a rote
    hypnotic, in sync with the moon and stars, that you
    would once lean over the gunwales to inquire just too
    far

And that I might hook and pull you, with a jerk down, to
    become a glistening pebble in time

at the gastric, elastic
    bottom of
        the Prison

where we would dance
    and make salt worlds
        a Prism.

The Piazza Senza Banco, Long After

James B. Nicola

How high the dollar soared, I recollect,
way back in 1984—so high
    I mustered the means, barely, and back
    I flew. A dollar rising, though, means
    a fall in what the dollar's being
    traded for, and all *that* means... One fall
    day in a Piazza famous for
    something Old Worldish as grand piazzas
    are, flagstone-paved and vast as it was old,
    I heard and noted, rising from the stones,
    CLOK CLIK CLOK CLIK then heard *Buona sera*
    in Italian, then CLOK CLIK CLOK CLIK...
    Now, everybody knew that Italians
    made the best shoes in the word; I knew
    each person from the shoes' plangent echoes,
    rhythm, pause—each personality.
    CLIP CLIP CLIP *Buona sera* [no pause
    this time, but instantly:] CLIP CLIP CLIP...
    CRUK CLOP CRUK *Buona sera* [An instant's
    hesitation] CLOP CRUK CLOP... But then:
    ...CLOP CLUK *!!clingggg!! Grazie!* CLOP CLUK... Each
    Buona sera sounded as if CLUKed
    by a sour bird whispering. The sound of
    Grazie, though, came from no sour throat
    but from the cold flagstone, even though
    the voice was neither cold nor sour for
    that one word. I watched the voice, then thought
    perhaps I was rude in watching. So:

!!clingggg!! (My sneakers had not echoed.) I
turned to go, forgetting what the *!!clingggg!!*
meant: *Grazie*, of course. So I turned
back, saw her nod, and resumed my course,
the Piazza's sounds reverting back
to CLIKS, CLAKS, and other-worldly sounds
of *Buona sera* breaking the CLIK-
CLAK, sometimes (*Buona sera* is the
Italian for *Good evening*).... Sometimes
I think, since Italians often wear
sneakers today, while I wear Italian
shoes, the sounds might be reversed today,
but that the coins would make the same sound—*!!clingggg!!*
—when collected, as *cento lira* coins.

Una Terra del Miracoloso
Robin Michel

Mr. and Mrs. Ewing are preparing for their Italian vacation. Mr. Ewing researches flight and hotel accommodations, the U.S. dollar to Euro exchange rate, various cities for both day trips and overnights, train schedules, and tickets. He cancels home delivery of their two newspapers, places a vacation hold on their mail, changes their cell phone plan to accommodate international travel, and visits a downtown branch of their bank to convert dollars into Euros.

Mrs. Ewing signs up for a few Italian lessons (lezioni in Italiano), purchases a volume of poetry written by an Italian poet she is unfamiliar with (the only book in Italian she could find at her neighborhood bookstore), and with the help of an English-to-Italian dictionary, manages to translate (she thinks) one entire poem. Trying to be more pragmatic, Mrs. Ewing does practice, without any real schedule or discipline, a few phrases her Italian teacher gave her useful for the trip:

> *Scusi, può ripetere per favore?*
> *Non capisco, non parlo bene italiano.*
> *Può parlare lentamente?*

Mr. Ewing tells his wife, a communications specialist, that she is responsible for communicating with the Italians. Mrs. Ewing happily agrees but does not bother to memorize numbers in Italian or how to tell a waiter she is vegetarian.

Getting a taxi from the Aeroporto di Roma to their Airbnb is easy, as the white taxis line up outside the terminal and take turns receiving passengers.

"Buongiorno," Mrs. Ewing greets the driver in an apologetic whisper.

"Buongiorno," the man responds with a big smile as if Mrs. Ewing were a competent student in la lingua Italiana and not the slacker she is.

Mr. Ewing shows him the address of their room on the reservation printout, and off they go, winding through streets narrow and wide, then narrow again, at a fast, crazy Italian taxi driver speed, narrowly missing cars, bicyclists—without helmets!—and pedestrians, while 1970's U.S. pop-rock music blares on the radio. Both Mr. and Mrs. Ewing stare out of the taxi windows, drinking in the tall buildings and cobbled streets, the sun-bronzed women in their breezy summer dresses and strappy sandals, the men in their tight white shirts, pressed jeans, leather shoes, and eye-catching belts, every third person smoking their cigarettes as if they were in a Michelangelo Antonioni film.

They spot the tourists, too, dressed in t-shirts produced in Bangladesh and carrying shopping bags filled with souvenirs made in China. "I want to tell people we are from Canada," Mr. Ewing had said before they left home.

"Mi chiamo Don," Mrs. Ewing instructed, "Io sono di Canada."

Mr. Ewing will not say this, of course, as he is an honorable, truthful man, but he will later tell Italians who ask where they are from that they are embarrassed to say they are from America. When this happens, many will look confused. "But why?"

"Our president embarrasses us." They continue to look confused, as if their English is inadequate in translating just what it is this strange man is saying.

Arriving at their destination, Mrs. Ewing thanks the

taxi driver correctly—she hopes—saying "grazie" and not "gracias," which is far too easy to do. She is now regretting all the time she spent translating some obscure poem from Italian to English that made little sense once finished. How much better to use those hours learning how to ask for the bathroom or working on the pronunciation of the few words she did learn. *Que sera sera*, she thinks, and then wonders what language *that* is.

Arriving is easy, but it won't take long for Mr. and Mrs. Ewing to learn that when it is time to leave, calling a taxi to pick them up at their apartment is much more difficult. The recording on the taxi answering service is in Italian, and there is no slowing it down by requesting it to *Può parlare lentamente?* When Mrs. Ewing finally does get a real live person, the taxi dispatcher does not speak English. Mrs. Ewing has not memorized their house number, 255, in Italian, remembering too late that the Italian teacher warned the students not to say each number in the one-digit format. Still, it's all she knows, and so she gives it a try: "Due—cinque— cinque," she keeps repeating, and the street name—she is apparently mispronouncing the name of the street.

Per Cristo's sake, Mr. Ewing thinks, what kind of a communications specialist is she?

"Che cosa? Che cosa?" The dispatcher answers in turn and spews a Mount Vesuvius stream of Italian words as undecipherable as the hieroglyphics on the ancient Roman ruins they have visited at various sites and museums. "Non capisco." *That* Mrs. Ewing understands. The dispatcher does not understand.

San Cristoforo, patrono dei viaggiatori, where are you when we need you?

Suddenly, the dispatcher says very slowly, "Text? Can–you–text–it–to–me–if–I–give–you–a–number?"

"Si! Si! Si!" Mrs. Ewing reassures her, writing down the

number for texting.

When the taxi arrives, Mrs. Ewing briefly toys with the idea of lighting a candle in honor of Saint Cristoforo at the next ancient basilica they visit. "Italia is truly a land of the miraculous," she tells Mr. Ewing.

He takes her hand and gives it a loving squeeze.

Arrivederci
Louise Turan

After it happened, the advice came pouring in. All morning, waiting for the plumber to arrive, family and friends called to tell her what to do: take an evening art class, join a book club, go hiking, change your hairstyle, sign up for yoga, redecorate the house. We have your best interest at heart, they insisted, but Stephanie wished they would just be less interested instead.

"Listen," Stephanie retorted. "I'm the one who's getting divorced. This is my decision. I made my bed, and now I'm going to lie in it."

The truth was her husband had been the one to lie in bed, only it was someone else's, a waitress named Jenny from their favorite take-out place. And it wasn't merely a fling. He had been seeing her, and no doubt sleeping with her, for over a year. Stephanie had found out the hard way. Not from some truthful, soulful, heart-wrenching confession but by seeing a text on his phone. He had been asleep when it rattled on his bedside table. She picked it up, thinking it might be his mother or something important at that late hour.

"SugarBear, is the coast clear? Call me, babe. Counting the minutes."

The text was followed by a number of symbols: red hearts, yellow smiley faces, and puckered lips. At first, Jeff, bleary-eyed from sleep, tried to deny it, but the evidence was clear: his mother called him Jeffy, his Dad called him Slugger, her sister called him Shit Head, and she, as well as his friends and teammates, called him JT—no one called him SugarBear. Her sister had got it right; no denying that now, either.

Stephanie calmly placed the phone back on the bedside

table, put on her robe and slippers, and went downstairs to the closet by the garage, where they stored all their athletic gear: his baseball stuff, wet suits, life vests, paddles, bike helmets. She grabbed one of his bats, the Hank Aaron signature series, and, tapping it on her palm like a drum beat, went back upstairs to their bedroom.

"Jesus Christ," Jeff cried, sitting up, seeing her in the doorway with a bat raised over her head, coming toward him.

"Get the *fuck* out, or I'm going to smash your *fucking* brains all over your pillow. Or, better yet, maybe I'll make you eat your phone, and you'll choke on it and die," she added, grabbing and brandishing the phone in her other hand.

Growing up, Stephanie had never been good at dealing with anger, not even when her mother smashed her thumb in the car door, or when her younger brother got all the attention, or when her dad relocated, and she was forced to do her senior year at a high school in the suburbs of Kansas City. But she found it now, like a hidden treasure, like diesel fuel setting her on fire.

It took less than a minute for Jeff to vacate. It turned out that he had already packed his suitcases in the trunk of his car, making her hate him even more.

"I never want to see you again, you *fucking* bastard," she yelled as his Ford Escort careened out of the garage, spilling skis, bikes, and the recycling bins onto the driveway. His tires screeched as he raced away. Good, she thought, let all the neighbors know. And then she was sad. They probably already did. She took off her wedding ring and threw it in the yard.

After many bourbons and a sleepless night, Stephanie got up and, not getting any hot water in the shower, went to the basement and discovered the water heater had burst. Everything—storage boxes, the washer and dryer, heater—looked like small islands; pieces of laundry floated on the surface like castaways.

"Shit," she yelled, throwing up her hands, and went back upstairs, cursing Jeff. This was the last thing she needed. She rummaged around the kitchen, searching drawers where they kept things like phone numbers and appliance warranties, but couldn't find anything related to plumbing—only the take-out menu, with a phone number penciled in on the back. Ha. That explained all those late nights Jeff volunteered to go pick up their dinner instead of waiting for delivery. No problem, he had said. Right. Big problem.

Stephanie, half-sobbing, half laughing hysterically, called her older sister, Susan, and recounted finding out about Jeff's betrayal. Her sister had, of course, suspected his infidelity all along, and you didn't need a Ph.D. from Harvard, either, she added, even though she had one. And after spending a good ten minutes raging about Jeff the Shit Head, another ten minutes chastising Stephanie for sitting on her ass in podunk Trenton and not doing anything about getting her dream job at the *Inquirer* or the *New York Times*, and another ten minutes telling her to stop wasting her time covering baseball, even though it was okay because even Gertrude Stein loved baseball, Susan said not to worry and gave her the name of the greatest plumber on the planet. Expensive but great.

"Great," Stephanie muttered and called the number, surprised to get him on his cell.

"Hello, Mr. Bello? This is Stephanie Talbot, I mean Stephanie Daly." It was always so confusing. For house stuff and credit cards, she used her married name, but at work, she always used her maiden name. Now, at least, that issue would get cleared up, she thought ironically. Her old name, down the drain, ha ha.

The plumber said he'd get there in an hour or so, after he finished his current job. In the meantime, with her pajamas hiked up and rain boots on, following his instructions, she turned off the main valve. She got dressed, made coffee, and called Beth, her boss at *The Times of Trenton*, who was very sympathetic. Been there, done that, she said sourly.

"Steph, I'm not usually the one to give advice, but I think you need more than a few days off. I think you need more like a month, or a couple of months."

Shit, Stephanie fretted. Now, on top of everything else, she was getting fired.

"This could be a blessing in disguise," Beth continued. "What I mean to say is, what we have here is a whole new ballgame."

Stephanie, a writer and journalist, appreciated her editor's use of idioms but had made a pact with God that if she got the sports desk assignment at the *Times*, she would never use them as a crutch, especially baseball ones. Over the past three years, covering the Trenton Thunder, when she had met Jeff, she encountered lots of opportunities but had kept her word.

It turned out Beth was not firing her. Beth was actually offering her a new assignment.

"Have you ever heard of the Tour D'Italia? Well, our dear publisher's son has become a cycling fanatic and will be racing in his first Tour. He wants me to send someone to cover it, and so I thought, why not you?"

Italy? She and Jeff had talked about going on their honeymoon, but his game schedule interfered, and they were saving up for the house. At the time, she had not minded much. She spent her day at the stadium, watching and writing about the team, and then, at night, they had had some romantic dinners, followed by sex, which he explained was just like baseball: dinner being the equivalent of the first inning, dessert the seventh inning stretch, and then the wind up into a grand slam 'round the bases to home plate. At first, his baseball and sex analogy had made her laugh and think that he was cute and funny, though occasionally, there was disaster: no score. But after three years of marriage, sex had become more like a straight shot home, without even touching the bases. Now she knew why.

"I guess you are thinking about it?" Beth queried. Stephanie took a deep breath.

"Beth, I appreciate you thinking of me and wanting to help with my, you know, situation, but I know nothing about cycling, let alone professional cycling. Why not send Jim? He's a biking nut, young, just out of school." Jim covered local high school sports.

'Steph, do me a favor," Beth replied. "For once, don't be yourself. Look, you'll be in Italy, for Christ's sake. You'll get to be outdoors, meet new people, see new scenery, and feel the history. So stay home today, get your pipes fixed, and think about it." Beth hung up.

Stephanie stared down into the basement, watched the water lapping on the first step of the stairs like it was a shoreline. Part of her wanted to redial the plumber, tell him not to come, and then go back into the basement and turn the valve back on. She fantasized about letting the water flow, filling up the basement, filling up the first floor, then the second and third until the house washed away down the street.

It took Tony, a nice man with white hair, big shoulders, and a broad chest, wearing a starched green uniform and shiny black boots, about three hours to hook up the pumps, drain the basement, and fix the heater. A temporary fix. She would have to buy a new one. Her kitchen floor was a mess from his boots as he traipsed back and forth from basement to truck.

"Sorry about your floor, Mrs. Talbot," Tony said, wiping his hands on a towel hanging from his belt. I'm gonna take my tools back out to the truck. Here's your invoice. I'll be right back."

Stephanie looked at the invoice. This is probably how much it costs to go to Italy, she thought, bemused. She had never paid the plumbing bill before and was mildly shocked, but she didn't say anything. She was glad he had not mentioned all the crap that was still sitting in the driveway from Jeff's hasty exit.

"Do you take credit cards?" She asked when he returned. He had removed his boots and put on clean, heavy black shoes.

"No, sorry. Checks only," he said apologetically, bending down, cleaning the floor with a rag.

Stephanie found her purse and took out her checkbook. She checked the invoice to read the billing name: Bello Plumbing.

"Bello, I'm guessing that's Italian?" she asked, smiling, thinking, ok, this is funny.

"My grandfather, Giuseppe Bello, was from northern Italy, the Veneto area. They came over in 1890, but I still have lots of family—uncles, cousins—living over there. We go to visit every year. You ever been?" He folded the check and put it in his pocket behind the plastic pen protector.

Of course you go, she muttered to herself, thinking about what she had just paid him. As far as she knew, there were no relatives in her father's ancestral Ireland. And he, being a department store manager his entire life, had never had enough money to take them much of anywhere, let alone Italy, Kansas being the only exception. That was kind of a foreign country.

"Are you thinking of going?" Tony asked, getting ready to leave. "If you are, that's good. Italy is nothing like anything you've ever seen. And the food! Mamma mia. Do you like Italian food?" Stephanie could see that Tony was getting very excited, his speech picking up speed. "If you go," he continued, his eyebrows dancing up and down, tapping his chest with a knowing finger. "Trust me, you'll never want to come back."

"Well," Stephanie paused, wondering if she should confide

in someone she didn't know, but he seemed very eager and genuinely interested.

"I may be going for work. It won't be a vacation. To cover the Tour D'Italia. You know it?"

Tony looked at her strangely, like she was speaking a foreign language, but then he brightened. "Oh, you mean the Giro. The Giro D'Italia! Of course, it is the most famous bike race in the world!"

Beth must have gotten it wrong, Stephanie thought. Now she was feeling even more doubtful about the assignment, especially if her boss couldn't even get the name right. Stephanie looked down at her shoes.

"I don't know anything about cycling. Baseball has always been my thing. You know, I wanted to be Roger Angell. My husband, Jeff, plays in the Minors, you know, the Thunder."

Tony cut her off. "Your husband is Jeff Talbot? The one who blew the Trenton High School Championship because he didn't hit the bases in the last inning on a grand slam?"

Stephanie stared at her shoes again, nodding, painfully acknowledging the truth. If Tony only knew.

"Look, I know this is coming out of left field," he continued as Stephanie cringed, "but if you need to learn about cycling, I think I can help you. Some of the kids are here visiting, about to head back to Venice. I call them kids, but they are your age, you know, young people," he smiled, adding. "Italians are practically born on bikes."

"I'm not exactly a young person," she stammered. "I got married later than most girls. I was pretty focused on my career and sports journalism—for the most part, a man's field—so I had to work pretty hard. I didn't go out much. I was always working," she added sheepishly, wondering why she was confessing all this to Tony, who had now, it seemed, transformed from plumber to therapist. He grabbed the cell phone on his belt and dialed.

"Marco? Ciao. Uncle Tony. *Senti*, listen, I know you were making a special dinner tonight. Would it be all right if I brought a guest? She wants to ask you all about the Giro." Stephanie heard a bright voice on the other line.

"*Si, si*. I'd like to tell her what you are making." Tony started to write on the back of the invoice. "*Arancini*. Uh-huh. *Tortellini in Brodo. Fritto Misto. Contorni. Dolce.* Got it. See you soon. *Ciao, Ciao.*" Well, at least she knew ciao, but had no clue what else Tony had said.

"Here," he said, taking one of several pens in his pocket. He scribbled an address and phone number next to the menu. "Come over at 7:00, okay? Marco is cooking for us, a going away present. He said he didn't mind one more. Especially a *bella signorina*," Tony said, winking. "With your fair complexion and blue eyes, you could easily pass for a pretty Northern Italian miss."

Stephanie felt her cheeks go red.

"Listen, it's okay. I see the mess in the driveway, you're not wearing a ring, and it's always the husbands who call the plumbers," he explained, this time transforming himself from therapist to sleuth.

Oh, God. Stephanie worried. What else could he see? That she should never have married Jeff? That she was glad they had never had any children? That she hated the house? That she wasn't even sure she really liked baseball that much anyway? Tony must have sensed her discomfort because he changed the subject back to his invitation and the dinner.

"You are in for a real treat. *Arancini* are fried rice balls filled with cheese, *tortellini* are these delicate little pasta stuffed with a mixture of chicken and veal. *Fritto misto* is a very traditional Venetian dish, fried seafood, and then he's making some kind of dessert. Something sweet, a dolce." Tony rubbed his stomach, stressing the last word, which sounded like *dolchay*.

Pizza she adored, and everything he described sounded

delicious, but she frowned. It all seemed a bit much, Tony, his family, the food. She felt like one of the pieces of laundry in the basement, floating, alone.

"Please," he said, putting a hand on her arm like a soft apology. "Besides, you will like him, Marco. He's quite a character, and he said he'd be happy to tell you about the Giro."

"All right," she sighed, relenting. Maybe she could pick up some good information to help her decide about the assignment. Besides, where was she going to go tonight, anyway?

"*Va bene*," he said, heading for the door.

"Pardon?" Stephanie asked, holding the kitchen door open.

"*Va bene*. It means all right. OK. Very good. Consider that your first Italian lesson," he said, waving.

Stephanie laughed out loud, a real laugh, a big tickling feeling on the inside.

"*Va bene*," she repeated awkwardly, but the words felt good in her mouth, like something sweet, like dolce.

Paul Explains Home
Ann Howells

Rush to your lighted home
evening after evening;
let bare feet slap.
Let nothing detain you.

In the city, people
cannot hear you. Their ears
fold closed; their tongues
are clipped.

There, consonants bounce
and tumble, clatter the walk;
you're pressed against bricks,
mouth a silent O...

mouth, not voice.
You don't have a voice,
barely exist, mere reflection
in shop windows.

Here, everyone who enters
is family or friend—
windows spill laughter
and doors are flung wide.

If you walk away, tires hiss
the freeway, windows blink,
doors crack. Turn back,
home flings open wide arms.

Landscaping at the Phoenix Airport
Ann Howells

Men rake and dig, plant sotol, ocotillo, cholla,
organ pipe, and prickly pear. I watch them
from the shuttle.

I'm late, and a wheel has fallen from my suitcase.
Dry stone walls cocoon in rabbit wire,
and saguaros stand

supported by wooden tripods, protected
against mishap—bump from heavy machinery.
Saguaros must reach

fifty years before sprouting stubby arms.
They are sturdy, resilient with spines
and tough hide,

but each of us is vulnerable in some manner.
Airport saguaros are venerable old men. Some –
called crested –

wear crowns that are really malformed arms
patterned in swirls, appearing ornate. When I
reach their age,

perhaps I too will grow a crown, be named queen.
Bearers will tote my broken luggage, pilots
hold the plane.

Bulkhead Seat
Mary Donaldson-Evans

I hadn't asked for a bulkhead seat, but really, the leg room in the Boeing 757 was just too inadequate for my long legs, and I was thinking, with despair, of the eight-hour flight ahead when, suddenly, I spied a vacant seat in the exit row in front of me, right behind the bulkhead toilets. The plane had left the gate but hadn't begun its takeoff roll, so I quickly unbuckled my seatbelt and moved forward.

Whew! I felt as if I had been upgraded to first class. Perhaps I'd even get some sleep. After a three-week trip backpacking through Europe, I was exhausted. I stretched out my legs, put my headset on, set it to the "Country Roads" channel, and settled back to enjoy the flight. Well, perhaps not to "enjoy" the flight. Who enjoys an eight-hour flight? But at least to relax and doze a little.

As soon as we had reached our cruising altitude, the seatbelt sign went off, and the parade of passengers to the toilets began, slowly at first, then with more regularity. I amused myself by trying to guess their age and nationality. I was flying USAir, so there were bound to be some Americans. And since the flight had originated in Amsterdam, there were no doubt quite a few Dutchmen aboard the plane as well.

The guy with the plaid shirt that gaped open between the buttons, stretching to cover a belly that had seen too much fast food and beer? Definitely an American. 50-something, I guessed. The double chin still had some elasticity to it.

The curvaceous young woman with the gauzy scarf and mini-skirt who left a trail of sweet-smelling perfume in her wake as she walked by? Her dark eyes and black hair suggested a southern European country, an impression semi-confirmed when she turned to the guy in the seat behind me and said something about "*los niños*." Spain, I guessed. Late thirties, with just the beginning of crow's feet around her eyes, those first lines that you actually welcome because they give your face character.

The college-aged student with the sweatshirt announcing not only that she had been to Amsterdam but that "Coffee Shops Rock"? Probably American. She was a well-weathered 22 who'd soaked up too much sun and smoked too many joints, probably at the same time.

The plump woman with her hair in a bun who smiled at the flight attendant as she passed, revealing long, overlapping, and discolored teeth? British, 60-something. Why can't the Brits get decent dental care? Guy de Maupassant, one of my favorite authors, once compared the teeth of an English woman to garden tools. One hundred and thirty years later, her compatriots are still smiling smiles that remind you it's time to plant the pansies. Yup. Definitely British.

I was beginning to tire of the game when an old man shuffled slowly toward the toilets, so feeble and unsteady on his feet that I feared he might fall. I noticed his feet first, and then my gaze rose to meet his, and my heart skipped a beat. It was my father! I nearly called out, "Daddy!!!" I'm glad I didn't. My father has been dead for 15 years. I was at his funeral, and even though I didn't see his casket lowered into the ground—it was only April, and in Minnesota, the ground is still frozen at that time of the year—I did see his waxen form at the viewing, and I had no doubt whatsoever that he had died. And yet, here he was, not just the spitting image of my dad, but *my dad* back from the grave. I tried to persuade myself that this was just a lookalike and that it was bound to happen sooner or later, that Mother Nature or God or some other Higher Power probably screwed up occasionally and forgot to change the pattern. It was inconceivable that in the billions of people who walked this earth, there were not quite a number of people who were true doubles, twins born of different parents. I mean, how many variations can there be on the human face? Two eyes, a nose, a mouth: how do you create billions of faces with these basic givens and not duplicate some of them?

But the fact is that he looked just as startled to see me as I was to see him. That has to count for something, doesn't it? I mean, if this old man wasn't my dad, why did he, too, have a look of recognition when he saw me?

I don't know if he looked away first or if I did, but I reached for the in-flight magazine and changed the channel to "Chill": "Close your eyes and take in the ambient sounds and chilled beats from a variety of artists, all designed to calm and relax," said the magazine in its description of this channel.

I closed my eyes. I tried to let myself be calmed by the music. It didn't work. When I looked up again, the man was fumbling with the lock on the toilet door. The word "Occupied" was illuminated, and this man couldn't have been my father because he obviously didn't know English. He kept pushing the lever up and down, up and down. He seemed almost frantic. Finally, a flustered-looking woman emerged, nearly knocking him over when she opened the door. He struggled to remain standing, managed somehow to get into the toilet, then had a hard time closing the door, but it finally snapped shut. I couldn't tell if he locked the door properly. If he didn't understand "Occupied," how could he understand "Please lock door"? Would the arrow be sufficient to clue him in? I resisted the temptation to get up and look, but when a teenager with a nose ring approached, I leaped out of my seat to check. Whew. The word "Occupied" was illuminated.

I waited for him to emerge. Five minutes passed, then ten. What was he doing in there, I asked myself. Was I the only one who noticed how long he'd been there? There was another toilet in the block, and passengers came and went too quickly to notice that one of the toilets had been occupied for a long time.

What to do? Get a grip, I told myself: he *looks* like your father. He's not your father. And whoever he is, he's probably fine. Maybe he's experiencing air sickness. Or brushing his teeth and washing his face. Perhaps he's reading a novel on the toilet and got caught up in the plot. I tried to remember if he had had a book in his hand when he went into the toilet.

I waited another ten minutes. Dinner was served. That distracted me for a while. Then, after a half hour or so, the trays were removed, there was another run on the toilets that must have lasted for another forty-five minutes or so, and passengers started to lower their shades and go to sleep. Still, my dad, or rather the old man, had not emerged from the toilet. By now, he'd been there for two hours. How was it possible that nobody but me had noticed? I decided to signal one of the flight attendants. I pressed the call button, the one that had a little red person icon.

"Yes?" she asked, a hint of irritation in her voice.

"Um, there's a man in one of the toilets," I said. "He's been there for quite a while."

"So?" said the flight attendant.

"I mean, *quite* a while," I said again, with emphasis.

"How long is quite a while?" she asked.

"Oh, a couple of hours or so."

"*A couple of hours?!*" she asked incredulously. "And you're just reporting it now?"

I felt a bead of sweat form on the nape of my neck and run down my back.

"Well, I didn't think it was any of my business," I said. "Except that..."

"Except what?" she asked, interested now.

"Except that I think it's my father."

"Come again?" she replied, sure that she had misunderstood.

"Oh, never mind," I said, worried now that I wouldn't be believed.

"No, tell me what you said," she insisted. "You *think* the man locked in the toilet is your father? Are you traveling with your father?"

"Hardly. He's been dead for 15 years."

I could almost hear her brain synapses firing as she tried to take in this new bit of information and decide whether she should force the door, potentially embarrassing a passenger who was in some kind of discomfort and had been occupying the toilet for a longer-than-usual length of time or to dismiss my observation out of hand as the raving of a delusional woman.

I tried to explain, but my mouth wouldn't form the words.

"We'll keep an eye on it," she said, and I knew she was also thinking, "We'll keep an eye on you."

The rest of the flight passed uneventfully. I dozed for an hour or so, and when I awoke, the word "Vacant" showed on the door of the toilet my dad had occupied. Had the flight crew "liberated" the man? Had he left of his own accord?

My stomach rumbled. I needed to use the toilet. I opened the door slowly, lest he still be there. It was indeed vacant. The image of the Empty Tomb flitted across my mind.

But he had to be on the airplane.

I decided to stretch my legs. I walked as far as I could to the front of the plane, i.e., just up to the "off-limits" Business Class section, where a curtain had been drawn across the aisle, and then retraced my steps very slowly, looking into every face as I made my way back down the aisle to the tail. He was nowhere to be seen, but I did notice that in the galley, at the back of the plane, two flight attendants were eyeing me with suspicion, watching my every move.

I did a second pass through the cabin. No sign of my dad.

It's like when you drop your contact lens in the sink. The trap is closed, so you know it has to be there, but it's not, and no matter how hard you look, you can't find it. Completely confused, I reckoned that there was only one other possibility: the man in the toilet had died, and the flight attendants had removed his body while I slept. But where would they have stashed it? Planes don't have morgues, do they?

I went back to the galley to have a look around, pretexting the need for a drink of water. I scanned the small room, noticing that the metal cabinets in which the dinner trays are usually stored were not big enough to hold a human body.

The flight attendants exchanged a look.

It was time to return to the bulkhead.

Sinking into my seat, I put my headset back on and changed the channel to classical music. The strains of Mozart's Requiem filled my ears and brought tears to my eyes.

"Bye, Daddy," I whispered. And then, unbidden, another thought came to me: Lack of sleep can make you crazy.

The words had been spoken many years ago by a psychologist in the course of a family session that followed my younger sister's psychotic break. It was a scary time for all of us, and, in fact, my sister had not slept in days.

I thought back to my trip. When was the last time I had had more than two or three hours of sleep at a time? I couldn't recall. First, it was the time change that put me off-kilter, then the overnight train travel, the food poisoning, the snorer in the next room of the two-bit hotel…

So that was it. I was sleep-deprived, and the man I saw wasn't my dad after all. Still, I shall always remember the thrill of recognition I felt when I first saw him and the rush of longing when we exchanged a glance that was more eloquent than the most eloquent of words.

I closed my eyes and summoned the sandman.

A Conversation with
Mary Donaldson-Evans
Lowestoft Chronicle

Mary Donaldson-Evans
(Photography: Lance Donaldson-Evans)

During a distinguished academic career, in which she was awarded a chaired professorship, received prominent teaching awards, and was named, "Chevalier" of l'Association des Membres de l'Ordre des Palmes Académiques, Mary Donaldson-Evans drew praise for her many scholarly essays on 19th-century French literature and culture. Her extensive examinations of the work of Guy de Maupassant, which began in the late 1970s, include the book *A Woman's Revenge*, which led academics to view her as a connoisseur of Maupassant's work. Recently, her biographical book, *Behind the Lines*, attracted warm reviews for its exploration of the era's social and historical circumstances and the hardships and personal sacrifices of military families and was named a 2022 Distinguished Favorite by the Independent Press Award.

In this exclusive interview with *Lowestoft Chronicle*, Donaldson-Evans discusses her father's deployment in Italy during WW2 and reveals her fascination with Maupassant and nineteenth-century French literature, the motivations behind her books, and future literary projects.

Lowestoft Chronicle (LC): Was *A Woman's Revenge: The Chronology of Dispossession in Maupassant's Fiction* your first published book? What is the backstory on how you came to publish this through French Forum Publishers?

Mary Donaldson-Evans (MDE): The editors of French Forum Monographs, Raymond and Virginia La Charité, also published a professional journal, *French Forum*, and it was there that I placed my very first article, which happened to be on Maupassant. Since they had welcomed my contribution to the journal, it made sense for me to submit my book to their monograph series. I had not tried my luck anywhere else, and I was thrilled when they accepted it.

LC: The book received high praise in academic circles, garnering many positive reviews. In fact, Allan H. Pasco, a distinguished Professor of Nineteenth-Century Literature, who considered you "one of the United States' best readers of Maupassant," asserted: "Donaldson-Evans has added considerably to our understanding of the Maupassantian universe." When did you first develop an interest in Guy de Maupassant, and why? Is it fair to say that your numerous essays on him and the extensive, learned author entry you contributed to the *Dictionary of Literary Biography* suggest you strived to become an authority on his work?

MDE: As a PhD student in the University of Pennsylvania's Romance Languages Department, I knew early on that I wanted to write my dissertation on nineteenth-century French literature. The late Frank Paul Bowman, an eminent scholar, was one of two specialists in the nineteenth century, and I approached him to see if he had suggestions for topics worth pursuing. He immediately mentioned Maupassant. I was appalled because, at the time, Maupassant was widely considered to be an author for adolescents, someone you put aside as you matured. This stemmed partly from the fact that his most successful genre was the short story, considered to be inferior to the novel. Now Professor Bowman used to say of his weaker students, "Well, we can't get any more blood out of that turnip," and when he proposed that I consider writing my thesis on Maupassant, I interpreted his suggestion as proof positive that he saw me as one of his "turnips." Nevertheless, I did begin to familiarize myself more thoroughly with Maupassant's work, and the more I read, the more I became convinced that there was more depth to his fiction than scholars realized. I wrote my thesis on Maupassant under the direction of Professor Bowman…and the rest, I guess, is history. At the time, most of the critics who chose to write on Maupassant—in France and elsewhere—focused on his biography, and particularly on the more lurid aspects of his life, for he was an impenitent womanizer. Apart from Edward Sullivan of Princeton University and Artine Artinian of Bard College, few American critics were actually examining the work. I didn't set out to be a Maupassant scholar as such, but once I got started, I found his stories and novels a very rich mine to explore.

LC: In *Medical Examinations*, you expose the textual duplicity in the narratives of late-nineteenth-century antimedical French literature—specifically, you study physician-characters and physician-narrators. A wonderfully precise scope and a fascinating study but quite a challenge to write, I should imagine. What made you research this unusual subject? Was it a challenge omitting works, or was the greater challenge finding eight suitable works?

MDE: I loved that project, and I learned a lot about nineteenth-century medical practice in researching it. I guess the impetus for that study came from my realization that nineteenth-century French literature was rich in depictions of physicians and that they were often portrayed as inept bumblers or downright charlatans. Charles Bovary is a case in point. I set out to find out why this was the case. Surely it was not coincidental that many writers of the era were victims of diseases for which there was, at the time, no cure. Maupassant offers a prime example here, as he was suffering the effects of syphilis for much of his adult life and succumbed to the illness at the age of 43. The challenge was in narrowing my scope. There were abundant examples from the fiction of the period.

LC: Your subsequent book, *Madame Bovary at the Movies*, an extensive study of twentieth-century film (specifically, the screen adaptations of Madame Bovary)—"an indispensable study" according to Professor Colin Davis—stemmed from an essay you contributed fourteen years earlier to the textbook *Approaches to Teaching Flaubert's Madame Bovary (Approaches to Teaching World Literature)*. What compelled you to write about film theory? Were you approached by a publisher to write this book, or did positive responses to "Teaching Madame Bovary through Film" encourage you to explore the topic in more detail?

MDE: *Madame Bovary at the Movies* was the third authored book of my academic career, and yes, it's true that my teaching informed my scholarship. We were pressured to boost enrollments in foreign languages, and one popular way to do so was to offer courses on film. We were also encouraged to teach foreign literature courses in translation. I designed a course on the nineteenth-century French novel through film, in which students read five well-known novels in English translation and, after each reading, watched a film based on the novel, and it was very enlightening to hear students discuss what novels could do that films couldn't and vice versa (to paraphrase the title of an article by film critic Seymour Chatman). It was around that time that I learned how popular *Madame Bovary* had been with filmmakers throughout the world, thanks to its pre-cinematic techniques (Flaubert's propensity for "showing" rather than "telling") and one thing led to another and, well, the book came out of that. There were over 18 adaptations of the novel, from several different countries and starting in the silent era, and I learned a lot about filmmaking simply by comparing and contextualizing them.

LC: As an expert on Maupassant, it begs the question: why not also analyze screen adaptations of Maupassant's works? In *The New Yorker,* Richard Brody writes: "Maupassant's stories are so cinematically fruitful because their loose ends invite adaptation and render even methodically faithful adaptations overtly interpretive." In light of the fact that Maupassant's hundreds of stories inspired many film and TV adaptations, did you consider analyzing the reception of some of his films?

MDE: Great question! This is something I would probably have considered doing had I remained in academe, but by the time I finished the book on the Bovary adaptations (published in 2009), I was winding down. I had accepted to do a critical edition of Maupassant's *Bel-Ami* for the French publisher Garnier towards the end of my career, and all my remaining energy went into that. For reasons beyond my control, that book never appeared (if I were an optimist, I'd say "has not yet appeared"), but that's another story.

LC: *Behind the Lines* is an engrossing account of your parent's life in the 1940s while your father was stationed in Italy during WW2. Actually, a book critic in *Kirkus Reviews* put it better, eloquently describing it as a heartfelt examination of "the work and worry that filled the lives of wartime families and the sacrifices they undertook for those they loved." As you sifted through your father's vast WW2 memorabilia (which apparently consisted of hundreds of exchanges between family and friends), was there a particular moment, a letter perhaps, that made you want to share his and your mother's memoirs with a broader audience?

MDE: Honestly, my brother Chuck and I (because he's the one who found the letters in the first place) were like kids in a toy shop when we opened that battered trunk and started reading those musty old letters. It was a "Back to the Future" moment, discovering our parents as they were as young marrieds. There was no particular letter that triggered the desire to publish a book based on this correspondence, simply a sense that we had a story worth telling here. Chuck left the project in my hands.

LC: In fact, Chuck contributes an interesting chapter towards the end of the book and might have featured more had he been able to join you on your Italy trip. Did you discuss chapter ideas with him while writing the book?

MDE: Absolutely! He gave me advice all the way through and was one of my first editors, along with his wife, Gail, and of course, my husband, Lance, who was my very first reader. Chuck has a wicked sense of humor, and he had initially suggested I entitle the book *Letters from the Rear*, but we thought better of it. I should add that my kids and their spouses also had important roles in the book's production. My daughter, a professional editor, was especially helpful; my son, an architect, designed the cover.

LC: WW2 narratives hold special appeal, but as you stated in your book, the focus here is not on military battles but "small acts of personal sacrifice" and the "insecurities and fears of wives left to fend for themselves at home." You had initial concerns about whether this volume would be a worthwhile addition to the legions of war memoirs already in print. Was there also a fear that this project shouldn't be a public work, that the correspondence between your parents was a private matter that ought to be confined to the family circle?

MDE: Certainly! This is something that all memoir-writers struggle with, and the book shuttles back and forth between history and memoir, exposing my parents' foibles in a way that might be embarrassing to them were they still alive. On balance, though, I think their humanity and their courage carry the day, and I've been gratified to hear readers tell me that they found my parents admirable. Above all, I wanted to describe the life of an ordnance soldier, and not just any ordnance soldier but one who was lucky enough to be assigned to the prestigious 10th Mountain Division. My dad's experiences, and those of my mom back home, reveal the challenges of what is now a bygone era.

LC: The sheer scale of work involved in reading, editing, and arranging the mass of letters must have been immense, and your careful research on the 10th Mountain Division and interesting but more obscure WW2 details are evident. How does this book compare with your academic books in terms of composition and research effort?

MDE: My academic books required hours and hours of library research. While I read perhaps 30 books in preparing *Behind the Lines*, much of my research was facilitated by the Internet. Admittedly, this would probably also be true today of academic research. The mental effort required to analyze literary texts was no doubt greater than the mental effort I expended here, but this was offset by the need to acquaint myself with WW2 history. I had been woefully ignorant of this era before I set to work on this book. As for composition, I would say that I had an easier time in the writing of this book than I had with scholarly articles and books. My thesis advisor (him again!) once told me that my style was "too chatty for the honorable genre of the PhD thesis" and I struggled to give more sophistication to my prose. That wasn't an issue here. For one thing, my thesis director, like my parents, is long gone (May They Rest in Peace). For another, I was hoping the book would appeal to a wider readership than had been the case with my academic writing, and a chattier style seemed appropriate.

LC: Ultimately, what might have become a mundane account of army life and everyday family frustrations is, instead, a rewarding examination of the era, enlivened by observations on things like teeth and tobacco, religion and rationing, and paper and Parker pens. In fact, your research takes you as far as Italy, following in your father's footsteps. How did your battlefield trip to Italy come about, and how important was it for you to see the places your father was stationed? Was this 2017 pilgrimage undertaken to help write the book?

MDE: (I like your alliteration!) I blush to admit that I had known nothing of the 10th Mountain Division before embarking on this project. I was aware that my father had served during the Second World War, that he had been sent to Italy, and that he had brought a doll home for me. And that was it. However, once I learned about this amazing unit, I joined the descendants' organization and proudly displayed a sticker on the bumper of my car. How not to succumb to the temptation to join the battlefields tour that was being arranged by the organization? While the pilgrimage was not exactly undertaken to help write the book, it certainly played a role in the whole "immersion" experience and provided me with material for the book's last chapter. My husband Lance accompanied me. Before we left, he had used his internet skills to put me in touch with an Italian family from Cividale who had befriended my father as the war was ending. Not the least of the thrills of the trip was meeting a woman of 80 who had fond memories of my father's visits to her home when she was a child. But yes, seeing the hill towns where my father had been stationed was also very moving. I quite literally felt his presence during the tour, and writing a book about his experiences—and my own—seemed not just appropriate but necessary.

LC: For the past ten or more years, you've concentrated on short fiction and memoirs, appearing in numerous literary journals—your travel exploits even show up in a column in *The New York Times*. Are you working towards a collection of travel essays or a story collection? What are your next literary goals?

MDE: This is a tough question to answer. I had not actually thought of gathering my travel pieces for publication as a book, but you've given me an idea! I do have two projects underway. The first involves assembling the many memoir-type pieces I've written over the years about various aspects of aging. That sounds depressing, I know, but they're mostly light-hearted and anecdotal rather than profound and probing. Everybody can relate, I think, as we've all had moments when we become acutely aware of our advancing years, whether it be that mental lapse that makes us fear Alzheimer's or the sobering moment when we spy our reflection in the window of a car door. I'm having lots of fun putting these essays together. The other writing project is based on a detailed record of dinner parties that I've been keeping since 1972. My husband and I used to entertain quite a bit—we've slowed down now—and we've had some memorable dinner parties, some quite hilarious and successful, others spectacular failures. I'm interspersing narrative with recipes. Time will tell whether I have enough material for a book. I also have a good number of stories, about half of them published, that I could gather for publication in a single volume.

LC: What's the backstory on your latest piece for *Lowestoft Chronicle*? Did "Bulkhead Seat" emerge from intensive research on your father for *Behind the Lines*?

MDE: I never made that connection myself, but who knows? It's true that I was deeply immersed in the book project when "Bulkhead Seat" was written, and I remember picturing my own dad as I tapped away on my laptop. I actually composed the first draft of that story on an American Airlines flight to Philadelphia from Amsterdam, and yes! I had a bulkhead seat!

Idlewild*
Joan Mazza

That feeling when your shoulders relax
and you slump in a molded airport chair
or waiting room, knowing you're
captive to time and others' plans
and schedules, trapped in one place
for days because of a blizzard or monsoon,
unable to go to commute to work, too late
to shop for more supplies. Your body
lets go, freed of the burden of errands
and meetings without meaning, allows you
to gaze out the window as snowflakes fall
and icicles march along the eaves.
With nowhere to go and little to do,
your mind wanders into cobwebby corners
where memories lurk, dusty and gritty,
with a soundtrack from an old kitchen radio
and a scent track with the fragrances of broiled
lemon and garlic chicken, Mother's voice near,
warning of the treachery in ice and frostbite.
Cut off from any demand or obligation
to do something productive but likely
unimportant, you are stuck inside
a warm space surrounded by books,
or marooned in a place equally safe, waiting
for the call of your name or flight number.

---

*Adjective. Feeling grateful to be stranded in a place where you can't do
much of anything. From *The Dictionary of Obscure Sorrows* by John Koenig.

I Circle Back
Joan Mazza

to old issues stuck in my core, concerns surrounding
domination, my easy abdication of the pilot's seat, to
let someone take the wheel and all control. I've been
too quick to say, *You choose. I'm fine with whatever
you decide.* How soon I complain. This isn't what I
want— this isolation, job, labor's paternal division so I
get all the chores of toilets, kitchen, serving while
everyone eats dinner. I seem to choose those who boast
of their trove of inside knowledge, who ooze
confidence, tell me what to think and how to vote. You
say my brain is out of whack? If I agree with your
interpretation, you're correct. Disagree and I'm
resisting, hostile. If I make a case for my view, I'll be
tagged defensive. Maybe your hypothesis is wrong.
Uneasy, unsettled, I have reasons for my anger, and
circle back to resurrect arguments with the dead. They
can't interrupt. This time I have the final word, no
more circling back.

International Arrival
Jennifer Swallow

The crowd in the international terminal of Moscow Sheremetyevo thickened. Status updates in bright red—canceled, delayed, canceled, delayed—covered the arrivals and departures boards. Dark clouds hung low in the sky above the airport as flights were diverted to Saint Petersburg, Helsinki, and Kiev.

At a bar, with only a sparkling water in front of him, sat a short, slender dark-complexioned man. The lines on his forehead implied the concerns of a man of forty-five, though he was only twenty-seven. He held a battered leather briefcase to his lap with one hand and flipped a mobile phone open and closed with the other.

The phone rang, and he answered it in accented but fluent Russian. When he hung up, he abandoned his glass of water and snaked around bodies and bags over to the arrivals board. His eyes scanned it for a moment and paused when they found New York. Delayed.

Blyat. The woman on the phone was right. Since the flight wasn't canceled yet, he'd have to keep waiting. Normally, he wouldn't mind. When he'd taken this job in the spring, the notion of waiting in the airport for hours, day after day, had struck him as idyllic. With three young children and a wife at home, he relished the thought of being able to sit and read mystery novels with no interruptions. And up until now, that's exactly how his workdays had gone. Delayed flights extended his literary enjoyment, letting him be shocked by the crime, work alongside the investigator, and discover the murderer all in one sitting. Tonight, though, he had a concert ticket, a ticket he had saved a long time to afford.

He knew this flight wasn't going to land. Everyone expecting it knew. But if the board didn't say canceled, he had to wait until more information was available. Missing a pickup would mean instantly losing his job.

Blyat, he muttered again. Some curse words were the same in Russian and Armenian.

"Privet," a voice to his right said.

Artyom turned and saw a standard-issue Russian thug. Buzz cut, black leather jacket, and track pants. The man looked moderately fit, yet still had a paunch. He didn't carry any luggage. Artyom nodded once and walked back to the bar. He sat down at a table without ordering anything and pulled some papers out of his briefcase.

Dana Mulrooney, 24, Nashua, New Hampshire.
Arriving Tuesday, September 17, 2002, at 3:40 PM on DL217 from New York City.
Instructions: Drive to m. Smolenskaya, st. Novy Arbat, 26 for the night. Pick up at 8:30 AM and drive to Paveletskiy station for the 9:30 AM train to Volgograd.

The papers included her train ticket and a photo, which showed a broad smiling face with white, straight teeth and brown, straight hair that came down to her shoulders. She was indistinguishable from the other young American and British women he had collected who came to teach English. Barely a decade since the collapse of communism, and it seemed like everyone had money to spend on luxuries like private language tutors. While Artyom couldn't afford to pay a foreigner to teach his own kids, chauffeuring these teachers provided enough money for a used car and a much nicer apartment than his family could have ever hoped for in Armenia. He could even treat himself from time to time, like buying this ticket to see the rock band Splean.

The concert. It started at seven and would take almost an hour to reach from the apartment where he needed to drop off Dana Mulrooney. With the time it would take for her to collect her bag and get through customs, and the time to drive to the apartment, he would barely make the opening act. If she was an hour late, he would miss at least part of the main act too. He was certain her plane was seven hundred kilometers away, circling Saint Petersburg at that very moment, waiting to land, the airline already having decided no flights would be heading to Moscow for the rest of the night. If only they would update the arrivals board.

"Beautiful girl," a voice said over his shoulder.

Artyom looked up. The thug from earlier stood behind him. Artyom snapped the file shut and stuffed it into his briefcase. "She's my cousin."

The man smiled, then pulled out an empty chair at the table and sat down.

"Vadim," he said, offering a hand to shake.

"Artyom." He shook the man's hand, then locked the clasp on his case.

"Your cousin, eh? Abandoned the Soviet Union, now coming back to spend her American money buying up all our property?" Vadim tipped his back chair onto two legs and hoisted an elbow across the backrest.

"Not at all. Only coming to visit family." Artyom knew about guys like this. He would find information on wealthy arrivals, get the driver or family member drunk and passed out, explain to the visitor that there was an emergency and he was the new escort, and then, after they got out onto the highway, rob the person. Or worse. It was a common scam Artyom's employer had educated him about and reminded him of every time there was a news story about another occurrence, which was frequently. In four months on the job, Artyom hadn't fallen victim to one of these guys. That felt like an accomplishment.

"In Moscow? You don't sound Russian to me."

"I'm not. We're flying back to Yerevan together as soon as she lands." Artyom had practiced this story many times. If this Vadim didn't think they were even traveling into the city, surely he would find someone else to victimize.

"That's a lot of travel straight from New York."

Artyom clenched his jaw. The man must have stood over his shoulder long enough to read at least some of the datasheet. He offered a close-lipped smile and then said, "Well, she doesn't have long to visit. Can't waste time in Moscow. Now, if you'll excuse me." He rose from his chair.

Vadim sat up straight and held out both arms. "Hey, where are you going? None of the flights are coming in for a long time. Let me buy you a drink."

"I don't drink."

"Every good Russian drinks!" Vadim threw back his head and laughed loudly.

"As you pointed out, I'm not Russian. And I have to go now."

Artyom strode over to the Delta Airlines customer service desk. The line was several people deep, but he didn't need to wait. He heard someone at the front of the line ask about the New York flight, and the agent responded that she had no information about the plane's whereabouts. Artyom stepped out of line and scanned the frustrated faces of people waiting for flights that were never going to arrive or depart. Vadim had disappeared. Still, Artyom didn't want to chance another encounter. He headed for the airport exit.

Beyond the sliding glass doors, dense clouds the color of steel rolled and collided, their shapes constantly changing from one gargoyle to another. Signage and small trees bounced back and forth stiffly. Plastic bags and scraps of paper swirled twenty and thirty feet above the ground. The people running toward him were nearly doubled over in their efforts to not get blown over. Artyom stashed his briefcase beneath his coat, clutched it to his chest, and ran toward the economy parking lot.

Seconds after he reached his car, the rain reached Moscow. Droplets the size of gumdrops plopped onto his windshield, randomly at first, but within minutes, in a deafening, impenetrable cascade that obscured the cars around him. Artyom kept the ignition off and let his breath fog the windows. He could have been completely alone in the world for the next ten minutes, and he wouldn't have known the difference. But when the worst of the storm passed, and the chaos of the airport came back into view, his phone rang.

"Oh, thank god you are alright," his wife said.

"Of course, darling, why wouldn't I be?"

"I thought you were driving in the middle of this apocalypse."

"The flight hasn't landed yet."

"Even if it lands, promise me you won't drive in this. You don't know how."

Artyom had only received his driving license a month before he applied with the language school, a fact he had successfully hidden from his employer. Driving in the rain did make him nervous, and the impending winter worried him greatly. Regardless, he sighed gently into the phone. "Anush, all will be fine. Safe driving is my job."

"And you do it well, my love." She sighed. "I guess you will have to miss the show."

"Yes, I think so." He glanced at his glovebox, which held the coveted ticket. Then he glanced at his watch, which read five o'clock. "I don't know when the flight is coming. There's no information."

"Well, if there's still no information by seven, you should go. If the weather has cleared, that is. You could watch them and then head back to the airport after."

Artyom hadn't considered this. He could. He could drive down there and check the flight status right before Splean took the stage. The venue was only forty minutes away.

He talked with his wife a while longer while the rain continued to ting heavily against the metal of his old Lada Zhiguli. When they hung up, he considered his wife's suggestion again. He'd never left in the middle of an unfinished job. Maybe he should call his boss and tell her his plan. Maybe he should ask her if another staff member might be free. Would she understand how important this show was to him? Probably not. Tatiana Gorevskaya was a shrewd businesswoman, capable of finding her niche and profiting off the transition to this new economy. However, she did not approve of the societal changes, like the growing popularity of American-style rock music. And with hundreds of immigrants pouring in daily from the former Soviet republics, he knew he was easily replaceable. If he was going to do this, he would be wise to keep it to himself.

He remained in his car, reading the latest mystery from Darya Dontsova. An hour later, he still hadn't heard a single plane overhead. He pulled an umbrella from the backseat and dashed back to the terminal.

The line for the Delta representative was now over a dozen people deep. Artyom joined it and looked around. Every inch of wall space was being leaned against. Hundreds of angry voices echoed in the great hall. The bar no longer had even standing room, and men with pint glasses full of beer spilled out into the walkway, cursing passersby who jostled their elbows and sloshed beer over the rims and onto their shoes. These men were a homogenous bunch, except for one.

Next to an overflowing trashcan stood Vadim. They locked eyes. Vadim raised his pint glass and winked. Artyom turned back around to face the agent's desk, his heartbeat racing. It felt implausible that, among all these bodies and despite all the hours that had passed, Vadim knew exactly where he was. Coincidence seemed unlikely. Artyom clutched the handle of this briefcase with both hands and remained facing forward.

"Flight 217 is on the ground in Peter, but the passengers have been instructed to wait at the gate. We still intend to bring that flight to Moscow this evening." The tall blonde spoke in monotone, looking him directly in the eyes as she did, not needing to consult the computer screen in front of her.

"But when?"

"When we know, we'll update the arrivals board." She gestured vaguely to the nearest screens and then looked past him to the next person in line.

Artyom stepped out of line. If the plane hadn't left yet, the passengers had to get on board, fly, exit the plane in Moscow, and go through customs. He had at least three hours of free time ahead, and it was nearly seven. He hesitated and then exited the airport again without looking back toward the bar.

✦

The rain continued, limiting visibility on the M-11. The downpour had waterlogged the highway, and dozens of cars, including the Lada, hydroplaned into other lanes, causing even the vehicles with decent tires to hit their brakes and further slow traffic. Artyom hadn't gone faster than thirty kilometers an hour since leaving the airport. At this rate, he would arrive just as the band was finishing. Not to mention he'd never make it back in time to meet Dana Mulrooney if her plane landed while he was still in Moscow's central business district. The risk of losing his job wasn't worth seeing the band perform only one or two songs. He'd have other chances to see Splean, especially if he didn't get fired. Maybe he could actually afford two tickets and take his wife with him next time.

He put his blinker on and slowly merged to the right to take the next exit. At the light, he turned left and then left again to get back on the highway, heading toward the airport. As Artyom accelerated, the massive tires of a tractor-trailer in front of him sprayed his car with rainwater. Even at the highest setting, his wipers couldn't fight off the deluge. Unable to see the lines in the road or the walls of the on-ramp, he tapped his brakes to let the truck pull ahead.

Something rammed into the back of his car. Artyom's chest rushed toward the steering wheel with his head whipping forward after it a second later. He pressed the pedal harder to prevent his car from smashing into the semi, but the taillights at eye level grew larger. He jerked the wheel, but the concrete on either side gave him nowhere to go. The continued force behind him pushed the hood of the Lada under the rear of the giant truck. When the windshield hit the bumper, it spiderwebbed, and when Artyom hit the bumper, he was decapitated.

—■ ✦ ■—

At 11:45 PM on September 17, a Russian customs agent stamped Dana Mulrooney's passport and waved her through to the arrivals hall of Sheremetyevo. A man with a buzz cut, black leather jacket, track pants, and a small sign that read "Dana" was waiting for her.

Irrational
David Shawn Klein

My Uber customer rating was somewhere between pedophile axe murderer and Trump supporter, so I decided to go on a quest to resuscitate my good name. Plus, to be honest, my feelings were hurt. I didn't even know I could get rated until the tiny animated cars on my app began to stop, spin around, and race away. It was like Tinder for taxis; I was being judged wanting by dozens of left-swiping Uber drivers. I was stuck at 4.55 and worried that Uber and Lyft shared the equivalent of a No-Fly List to banish incorrigibles to ride-app purgatory, where lost souls wander around in search of a yellow cab during the worst rainstorm in recorded history.

It made me regret driving my regular Uber guy Jesus so crazy he started drinking out of a brown paper bag. Jesus was the only melancholic Dominican I'd ever met. I liked him because I'm the world's biggest introvert, and he never made eye contact. Instead, he always greeted me with a grudging hello that sounded like air escaping from a flat tire. He constantly wore a bright blue Moana baseball cap and the same jacket with the logo of the Jackson Heights Stingrays. It was great to have Jesus as my regular driver because he played Arturo Sandoval and Kenny G on an endless loop, and if you're like me and find it easier to binge-watch a C-SPAN senate hearing than ask a stranger if he'd mind turning down his music, even Kenny G is a lot less traumatic than bands like "Hammer On My Thumb," or "Driven By Spite," after a long day's work.

And I really wanted to have the same guy take me around the city. Part of the reason was that I'm so addicted to routine that I need to pop half a Xanax just to change toothbrushes.

But also, to pay the rent, I have to lug these giant suitcases filled with marketing stuff across the five boroughs. At first, using a car and driver seemed like the kind of extravagance reserved for Instagram stars or sixteen-year-old tech billionaires, so my suitcases and I hoofed it on the subway.

But even though they were on spinners, the suitcases seemed to have a life of their own, and the central purpose of that life was to humiliate me in front of as many people as possible. I regularly brightened the commute of thousands of over-stressed New Yorkers who stopped to watch the giant doofus get hopelessly stuck trying to force two suitcases through a turnstile. And God knows how many cell phones were switched to camera while I flailed after man-sized Victorinox as they rode further and further out of reach down the up escalator. So it was clearly time to retire from YouTube's "Idiots on Subways" and spring for an Uber whenever I needed to hit the road.

It was also a trust issue, wanting the same driver. Trust and anxiety. There are places in Staten Island so remote they have their own weather systems—would Uber really have a car ready at the tap of an app? Could I have faith it wouldn't leave me stranded on a frigid night in an outpost of Queens, a mile from the nearest subway? So I made a private arrangement with the first driver, who seemed to be inclined toward a touch of larceny. That was Jesus. The deal was that Jesus would take me to my destination, wait off the app, and I'd give him cash for hanging out. It was a small price to pay for the assurance that, when I needed him, Jesus would be there.

But he turned out to be the start of my dismal customer rating. It probably had to do with my traffic-induced meltdowns and the effect he thought they had on Liz of the Purple Heart. My Victorinox and I travel the city teaching free legal clinics for unions and day labor centers. Many of the people I teach are Spanish-speaking, and my Spanish is limited to "Soy abogado," which would make for a very brief evening if it weren't for Liz. But Liz does more than translate—though, in truth, she barely does that. You might say she freely interprets, but it's more like she says whatever she wants and I'm just along for the ride. She does it to make me "less boring." The class will often laugh after I've said something like "severe injury" or "prolonged hospital stay," so I know she's told a joke at my expense, usually about my age or how boring I am. Liz's wardrobe is from the house of Carolina Herrera, and she wears it like Carolina designed it exclusively for her. She's great with people: warm, earthy, and outgoing. It makes a welcoming contrast to my personality, which is closer to that of the lost tribe of Scandinavian Jews. I tend to look like I'm thinking deep thoughts about how to roll back global warming or fend off the zombie apocalypse, when in truth, I'm fretting over my Uber customer rating or how my Facebook photo makes me look like Gollum from "Lord of the Rings," or why my Twitter campaign for a national Lawyer Appreciation Day got only four likes and one follow. In short, Liz has the charisma that says give me a hug, pull up a chair, and let's shoot the breeze, while I have all the approachability of a crime scene.

In my early days with Jesus, I didn't know about Uber's rating system. I believed he and I were on good terms. But I was living in a fool's paradise because trouble was brewing in his Lincoln Navigator.

That trouble was me. And I had no clue until the day Liz gently persuaded me to help her find all the tropical fruits in her kid's version of *Dell's Official WORD SEARCH*. "Look at you," she said. "How did you manage to find 'guava' so easily? And on a diagonal!"

Suddenly it hit me that I was being played by a master.

The reason Liz had to treat me like the Bengal tiger that ended the career of Siegfried and Roy was this fetish I have about never being late. I'll get to the airport two hours before my flight leaves and nurse a twelve-dollar cup of coffee while men in yellow vests wave in the airplanes. If I have a doctor's appointment at ten, by nine-fifteen I'm in the waiting room, flipping through *Colostomy Bag Monthly*.

But Jesus's dicey grasp of his GPS and the tendency of New York City drivers to park their cars in the middle of major thoroughfares meant that we faced the threat of being late on a regular basis. I handled it with my usual grace under pressure.

"We're not going to make it! This city is *hell*. It's literally like living in hell."

Liz would brush me off with a wave of her hand. "We have plenty of time."

That would mollify me for ten minutes while I stared out my window at the same burly dude in a Bob's Furniture truck texting and sipping from a keg-sized container of Coke I'd been staring at when Liz first assured me we had plenty of time. At that point, sweat would begin to ooze across my hairline. "God *hates* me. I'm like Job, only worse."

Meanwhile, Liz never faltered from her serene belief that all would be well. "Calm down. You're going to give yourself a heart attack," she'd say, with the tone you'd use to pacify a colicky four-month-old.

In my fever of claustrophobia and cuckoo-clock anality, I was lost in a dreamscape where we were buried under an avalanche of motor vehicles. That usually signaled my inventory of fucks. "Fucking city!" "Fucking traffic!" "Fucking *life!*"

Then the two imperturbable Dominicans and the histrionic Jew would have a cultural-philosophical exchange concerning the true substance of time.

"Look," Jesus would say, pointing to the GPS that often led us to a highway in northern Queens when we were shooting for the Bronx. "We'll be there ten minutes."

"Only ten more minutes," Liz would add as if she were feeding a piece of fresh liver to a German Shepherd.

At this point, I'd glance over to catch the guy in the Bob's Furniture visor giving me a thumbs up.

"How can you say we'll be there in ten minutes," I'd ask with a strangulated cry. "If it was also ten minutes, ten minutes ago?"

It was abundantly clear that, on this trip, there would be no crossing of the cultural divide.

I never imagined that, through it all, poor Jesus thought I was blaming him for the traffic or that he was harboring a chivalrous concern for the unfailingly gracious, exotically perfumed psychiatric nurse trying to calm the maniac in his back seat. It was around that time, I believe, that Jesus began to picture, the way an insomniac counts sheep, a long row of liquor bottles in various shapes and flavors, sized to fit your standard brown paper bag. I'd especially never imagined that he might be right about Liz: in her private thoughts, she was, like Jesus, measuring brown paper bags and humming under her breath, "Stolichnaya, Tanqueray, Chivas Regal, Captain Morgan."

Not, at least, until the day she opened that *Dell's Word Search* and, with a tone that resembled a scale played on a child's xylophone, said, "I'm really having trouble finding the word pineapple; wouldn't you like to help me?"

All at once, I understood that, like Oedipus In a Lincoln, I was the cause of my plunging Uber rating. And that, much worse, I was driving poor Liz of the Purple Heart to nervous distraction. It was too late to salvage my relationship with Jesus. He took her aside one evening to plead, with tears, I imagined, of chivalry and madness, "How can you work for that guy? He's *irrational.*"

But he hadn't reckoned on her loyalty or my affection for

her Purple Heart.

And that brings me to my plan for joining the world of perfect fives. Liz suggested that I should simply ask my Uber guy for a good rating, but she didn't understand that there are two things men don't do: ask for directions and beg for Uber ratings. What Liz's *Word Search* gambit and Jesus's meltdown taught me was that an hour in the back seat of an SUV in New York City traffic is a pretty short prison sentence when you think about it. And how all memory of your suffering disappears before you know it. If not a trace of misery gets recorded in your hard drive, how important can it be?

So now I'm docile as an old dog. Also, I always remember to be courtly and solicitous toward Liz. In fact, I make a parade of it—with one eye on the driver to gauge his reaction. And as for the men and women who shuttle me around the city in place of good old Jesus, I had this idea that groveling might work. I thank them profusely, even when they take me from lower Broadway to Times Square by way of the Bronx. I tap my jacket pocket, "I'll get your tip on my phone," I assure them. And I do, big time, and give five stars, always five stars. And watch, with a small measure of relief, as my rating climbs another tenth of a point.

Even at a Distance
J.L. Austin

Even at a distance, there was something about that Caltrans worker that made the mid-afternoon air feel hotter.

Perry thought this to himself as one would say it aloud and instinctively reached for the Starbucks cup, which was already glazed with condensation 90 minutes into the drive. Part of the issue was that it was actually objectively warm. The steering wheel was uncomfortable to touch. He could even smell the heat coming off the vinyl armrest. Perry took a sip from the cup, wiped his mouth with the back of his hand, and tried to scan the road ahead of him for signs of movement. He was four cars behind the pilot vehicle, which idled like a predator in wait. Mr. Caltrans was a bored-looking speck of orange on a shimmering highway reduced to one lane. He kept raising his arm up and down, checking what looked to be his phone. Behind Mr. Caltrans, a cluster of tractors and diggers were parked in the shade; behind the equipment huddle, an enormous pile of rocks, mud, and a tree or two had pooled impressively onto the road from the nearby slope.

Highway Patrol had reported the slide at 6:35 AM—too early for Perry but perfect timing for Ma, who was already well into her third cup of coffee and second round of online poker. Ma paid attention to things like road conditions. She had paid extra special attention today, however, given that Perry was finally set to leave for good. Her scrutiny—over the weather report, the Highway Patrol feed, even the oil change sticker on his car—made him nervous. More than once, he thought about staying put. Riley was always moaning about the rent in the city. He claimed that people there never looked at you directly, that people made you feel like some kind of pervert for just saying hello. But Riley had always been prone to exaggeration and resentment—qualities that never would have thrived in a household kept by Ma.

What mattered was that Perry was finally on the road. Between the boxes jammed in the back and a blind spot that could only have been approved by 1980s automotive engineers, the rearview mirror was virtually useless. Peering into the driver's side mirror, however, Perry was able to see the growing number of cars snaking around behind him. His own car made a brief sighing sound but dutifully continued to chug along in the heat. Suddenly chagrined by his lack of car knowledge, Perry checked the temperature gauge on the dashboard. It wasn't yet at the midline, which he assumed was a good thing. However, it occurred to him that he had been sitting on the highway now for a good fifteen or twenty minutes. Even at a steady idle, surely he was burning through the gas— paid for in half by Ma. Looking up, he narrowed his eyes at the other cars in front of him. No brake lights. Just stillness. Hesitating for a moment, Perry set down the Starbucks cup, reached up, and turned off the ignition. The churn of the engine cut to a quiet tick.

Further ahead, Mr. Caltrans seemed to be texting with one hand while holding his stop sign in the other. Perry briefly wondered how much the roadside worker was paid per hour. He would never have told this to Ma, but there was something visually appealing in the worker's stance, even at a distance. Something jaunty, like a modern-day roadside cowboy— equally at home with a shovel, a sign, or a cellphone. At one point, Mr. Caltrans kicked a rock, which pinged off a nearby backhoe. The heat didn't seem to bother him at all. For the first time since he'd left, Perry began to relax a little.

Just then, the car in front of him—a sporty little coupe— rocked back and forth. The doors opened, and a man and woman got out, stretched, and met each other on the gravel shoulder. The two of them seemed to have brought their ongoing conversation with them; the man gestured dramatically as he spoke while the woman interjected with small, forceful remarks directed at the ground. The man lit a cigarette, and the woman said something sharp. The man issued a retort and turned to scan the horizon. After a minute, the woman, shaking her head, marched back to the car and wrenched the vehicle's door back open. A small, wiry-haired dog dropped to the ground—a sweet-faced mutt, Perry thought—and excitedly sniffed at the surroundings while the couple resumed their exchange.

Three cars up, Mr. Caltrans was putting away his phone and fumbling for a walkie-talkie. He held it up to his ear, then spoke a quick word into the receiver. Craning up in his seat, Perry saw a brilliant flash in the distance from the southbound direction. That would be the pilot vehicle, he thought, making its way slowly toward them on the other side of the slide. Although it was probably too early still, Perry turned the key in the ignition, and the engine rumbled back to life. A box in the backseat dislodged itself, slid forward, and deposited two cookbooks directly onto the center console.

Perry's head jerked at the sudden sound of shouting. A string of profanities filtered in through the passenger side window. The couple's argument seemed to be gathering in intensity. Battling the stubborn pile of cookbooks, Perry spotted the action through the dirty windshield. The man and the woman were screaming at each other in a way that felt inhumane to witness. The highway dust began to whip up around their figures, stirred by the slow procession of incoming traffic. Both of them resembled cobras coiled in a desert showdown. Startled and unleashed, the dog bolted for a nearby bush, but the man snatched him up by the collar. The poor mutt yelped in pain, but the man continued to grip him tightly as the shouting match reached a crescendo.

Perry, who did not make a habit of confronting strangers, suddenly felt stirred to action. He did not want to get involved in other people's business—and this definitely counted as "other people's business"—but the dog's cries raised the tiny hairs on the back of his neck and even roused the sly, thick hairs that sometimes grew up on his shoulder blades. Perry, who was forced to pluck them alone with only the aid of a mirror, did not like to think about these hairs.

So he rolled down his window. His palms slipping awkwardly on the hot steering wheel, he clambered up from his seat to stick his head out of the car.

"Hey!" he shouted directly at the man.

His cry was drowned out almost immediately by the horn blast of the pilot vehicle, which swept by Perry's car in an ugly cloud of fuel and red dust. Perry's eyes instantly watered as he was forced back down in his seat, sputtering. Guided by that familiar siren known to all highway voyagers—a tattered banner that read FOLLOW ME—car after car glided past. Perry hit the button to roll up his window, which complied with a sad, wheezing sound. An eighteen-wheeler guttered by, throwing a rock into the corner of Perry's windshield that connected with a loud crack.

The final car passed with a brief lurch of acceleration that felt decidedly smug to Perry. Putting on his wipers, he watched as the couple reappeared before him in a grimy tableau. The dog was no longer yelping but continued to twist helplessly in the man's grasp. The woman was shaking her phone an inch from the man's nose, screaming at a volume that would have given the horn blast a run for its money. Within a single moment, Perry felt a kaleidoscope of emotions: embarrassment at having been sandblasted in front of the Caltrans employee, pity for the sad mutt, and relief that no one—not even Ma— had ever yelled at him in such a way.

Just then, the floorboards beneath Perry began to vibrate

in an unfamiliar way. Assuming the old car had been idling for too long, Perry moved the shifter to DRIVE. The vibrating increased. The rock from earlier slid off the roof and down the windshield on a trembling path toward the hood. Looking through the windshield, Perry spotted the couple frozen in place, staring up the slope to the left. Even at a distance, Perry could tell that their eyes were filled with fear. With one last twist, the mutt bit the hand of the man, shrugged off its collar, and sprinted away southbound at an exhilarating clip.

Something like a groan issued from the slope, and the sparse trees began to lean forward. Instinctively, Perry put his foot down hard on the gas. The car whined as it attempted to turn 10 m/s into 6 but jumped forward with surprising urgency. The cars in front of Perry had already put 25 meters and counting between them. Trying to ignore the growing roar from the slope to his left, Perry swerved and barely missed a small boulder that came bouncing from the adjacent lane. A mangled traffic cone rose up to add another nick in the windshield. The car was quickly gaining speed, but Perry was struck with the sudden fear that his mother would soon be reading about him on the latest Highway Patrol dispatch, buried in a sad grave beneath the mass of an entire hillside. Son moves away, never to return alive.

But another bright spot of orange was growing in the windshield, and Perry instinctively flinched. No, not a traffic cone. The Caltrans man.

"Shit," Perry said simply. He braked hard. Reaching over, he flung open the passenger door. The Caltrans man threw himself in, followed quickly by the mutt.

"Go," said the Caltrans man. Perry floored it, and the aging sedan shot forward. Cookbooks slammed into the boxes behind their heads; just beyond the inadequate rearview mirror, the mountain advanced onto the highway with the slow, awesome power of a god. The sound of tree trunks snapping was keenly heard. The ground continued to tremble, even at 100 yards. Or maybe that was just Perry shaking.

His foot remained pressed to the accelerator until a gentle hand clad in a work-issue glove fell on top of his own, reminding him that he had passengers. Perry forced a glance to the right. Up close, the Caltrans man was the most beautiful sight he had ever seen. His eyebrows, bushy and powdered with mud, were wrinkled in a look of earnest concern. His jawline was dotted with a mix of stubble and the occasional acne spot. People probably thought he was younger than his actual age, Perry thought. The man took off his other glove and rested it on the mutt, who sneezed but consented to be held.

"Wow," Perry found himself saying. "Just wow." Two fire engines approached in the opposite lane at high speeds, whipping past in a flurry of noise and lights. Probably from the mountain station near the summit. Perry chanced a glance in the mirror and watched them recede in the distance.

"I know," the man said. "For more than a second there, I didn't think we were going to make it." He looked at Perry; for a single instant, all Perry could see was a halo of Day-Glo orange, and he knew that the familiar logo on the California roadworker's vest would remain burned into his memory like the indelible spell of a religious icon. When the man smiled, no amount of dome lights manufactured by 21st-century automotive engineers could compete.

"We did, though," Perry said. And then— "I think we're going to be alright."

Round the Bend
Warren Merkel

"Everything in Norway is either obligatory or prohibited," quips my neighbor Ingvild, a woman in her sixties with a thin swoop of hair dyed rust red. A wry grin slicks her face, one that tells me she's accustomed to the regulations of life in a socialist country. That's not the case for me. I've been in Norway with my family for eight months, having moved here in the thick of the December darkness for a professor position at a university. I am American, and my wife is South Korean; our two young daughters straddle these worlds and are acclimating to a third.

It's a late August afternoon, temps in the mid-50s. Ingvild and I are at the end of our narrow gravel driveway, which lollipops into a small parking area for residents. We're talking about driving in Norway. I inform her I have my Norwegian driver's license test next month.

"Theory or road?" she asks.

"Road," I ask her whether her husband, Jan, wouldn't mind my poking around his car. He drives a Ford Mondeo station wagon, the same type of car I will borrow from my driving school to take my test.

"Not at all," she says.

Raindrops begin to stripe my glasses. I'm wearing jeans and a T-shirt. Ingvild, like all Norwegians, is prepared for whatever weather is thrown at her. She's ensconced in Gortex. I'm reminded of the lone Norwegian maxim I know: *Det fins ikke dårlig vær, bare dårlige klær.* There is no bad weather, only bad clothing.

Mere weeks after our arrival, my wife and I relinquished our US licenses, which are valid in Norway for only three months. At the time, we thought little of a carless existence, as the city where we live—Trondheim, at 200,000 residents, the country's third-most populous—offers reliable public transport. The apartment we rent is one of six in a two-story wooden house painted mulberry red. It sits atop a steep hill overlooking the Trondheim Fjord; to the west lies Bymarka, a nature reserve of thirty square miles dotted with lakes and laced with countless walking and skiing trails. Despite our proximity to nature, we can be downtown in a flash: the walk is about twenty minutes, and the bus ride is about ten. Trondheim also boasts the world's most northerly tram, an 8.8-kilometer-long steel stitch that begins in the city center and, at its terminus, drops passengers at Lian, a popular recreational area stippled with charming cabins.

For six months, public transport transported us. We rode it to and from grocery stores and pharmacies, cafes, and museums. It took us to Leo's Lekeland, a gargantuan indoor playground where are 5- and 2-year-old daughters ran wild for hours. It sheltered us from the rain and the cold and let my older daughter press the stop button as we approached our point of departure. But after six months, my wife and I began to itch for new views.

Once the spring semester passed and we settled in, we looked into getting Norwegian licenses. We slowly began to entertain the idea of owning a car and exploring the countryside on our own schedule. But the more we learned about the costs and regulations of road travel, the more we questioned whether the effort was worth the bother. It soon became evident that it was easier to move to Norway than through it.

In the summer, I started the process of obtaining my license by paying $30 for week-long access to the website of a company that provides an overview of Norwegian road rules via a series of videos and tips. I have had a US license for thirty years, yet decided to part with $350 for two one-hour driving lessons. If I failed the one-hour road test, I would have to take the theory test before retaking the road test; coursework costs, taxes, and fees can be shockingly expensive. This was all the coaxing I needed.

Because of the strict road regulations in Norway, driving schools are a legitimate and healthy business; in my online search for one, I count eighteen in Trondheim (there are roughly 600 driving schools in Norway). Their offices are tucked away throughout the city, and the cars that drivers borrow for practice lessons are decked out in colorful advertisements with the school's name, logo, and contact information. I called several schools to inquire about prices, but they were roughly the same, so I settled on one within walking distance from my university office.

———— ✦ ————

Centrum Trafikkskole is squeezed into the Trondheim Torg, a three-story mall located in Kalvskinnet, a neighborhood near the city center. I climb the steps to the second-floor office, where I meet Christer, Centrum's co-owner and my designated driving instructor for my lesson. Christer is tall and stocky. A thatch of gray hair sits atop his head; the same gray hair muzzles his face with day-old growth. He's wearing a sweatshirt, white sneakers, and jean shorts.

"I wear these until October," he informs me, ostensibly proud to be the last citizen of Trondheim to put on pants as summer comes to an end. I'm tempted to tell Christer he's wearing jorts, a sartorial portmanteau beloved by clothing-conscious Americans, but I reckon the humor—if he finds any—would be lost in translation.

We head down to the basement, where Christer's car awaits us. It is a recent model Ford Mondeo station wagon, dressed up with bright green letters and yellow piping that advertises Centrum Trafikkskole.

"You can drive standard?" Christer asks.

"Yes," I respond. I want to keep my options open: if I take my driver's license test in Norway on an automatic, then I can only ever drive an automatic.

"That's good," he says.

—— ✦ ——

The lesson starts inauspiciously: I cannot locate the emergency brake. I was raised on used cars, all standard: a 1986 Toyota Corolla, a 1990 Audi 80, and a 1982 Honda Accord, the latter of which—as it neared death—my parents sold to their mechanic for fifty bucks. In all of these vehicles, the emergency brake was a slender black rod that the driver would yank up like a carnival ride lever. But on a new model Ford Mondeo, the emergency brake is a misplaced switch for a power window, stashed behind the gear shift. Christer points at it, then looks at me.

I pull out of the garage and begin navigating Trondheim's downtown area. The radio station commemorates 80's metal; I temper Christer's instructions and small talk with Alice Cooper lyrics and a Scorpions guitar solo.

"I'm going to be strict with you, Warren," Christer says. "It will make your test easier." His driving countenance is instantly palpable. Within the span of one lesson, he instructs me to brake slightly before I depress the clutch, make wider turns, enter roundabouts slower, check the rearview mirror before I brake, check the side mirrors for cyclists before I turn, signal earlier, signal later, and not grip the steering wheel underhanded when I turn. I feel sixteen again, a high school student in driver's ed class, armed with a flaccid learner's permit. But I know Christer is doing his job—I am paying him to help me pass my test. Despite Christer's matter-of-fact demeanor, he also lays bare a welcome lightheartedness. When he asks me to take a right or a left at a sign for Leangen or Lerkendal or Høgberget, I repeat the name, approximating it as best I can. But Christer laughs as I swing a phonological axe, butchering his mother tongue.

During my first lesson, my Achilles heel is the roundabout, a circular intersection uncommon in the US that serves to keep traffic moving and minimize the frequency and severity of collisions. I know I must yield to vehicles already in the roundabout, but the other fundamentals, second nature to Norwegians, blow my mind. If I plan to turn right in the roundabout, I use my right turn signal both to enter and leave the roundabout; if I intend to go straight through the roundabout, I begin with no signal but must use my right turn signal once I have passed the first exit; if I leave the roundabout to the left, or after three-quarters of a circle, I must signal left when I enter the roundabout, then indicate right after I pass the first two exits and approach the third. These rules are standard for a roundabout with one lane; life intensifies if the roundabout has two. Christer forces me through five or six roundabouts until I get it right.

We also spend some time on the highway. In the US, I am accustomed to entrance ramps the length of a diving board, which force me to gun it in the hopes of another driver letting me squeeze in. In Norway, I am surprised to see the driver in the rightmost highway lane yield. Every time. Christer educates me on the meaning of the three types of white lines for merging traffic: a solid white line must not be crossed; a white line with long dashes means a merging driver can enter the highway but must yield to other vehicles; a white line with short dashes means a merging driver has the right-of-way, and vehicles on the highway must allow them safe passage into a lane. If road rage exists here, Norway has likely regulated the shit out of it.

———— ✦ ————

At the end of the lesson, I pull into the car garage and cut the ignition. Christer asks me what I feel went well and what went wrong. I don't care about what went well.

"The roundabouts," I respond. Christer nods. "And speeding?" He nods again.

"If today had been your test, you would have failed," he says. "You went eight kpm over the limit. More than once." This is less than five mph, roughly the top slithering speed of your average snake. I fret about failing the road test, so I ask Christer details about the theory test and retaking the road test.

"Don't worry about it," he responds, slapping my shoulder. "Take another lesson with me, and you'll be fine." But my mind wanders, and that evening at home, I investigate the protocol for the worst-case scenario. I locate the website of a driving school that lists the estimated costs for obtaining a Category B (passenger car). These include a 14-hour course in basic road traffic knowledge ($150); night driving ($225); first aid ($100); a 20-hour driving theory course ($200); a 45-minute driving lesson ($85); two evaluation lessons ($175); a safety and flat tire course ($575); an on-the-road safety course ($975); a review ($30); and car rental for the driving test ($285). In Norway, the total cost can run up to $3,000—a fair price for a cheap used car in the US.

———— ✦ ————

I start my second lesson by popping the hood. During our

first lesson, Christer informed me that the examiner could ask me any number of questions about road safety or car maintenance. Though I'm not overly mechanically inclined, I can change a tire, so I found this facet of the test a bit absurd. Still, then I remembered all the stranded cars I had passed in my life in the US, a white T-shirt or a strip of orange tape dangling from a driver's side window like a flag of surrender: *I couldn't hack it on the open road.* Then I thought of how many Americans would have failed the Norwegian driver's license test and how many would have benefitted from this type of training.

"Where does the oil go?" Christer asks. I point.

"Where's the battery?" I point.

"Where's the windshield wiper fluid go?" I point.

"Where's the coolant go?" In a flash, all I see is an engine—a tangle of tubes and wires.

"That one?" I say. Christer shakes his head, redirecting my finger. "You should know this stuff." I thank Christer and reach my hand to close the hood, but Christer stops me. Apparently, I'm doing that incorrectly as well.

My second lesson goes smoothly. I relax a little and am momentarily able to steep myself in Norway. As we work our way from the city, we pass Nidarosdomen, the oldest Gothic cathedral north of Hamburg, and Gamle Bybro, or Old Town Bridge, a 17th-century pedestrian bridge that crosses the Nidelva River. Out in the country, we weave through two-lane roads that splice the quintessential Norwegian landscape of rolling hills and houses painted deep red. It is torture to possess a car and the freedom that accompanies it for only one hour. For the first time in eight months. In Norway.

I want to keep driving. To the next town, and then the next; to the ruins of a medieval abbey I'm sure must lie ahead somewhere; around one more corner, just one more.

And then the lesson is over. I have botched turn signal

protocol in one roundabout and pulled shamefully into a bus lane before turning right, but Christer tells me neither of these blunders would merit failing the exam. He is confident I will pass.

◆

On the day of my test—September 27, which my driving school had reserved for me four months in advance—I meet Christer at his office. He is wearing a gray hoodie and jorts. We do a 45-minute lesson, then drive in the Ford Mondeo to the Statens Vegvesen, or State Driving Authority, where I will be paired with a driving examiner.

Before we walk in, Christer asks me if I am familiar with procedures in the case of an accident. I shoot him a blank stare.

"Do you know where the orange safety vest is?" In Norway, the driver must wear an orange safety vest when exiting the car unexpectedly—for instance, in the case of an accident or breakdown. Something orange had caught my eye earlier in the lesson, tucked away in the driver's side door. I pull it out.

"Good. And where is the safety triangle?" We get out of the car and pop the trunk. Christer shows me how to set up the triangle. He tells me the distance from the vehicle that the triangle should be set on the road in the city, in the country, if there is a blind spot. I stuff my skull with the extra information, wondering if it will be on the test.

"Alright then," Christer says. "Let's go in." We traipse across the parking lot and enter the building. I take a number from a machine like I'm at a deli.

"I hope your examiner speaks English," Christer adds.

"What's that?"

"You didn't mark that as a preference on your application." I try not to piss myself. Christer sees I'm trying not to piss myself and laughs. "You'll be fine." He pats me on the shoulder.

———— ✦ ————

The name of my driving instructor is Martin. He speaks English—he tells me how he and his family vacationed in California a few years back. Before I start the engine, Martin asks me where I would place the safety triangle: I respond with the proper distance in the country, and the city, and also note that blind spots on the road would determine whether I place the triangle in front of or behind the car. He nods in kind, and I breathe a sigh of relief.

Martin looks to be in his thirties, and he is fighting a cold. He is kind—he asks me whether or not I would appreciate small talk during the test or concentrate on the road.

"A little small talk is fine," I say, trying not to seem uptight.

We drive along one of the dozen or so routes that examiners must follow. He guides me through roundabouts, along two-lane roads and highways, and into the parking lot of a shopping center, where I must back into a parking spot. For the first time in my life, I use the rearview camera to guide me. On the highway, I watch my speed, not passing one car. Everyone passes me, and I remember what it was like to drive with my grandparents.

As the exam ends, we pull into the parking lot of the Statens Vegvesen. Martin is silent and taps notes into his tablet. The suspense in the car—at least for me—is palpable.

"How do you think you did?" he asks. I reply honestly.

"I made a mistake with one turn signal through a roundabout, and I drove too slowly at times. Otherwise, I think I was safe and abided by the rules."

"I agree," Martin says. "You did drive too slowly. But you did fine. You've passed." I'm elated. Once we step out of the car, Martin and Christer chat in Norwegian. Then we head back inside, where I have my photo taken and provide a signature. I stay in the booth for five minutes, snapping the picture to my satisfaction. I am proud of my accomplishment; besides, this mugshot is valid for fifteen years.

———— ✦ ————

In Norway, I hear a horn honk once, perhaps twice a month. I've never seen anyone peel out, kicking up plumes of smoke as the stench of blazing rubber fills my head. No raised fists in rear views, no road rage between drivers who emancipate their life's problems on the road. When I cross the street with my daughters, the drivers stop. I am forever tempted to smile or nod as I would in the US, to raise my hand in gratitude. But the drivers are stone-faced. They do not stop because they have the time or because they feel the urge to extend me a courtesy. They simply approach the crosswalk with care, then wait. It is as if, for the briefest of moments, my children are theirs. Norwegians drive the way the system wants them to. It's a high price to pay, and one I am at peace with.

Point A to Point B
Melissent Zumwalt

The morning of my sixteenth birthday transpired at the DMV. For a rural kid, life without a driver's license resembled imprisonment—and I sought to capture my freedom at the earliest possible moment.

My family lived fifteen miles from the high school, with only two stop signs between these locations, down winding stretches of two-lane highway in the Willamette Valley of Oregon. Roads surrounded by fenced pastures of horses and cattle and expansive fields of commercial hops and berries, the ripe, putrid stink of manure permeating the air. With few other vehicles and sizable distances to travel, cars hurtled forward at upwards of seventy miles an hour, stopping abruptly behind tractors crawling along the asphalt. Ramshackle houses and barns intermittently dotted the landscape, and at night, rich darkness encompassed all due to the complete lack of streetlights or buildings. Unlike me, most of my friends lived near the high school, within town limits, but some resided further past the school in the opposite direction, meaning as many as thirty miles away from my home.

The ability to get a ride somehow from someone was the conduit to existence, to being a participating member of high school society. My parents certainly weren't going to continue to chauffeur me around—they had neither the time nor the interest for that. And truth be told, I wouldn't have wanted it anyway. Being driven around by Mom or Dad made you look childish, immature, like you couldn't take care of yourself. And I planned to be anything but that.

———◆———

The next day at work, a nondescript diner, one of the career waitresses, asked about the outcome of my driver's test. My mouth widened into a beaming smile radiating with affirmation.

She followed with, "What was your score?"

I held zero shame in admitting the receipt of a seventy-five, which she quickly acknowledged with, "Just barely passed, huh?"

Who the hell cared? It's not like my license came with some sort of contingency because of receiving the lowest possible passing score (although, in retrospect, maybe it should have). Prior to the test, I'd driven a car a total of exactly four times. Once, when my dad taught me how to drive a stick and the other three times with Mom, going into town on regular type errands like grocery shopping.

My novice driving skills frazzled her. Driving together deteriorated into her panicked voice, yelling things at me like, "There's a kid! See him? Do you see him? Slow down. Slow Down!" With me already plodding along at least ten miles under the posted speed limit and said kid being located fifty yards away, nowhere near the road. These episodes produced so much anxiety for both of us; I didn't last more than fifteen minutes behind the wheel until my requests to practice driving turned nonexistent.

But standing there in the diner, holding that beautiful plastic card in my possession, none of it mattered. The door to the world just cracked open.

———— ✦ ————

But in order to achieve full liberation, one needed not just a license but also a car. My parents decided I would drive a Volkswagen Beetle, or rather, Dad decided.

After my parents filed for bankruptcy and all their

best-functioning cars were repossessed, Dad developed an inexplicable interest in Volkswagen Bugs. He probably met someone who restored them and sold them at a profit, then figured he too could purchase cheap, decrepit Volkswagens and fix them up.

His assumption that he could find crappy cars and (sort of) afford to buy them panned out. Dad procured several Volkswagens in various states of disrepair—a black one with torn upholstery, a rusted-out red one, a sort of yellow one with a baby blue fender, and the surprisingly intact 1973 Crayola green Beetle with an uncommon automatic transmission designated for my use.

Unfortunately, the dedication required to refurbish the Volkswagens did not mesh with Dad's work ethic. On the day of my sixteenth birthday and the acquisition of my driver's license, the car still didn't run.

———— ✦ ————

About a month later, Dad left a note for me at the school office. Apparently, he'd resuscitated my Volkswagen into an operable state and somehow figured out a way to bring the car to school and leave it for me to drive home.

After reading that note, a wave of endorphins surged through my veins. Anything, everything, became possible. My energy bubbled over; I needed to get out there and experience...something.

I sought out my friend Jill so we could skip our last class periods and go joyriding through the tidy side streets of the town, being careful to keep several blocks between the school and us to avoid being spotted by anyone.

That escapade, bumping down the road at twenty miles an hour, the sheer thrill of our bodies moving unassisted through space, was akin to a magic carpet ride.

But thirty minutes into our euphoric freedom, the car sputtered, then wound down to a complete stop in the middle of the street, even as my foot jammed the gas pedal.

"What's going on?" Jill asked.

"I have no idea," I replied, turning the key back and forth in the ignition, hoping to restart the engine, praying for the sound of it revving. "I guess it died. We'll have to push it to the side of the road."

"Are you serious?" Jill laughed, "You want me to get out and push?"

Just then, two young boys, towheaded cherubs with freckled noses, no older than ten or twelve years old, approached the car. They appeared intent on speaking with us, so I rolled down my window.

"Did you break down?" one asked, "Do you want us to take a look at it?"

Jill and I glanced sideways at each other, trying to figure out their angle. Were they playing a joke? Did they think they were hitting on us?

The other boy chimed in, "We fix go-carts."

Well, what could it hurt? We didn't have any better solutions, so I told them to go ahead.

In under ten minutes, the engine stuttered to a steady purr, the sprung driver's seat vibrating beneath me. The car inched forward of its own volition, carrying us on down the road, our arms waving thanks to the young mechanics.

I had no idea that afternoon would be a harbinger of all that was to come.

———— ✦ ————

The first day driving my car was not my first experience skipping class. Perhaps it was my second time, maybe the third. But once the car ran, it enabled me to turn cutting class into an art form. I knew exactly which classes to skip on which days when my presence (or lack thereof) would go unnoticed and what types of excuses worked with which teachers. It's doubtful I finished one full day of school my entire senior year.

Sitting in econ or government felt like being burned alive from the inside. There was so much energy within me, so much desire to experience *life* as my sixteen-year-old mind imagined it. Escaping from the confines of the school walls kept that fire from consuming me.

I skipped class to lounge by the river with my friends, to be outdoors, inhaling the sweet, warm air of spring, feeling the heat of the sun kiss my face, invigorating my spirit. Or we drove into Portland to walk the sidewalks, to allow the vibrant pulse of cars and people and electricity to rush through our veins. With especially beautiful weather, we might cut the whole day and head to the coast, a hundred miles away, where we jumped into the churning coolness of the Pacific Ocean, refusing to allow a single moment of our young lives to slip away uncelebrated.

There was only one caveat I made with myself. I could skip school as much as I wanted as long as I kept getting good grades. I actually enjoyed learning, but memorizing rote facts didn't feel like learning. It felt like busywork, like being trained to squelch the hunger in one's soul in order to prepare for lackluster adulthood. That wasn't how I planned to live.

⸻ ✦ ⸻

I enjoyed experimenting with new types of make-up and clothes—things like 1960's hippie dresses, 70's bell bottoms, combining grunge-inspired thermals with floral skirts or donning blue eyeshadow circa the golden age of disco—anything to keep life colorful.

About a month after the little boys came to my rescue, inspiration struck me to show up at school looking absolutely fabulous. My outfit consisted of a skin-tight, long sleeve black leotard, a black A-line mini-skirt, and three 3-inch platform heels with epic cat-style eyeliner and curled ringlets framing my face. The effort this required created a delayed start to the day. A day in which winter made its arrival known by turning the car's windshield into a kaleidoscope of frost. I fumbled around the car, scraping at the icy windows in haste.

Driving down the road, the windshield kept fogging up. I knew the car didn't have to defrost—Dad gave me an old rag to keep in the car to use for this purpose—but until then, rubbing feverishly with that rag, I really hadn't understood its critical role.

Fog in that part of the valley grows thick like moss. Visibility was reduced to less than twenty feet that morning. Through the gauzy haze, two pinpricks of red appeared, so small as to seem they were perched on the distant horizon. It took a fraction of one second for my mind to recognize these dots of red as brake lights. It took another part of a second to comprehend that they were growing larger at an exponential speed, rapidly transforming into throbbing red orbs. I braked hard, heart palpitating, digging my platform heel into the pedal, grinding it to the floorboard.

And then, Impact. The Volkswagen crashed into the back of a flatbed trailer. My whole life altered in the flash of a microsecond. Already responsible for an accident, only two months after obtaining my driver's license.

Stepping out of the car—shaking, tears staining my face, the pervasive stench of burning rubber filling the air—I kept stammering apologies (clearly, my parents never gave me the lesson about not admitting fault in an accident). The industrial-size flatbed trailer belonged to a middle-aged farmer. His trailer looked like a tin can launched at a high velocity and hit his rear bumper (which, essentially, it had). My car looked like said tin can, crushed, mangled, deformed.

The farmer took photos of the scene with a disposable camera. He told me it would be okay, then put his arm around my shoulders and took a photo of us together. At the time, it seemed he was trying to make me feel better, but in retrospect, I realize it was probably for insurance purposes. (*See how young this girl was? No idea how to drive. And she kept apologizing…. So guilty!*)

If my car didn't run, it meant walking five miles back to the house, stumbling through the gravel ditch on the side of the highway in three-inch platform heels and a mini-skirt, the chill of fog biting at my exposed legs, and then telling Dad about my colossal error in judgment. But when I slunk back into the driver's seat and tested the key in the ignition—and the car started!—a flash flood of relief overwhelmed me.

Even though the car looked totaled, since Volkswagen engines are in the rear instead of the front, it remained driveable. The Volkswagen chugged along the final ten miles to school, a shell-shocked driver at the helm.

Hiding the accident from my parents presented an impossible feat. Mom expressed anger about the accident's projected effect on their insurance premiums. The safety features of the car never entered into the conversation.

Dad pounded the hood back into place as best he could, but several pronounced dents survived, and a significant portion of the paint chipped off. Since the hood no longer latched after caving in, Dad tied it down with a piece of rope as a precaution - to ensure it wouldn't fly up while driving. I knew I would need to live with my mistakes.

———— ✦ ————

When Kurt Cobain appeared on TV wearing a dress, it

changed things. Even out in our rural high school, the paradigm shifted.

The more well-to-do kids who once drove to school in their parents' old BMWs started showing up in battered pick-up trucks. They slouched through the hallways in flannel shirts and Doc Martens scowls on their faces. They listened to Pearl Jam and Soundgarden, pretending their lives contained enough angst to understand the gravity of the lyrics.

Being flawed was in. Although I never let on what my home life was like, surely a girl who rolled up to school in a half-smashed car held together by a rope must have something angsty-enough-to-be-interesting going on. My popularity was sealed.

———— ✦ ————

The Volkswagen died. Often.

Sometimes coming to a stop killed it (like at a stop sign). Sometimes no indication of a problem existed until I found myself immobile, stranded in the middle of the road. These instances required that I attempt to push the car out of the way. My attire never seemed suitable for this activity. Sometimes I'd be wearing a vintage dress; sometimes, I'd already be in a stage costume, preparing for a dress rehearsal; often, the rain poured down, creating a sloppy, slippery mess. But inevitably, someone (almost always male) materialized and helped me.

Dad, seeking the easiest fix possible, proposed a simple solution to the ongoing problem, "Looks like the battery can't hold a charge. You're going to need to plug it in every night."

And so, every day the car returned home successfully, I pulled out the jumper cables and plugged my car's battery into an electrical source. However, even that approach wasn't foolproof.

But I did become a pro with a set of jumper cables.

The car went in reverse until one day; it just didn't anymore. On the ever-growing list of problems with the Volkswagen, losing reverse was pretty insignificant. It just meant leaving extra early for school in order to be able to pull through a parking space. I had to beware of getting stuck in places I couldn't back out of.

One afternoon the Volkswagen stumbled into the gas station on fumes, the gauge indicating a nearly empty tank. With a few days left until payday, my wallet was empty. But I did manage to scrounge up a few dimes.

When the lanky attendant sidled up to my window, I said, "$2 in regular."

He scoffed at my meager request, his eyes rolling so far up into his head it was audible. But he sauntered to the rear of the car and completed the two-dollar fill.

"Ok," he returned, "Two dollars."

Conscious of his annoyance, I lined up the twenty dimes into a tidy stack and handed them out the window.

He glared at the change in his palm and shot back, "Get a job, why don't you!"

"I have a job," I muttered to his back as he walked away.

It was particularly insulting since independence comprised my identity. Sure, I didn't work a ton of hours like some kids, but I wasn't going to let myself accrue any debt, and I was going to be able to provide for myself no matter what.

The Volkswagen's heaters blew scalding hot air from underneath the two front seats. On the peak of a summer afternoon, with temperatures escalating, driving around with a good friend in the passenger seat, she asked me, "Mel, can you turn the heat off? It's burning my ankles."

My response came with a smirk of my own discomfort, "Um, no. The heat doesn't turn off." The Volkswagen was rife with quirks that my passengers had to accept. The only people who would ride with me were those who didn't own cars or licenses of their own. My car was the last resort of the desperate.

Sometimes, turning a corner with enough speed, liquid (hopefully, it was water, but I couldn't say for certain) flew out of the dashboard vents and sprayed my passengers.

A period also existed when the car hit forty-five miles per hour, and it shook violently, necessitating a stern grip of the steering wheel to maintain control of the car. If any passengers happened to be with me, the look on their faces grew troubled with concern. Once a friend asked if everything was okay and if we needed to pull over. "It's fine," I said. "Once I reach fifty-five, the shaking stops."

I just had to hold on when things got tough.

———— ✦ ————

At the end of each school year, a Senior Awards Ceremony honored academic achievements and those headed off to four-year universities. They also doled out something called the President's Award for Educational Excellence to students who kept a minimum 3.5 GPA and did well on standardized tests. It wasn't any big deal. Lots of kids got it. But when my name was called as a recipient, the friends around me at the assembly turned my way in utter shock.

"You?" one asked.

"So?" I shrugged.

"But you're always out skipping class with us!" another said, "How did you keep your grades up?"

One guy in our graduating class received acceptance to Yale. It was unprecedented for our school to send someone to the Ivy League. The whole auditorium erupted into a standing ovation. Although I would not be receiving any standing ovations, I accomplished an unprecedented achievement of my own. I would be the first in my family to attend any college, the state university a hundred miles down the interstate.

I was always going to go places, no matter what vehicle I had to use to get me there.

Lost City
Robert Wexelblatt

The sun had just touched the steppe when we climbed out of the Land Rovers, beating dust off our clothes, a gesture that had become second nature. Our shadows stretched jaggedly over a low heap of rubble. Because of the rosy light, the damage looked fresh, as though the city had been razed a mere six hours ago and not six centuries.

Krueger squatted and picked up a pebble. "Right where you're supposed to be," he said, addressing either the stone in his hand or the hillock of gravel.

The last week had humbled even Krueger. He didn't crow about his navigation; on the contrary, he spoke as if the city were to be congratulated for not having relocated.

We could tell he was moved, and so the rest of us held our tongues. This was having his moment of triumph, and anyway, the steppe had abraded the enthusiasm of the rest of us, worn down to our dendrites. Nice for Krueger, we thought. Though he hadn't promised us anything more than this tumescence of debris, who could have helped to hope for something richer, grander, stranger? The phrase *lost city* tends to stimulate the imagination.

On the far side of the rubble, hundreds of yards away and halfway up a swale, we could make out several huts and three cultivated plots marked out by stones. Nothing was moving over there, not even a goat.

"That's a surprise," somebody said. We had grown used to seeing the black tents and beshitted flocks of the nomads whose paths we occasionally crossed but nothing resembling huts.

"Suppose we could get a beer over there?" Krueger joked.

And, to raise our spirits, we laughed.

We picked our way gingerly over the ruins. It was impossible to make any sense of them; that is, to see them as an ex-city. Where once, according to Krueger, there had been an ornate mosque, four wide boulevards, a marketplace, cisterns, and gardens, now there was nothing at all. Not so much as two joined bricks, no trace of the twelve-foot-thick walls that were supposed to have surrounded but failed to protect the place. The destruction had been methodical and thorough. Modern artillery is haphazard by comparison. Even a bombed-out city still has a skeleton; you can make out where the streets ran, where the foundations had been dug. But here, the pulverizing had been retail, not wholesale.

By noon it was too hot to do anything but make camp by the Rovers and eat a meal of corned beef hash. We still had plenty of water, but it was warm, and our mood was glum.

———■ ✦ ■———

Krueger had organized the trip, promising us a kind of working escape, a vacation adventure to take us away from our humdrum lives. He called us, the most bored of his college chums, sold us on the idea, pried a couple thousand dollars out of each of us, and eked out the expenses with an advance on his photographs and a small grant from an obscure educational foundation where his wife had contacts. His plan was to retrace a forgotten trade route in Central Asia, a minor spur of the Silk Road. We were to travel from West to East, pick up a pair of Land Rovers in Germany and stop well short of the Chinese frontier. Krueger had it all worked out. We could pack everything we needed, he said. Language would be no problem, as he'd learned some basic Uzbek and spoke fluent Russian. He had a good idea of where the city had been and reckoned it would take less than three weeks to get there, allowing for a little searching and no more than a couple more to get back. The site was somewhere in the middle of blank space on the map rather forbiddingly named the Hunger Steppe.

According to Krueger, even in its halcyon days, Suzam-Ord was no metropolis. It probably housed only a few thousand people. For a few decades, though, it had been fabulously rich. Then, a Mongol khan, who was busy pillaging up north, sent three messengers down to the city demanding tribute, a routine transaction for the time. But the caliph of Suzam-Ord, despising the nomadic infidels and puffed up with hubris, had the three messengers beheaded. For six months, nothing happened, and Suzam-Ord rolled on, fat and happy. Then one morning, the city awoke to find a swarm of barbarians on its doorstep, ferocious, foul-smelling men on fierce, tiny horses. They took the city, slaughtered its citizens, sealed up its springs, and razed every edifice. Before riding off, the khan is supposed to have laid a curse on the place. After that, there were no more caravans, and Suzam-Ord vanished from the maps and almost from memory.

Krueger had learned all this from an old manuscript he got from some professor pal of his wife's. We met in New York. Over dinner at an Afghan restaurant, he unrolled a copy of the manuscript. Were we in, were we up for an adventure? Were we bored with our lives? We were. The five of us drank to the discovery of Suzam-Ord with neat vodka. Why not? We had all looked up to Krueger in the old days. He had been our motivator, our idea-man. He organized our parties, talked us into going to New Orleans for Mardi Gras, found us tickets to *Hair*, bought the beat-up Chevy that got us to Fort Lauderdale for Spring Break and halfway back. Now he was rescuing us a break from the ennui of our careers and the monotony of our marriages. Why shouldn't we follow him, even now, even to the lost city of Suzam-Ord? No doubt we were rescuing him as well. Krueger was the hyperkinetic sort; he couldn't bear idleness.

He was just the kind of man to take improbable vacations, to order a bucket of oysters, to look for the best trout stream in Scotland, change careers and marry three times.

———■ ✦ ■———

We dug a latrine and spent the evening reminiscing. We turned in early, slept fitfully, and were up at first light, making use of the latrine. As for Krueger, he was already at the highest point of the rubble, snapping photographs.

"The ruins at dawn," he cried down to us dramatically.

"What ruins," we shouted back.

Considering the emptiness that stretched to the horizon, it was hard to believe there had ever been enough here to support even a small village. Yet there must still have been a trickle of water that escaped the Mongols' seals, enough to sustain those little gardens over by the huts.

"How long are we going to stay here?" one of us asked.

Krueger made a dismissive motion with his arm as he peered through his camera, clicked, then shrugged. "We can head back tomorrow."

This was welcome news. We had had an uneasy night. It wasn't quite homesickness we felt, and it wasn't superstition; it wasn't even the diet of canned goods, but it was something. Nobody had mentioned the story of the curse; nevertheless, there was no denying the place had a bad feeling about it. We had grown accustomed to the vacancy of the steppes, but this was something else. The utter destruction, the finality of it, the story of massacre, perhaps all that made us sleep badly, gave us bad dreams.

Once he had all the pictures he wanted, Krueger suggested we go over to the huts.

"What for? There's obviously nobody there."

Krueger looked at us over his reddish beard. "Hey, we're

explorers. Remember?"

It wasn't yet nine o'clock, but the heat was already oppressive. To get to the huts, we walked around the ruins rather than trying to pick our way over the debris. The sun would have heated the stones, and it was safer; nothing easier than to lose your footing on a pile like that, to twist an ankle, or worse.

The huts turned out to be ramshackle affairs of lath and tarpaper, but they were reinforced against the wind and weather with milled two-by-fours linked with steel strips. The roofs were corrugated tin and looked surprisingly firm.

The first hut had a proper wooden door. Krueger knocked three times.

We waited, expecting nothing. But then the door was opened by an ancient fellow with facial hair that made him look like a Tartar out of a painting. He wore a kind of sheet over a t-shirt and shorts and invited us to come in. He greeted us in Russian.

Krueger answered him, then translated. "He said welcome, and would we care for some tea." We filed in. The floor was covered with two rugs that must once have been handsome.

A second man was seated on a folding chair at a card table. He looked even older than the first one. Six more folding chairs were scattered around the room. The old man at the card table nodded at us but said nothing. The other one, though, made a little speech.

"We saw you arrive last evening," said our host. "Forgive us for not coming to welcome you to our city. We didn't think you'd be staying the night. Please make yourselves comfortable."

We arranged the chairs in a semi-circle.

"Where are you from?"

Krueger spoke for us. "We're Americans, from the United States."

"Ah," said the man evincing no surprise. "Sooner or later, Americans go everywhere, even to the moon. Like your Lewis and Clark," he chuckled.

Krueger was amazed, and he translated. The crack about Lewis and Clark astonished the rest of us too. Krueger asked the old man why he called the place his city.

"Because this is our city. We belong to it," the old man answered and treated us to what may have been a smile but looked like a grimace.

"I don't understand," said Krueger.

A faint whistle issued from the teapot. Our host motioned for his silent companion to see to it, and when the older man made a face at him, our host gently raised a finger.

Then the door opened, and two more human antiquities shambled in. Unlike our host, who could still stand upright, they were stooped. One was wearing a Chicago Cubs cap. When he heard that we were Americans, he laughed as if this were a terrific joke and had to shake all our hands.

He kept pointing to his cap and nodding. "Cups," he said. "Never win."

The other newcomer was less voluble but managed a bitter little speech, quickly translated by Krueger. "Welcome to Suzam-Ord, once the diamond of the steppe and the wonder of Asia, but now a corpse on a dry mattress."

The three others scowled at him.

Krueger translated.

We were each handed a glass containing about two fingers of some kind of tea. It was black and thick with sugar.

Another old man showed up. More nodding, grimaces and/or smiles. Suddenly, all of them had something to say. It was too much for Krueger to translate, and he gave up. More tea was brewed, more chairs occupied. The already overheated hut was soon stifling. Krueger fell into deep conversation with two of the old men and apparently forgot about us. Our host did most of the talking. The others had a lot to say, too, but to each other rather than Krueger. Their speeches grew longer, more emphatic, and, apparently, polemical. Eventually, they ignored us and began arguing with one another. Kreuger took out his notebook and a pencil.

After fifteen minutes of this, we were all bored and dripping with sweat.

"For God's sake, it's unbearable. Let's get out of here," one of us whispered.

"Come on, Krueger, we're taking off."

"What?"

"We're dying in here. And we don't know what they're arguing about. Let's go."

Krueger told us to shut up and turned back to listen.

As soon as we got to our feet, everybody fell silent. They looked more embarrassed rather than offended, as if they had forgotten us while they were arguing.

Krueger offered some excuse for our departure, but we weren't permitted to leave until we had shaken hands all around. Krueger stayed.

"Maybe they're ghosts," one of us joked on the way back to our camp.

"Oh, sure. A ghost with a Cubs cap."

"Caretakers then?"

"Of what? Gravel?"

"Hey, what do you suppose those codgers were going on about?"

"The prudence of leaving heads on strangers."

"Odd, wasn't it?"

"What?"

"That business about this being *their* city."

"Well, old men. You know."

"*Really* old. They all looked at least ninety."

"Everything dries out here. Maybe they're only thirty-five."

—— ✦ ——

While we waited for Krueger to return, we stowed most of the gear in the Rovers. We left the largest tent up and, in its shade, played poker for Cohibas and Partagas. We'd picked up the Cuban cigars in Poland and, even those who'd give up tobacco smoked them. A cigar became a postprandial ritual for us each night, mulling over our lives with words as light and thick as smoke.

Someone asked if we ought to check on Krueger. We made jokes. "What if those ancient guys are being the last of the Golden Horde?"

"What if they're ghosts? They may look bloodless, but what if they're still bloodthirsty after half a millennium?"

Krueger sauntered in around four-thirty, red and sweaty as though he'd been in a sauna. He downed half a canteen of water. We had plenty of questions, but he said what we were asking was a little crude and promised to read us his notes after dinner. "I tried to get down everything I could," he explained. "I wrote it out like it was a monologue. I couldn't keep the speakers straight."

"So, they didn't even try to cut your head off?"

Krueger made a peevish face and finished off the canteen. "After dinner, okay? Give me a little time to rehydrate and look this stuff over."

"Okay. We'll eat early, then. What's on?"

"Beef chili over noodles."

"Let's have that last bottle of Montrachet. We can drink to lost cities."

"And the ones waiting for us."

The temperature drops like a guillotine at night on the steppe. What clouds there are vanish, and you feel like you're floating through outer space. The infinitude of stars made us feel like a bunch of astronauts.

Seeing how it was our last night before turning back, Krueger pulled a burlap sack out of his pack and took out a bottle of Remy-Martin. He poured us all a dram and sat by the lantern to read. Later, after we were all back home, he mailed us each a spruced-up copy.

—————— ✦ ——————

He began in a low voice and read steadily.

"We were all born in a village twenty kilometers to the East of here. Everybody in our village is descended from the few who escaped from Suzam-Ord. The story of the survivors was passed down to us. They hid under dead bodies for two days waiting for the ruthless horsemen to leave. Then they scraped a living from the steppe through small farming and trading with the nomads, to whom they sold some of their daughters. Always our fathers kept the memory of Suzam-Ord alive, even maintaining something of its traditions too, though in a fitful and probably deformed fashion. We had no Koran, only a few verses that we boys all had to learn by heart:

> So, when the trumpet is blown with a single blast
> and the earth and the mountains are lifted up and
> crushed with a single blow,
> then, on that day, the terror shall come to pass,
> and heaven shall be split, for upon that day it shall be very frail...

"And that's how our lives went for generations until the Revolution, then collectivization, the Terror, and finally the Great Patriotic War. All of us were of fighting age when the war broke out, and when we learned of it, we met together and decided to volunteer together. We were full of dreams, sick to death of our village, fed up with the steppe and poverty.

We wanted to go somewhere else. This is how we became good Soviet citizens, men of the future. We fought for four years, though not in the same unit. Those of us who survived didn't want to come back. We stayed on in Russia and started families and were sure we were free of the past. Not one of us told his wife or children about Suzam-Ord. The truth is that we were ashamed of our ancestors. They were backward and for generations clung to the tatters of a vanishing religion and memories of a dead, once-rich city. They were superstitious and unimaginative. We all believed we had gone well beyond them, that we had slogged through the horrors of war into a new dawn, free of curses and prophecies. Without us, without its young men, the village slowly died. The population drifted off—joining the nomads or into Siberia, who knows where?

"One May Day, the three of us ran into each another in a parade of veterans. We threw our arms around each other's necks, overcome with emotion. We resolved to see if anyone else from our village had also made it through the war. It took two years for us to find each other. First, we exchanged letters, then made visits on holidays. Maybe it's just the nature of old men, but the more decrepit we grew, the more the old ways seemed to reassert themselves and the more the new ways that had appeared strong as iron began to rust. We found ourselves talking about Suzam-Ord and our fathers, who insisted the city would be reborn when the curse was raised. Perhaps, we began to think, it is up to us, up to us to lay that curse. After all, who else was there to do it?

"How much did we actually believe? Well, it would not be misleading to say none of us believed with a whole heart. But even a provisional, far-fetched faith was better than the emptiness we all felt. Perhaps you, too, have felt this need? What else could have made you and your friends travel halfway around the world just to look at that pile of stones over there? It's hardly attractive, that quintessence of nothingness.

I don't say that you share our longing, but you may at least sympathize with it. I imagine that, for an American, such yearnings express themselves in the wish to be in motion. That's how it was with us when we were young. Isn't it true that you all dream of riding into the West and never stopping? No doubt, as a people, you Americans are still too young to feel what six centuries of irrationality and stasis mean. Well, we, too, felt restless. For us, though, the way lay to the East.

"So we agreed to move back. Now we are all here, without our wives, children, and grandchildren. When we left, we told them our intentions and begged their pardon. We had to endure their tears, their reproaches, their worries, anger, and at last, their mockery. That was terrible, but we had each other. You too have your friends and will know their value, how they bear you up, even when they argue with you.

"As for us, we miss our families, and we argue all the time. Everything is a matter for dispute, everything. Is there anything in the prophecy? Are we fools? Was Stalin a monster or a hero? To argue has become, in a sense, our calling. Perhaps if we were young enough, we might attempt to rebuild the city. But, as you see, we are too old and too few. Our lives have given us many experiences and opinions, with much to disagree about. Above all, though, we disagree about Suzam-Ord. For example, if the curse is real and, if so, how it can be ended. Some of us say they believe in the prophecy that the city will again become great; a few go so far as to claim that it is destined to become the center of an empire extending to the Banda Sea. Others believe in the prophecy too, but more modestly; they think that the city will someday be rebuilt and that it's rebuilding that will lift the curse. The curse itself is a great cause of dispute among us because no one knows its exact nature. Those who don't believe in it at all say it was just a Mongol trick to frighten off trade. Others say that not only that there is a curse, but that to remove it will require some special sacrifice—three beheadings, for example, to make up for those of the khan's emissaries. Oh yes, last night there was even some talk about you and two of your friends in this regard. No, please don't be alarmed! I assure you that this proposal came from the very smallest of minorities, and even he was just making a joke, though in the way men joke about holy things. Anyway, most of us believe in the curse and that the prophecy is tied to it, that one is entangled with the other. They say they have to believe in the one for the sake of the other. Underneath this wishful believing, however, is the suspicion that there is no curse to expiate and no prophecy to be fulfilled, that the only truths are the dictates of geography and the unrepeatable events of history. Geography is obviously against us, while politics and commerce have long ago passed Suzam-Ord by. If we were to credit only facts, we would have to admit our city is dead three times over, that it is impossible to build even the humblest of expectations on this stony ground. You can see that for yourself. Yet some have an answer even for this. They argue that, because time moves in cycles, every past is bound to become some future, as the present will soon be that past and, again, a still more distant future. The most pious of us argue that our best course lies in silence, practical activity, and fulfilling the commandment for daily prayers. He declares that everything lies in the hands of Allah.

"Well, who knows? Perhaps Allah does watch over the steppe and long ago counted every pebble in Suzam-Ord. Where one has faith in nothing, it becomes easy to believe anything. If, after all, we have seen, even one of us can believe, then why shouldn't we all? Why shouldn't the city be rebuilt? With Him, everything is possible. It is even possible that you and your friends have come here as Allah's instruments. The world, we know, is changing. What we thought was history, what we thought were our true lives, turns out merely to have been history holding its breath. We have come back to die.

Why shouldn't our city come back to life?

"The steppe is a lonesome place. It's hard to put down roots here. Only the nomads are truly at home on the steppe because they are always on the move, and the steppe was made for them. A city on the steppe, isn't it an absurdity? And yet there once was such a city. And here we are, you and we together, because of this city.

"We're content to end our days in each other's company and to be buried here beside our city. Who knows? Perhaps we are the sacrifices that will end the curse. Maybe the emptiness of our lives will be exalted by the fullness of our deaths."

———◆———

It's been more than a year now, plenty of time for us all to get back in harness, steeped again in the routines of our lives. Even Krueger seems finally to have settled down. We don't keep in close touch, just a phone call from time to time. We all say we're fine, families doing well, work going all right. We make jokes about the ready availability of lettuce and oranges, and if any of us still smoke cigars, we smoke them in solitude, on the deck, at night, beside our gas grills. We are clean-shaven, take regular showers, and everything that happens to us is in accord with normal laws. We feel only what one ought to feel, including boredom, and our sleep is untroubled.

A Conversation with Robert Wexelblatt

Lowestoft Chronicle

Robert Wexelblatt
(Photography: Boston University Photo Services)

More than twenty-five years ago, a fascinating footnote in an essay concerning a Chinese general deploying an illiterate courier with a secret message inscribed on his scalp inspired author Robert Wexelblatt to concoct an ingenious account of the fictional life of famed itinerant peasant poet Hsi-wei. Having accrued over forty tales in the intervening years, this inspirational character continues to entertain and intrigue, with no end in sight to his remarkable wanderings.

In this exclusive interview with *Lowestoft Chronicle*, Wexelblatt discusses his latest collection of Hsi-wei tales, his interest in the Sui Dynasty, and the origins of some of his many inventive stories.

Lowestoft Chronicle (LC): Your newest story collection, *Other Places, Other Times*, contains twenty-six historical fictions, half of which feature the fictional peasant poet Chen Hsi-wei. I've been an admirer of your Hsi-wei stories for quite some years, savoring periodic new installments and speculating if there would be a second collection. What made you decide on this combination of thirteen Hsi-wei tales and thirteen diverse narratives across dissimilar periods and places? How did this book come to be published by Pelekinesis rather than Regal House Publishing?

Robert Wexelblatt (RW): This is a question to provoke both reflection and confession. I'd like to say *Other Places, Other Times* was meticulously premeditated, that I conceived of the plan then executed it as best I could. The truth is that I wanted to do a new collection, compiled a list of published but uncollected stories, then realized that I had a bunch of historical fictions about the same in number as the Chinese tales written after *Hsi-wei Tales* came out. The symmetry felt fortuitous, and so I organized the book, alternating thirteen stories featuring Hsi-wei tales with a baker's dozen that didn't.

I have no regular publisher but have been exceptionally lucky in finding ones willing to publish my work. A colleague of mine from Southern California is a friend of Mark Givens of Pelekinesis Press. This colleague suggested I get in touch with Mark and submit a manuscript. I sent *Mark Heiberg's Twitch* which he published in 2016. Mark is a delight to worth with, and things went smoothly. Two years later, I asked if he might consider another book, and he said yes. I offered more than one possibility, including the long and decidedly peculiar collection, *The Posthumous Papers of Sidney Fein*. To my surprise, Mark wanted to publish it rather than a shorter and more conventional book of stories. I cautioned him about it and said that I wouldn't accept his generous offer until he'd had two weeks in which to come to his senses. He took the two weeks but still wanted the book. It came out in 2018. So, my association with Pelekinesis preceded the one with Regal House. Because of the Hsi-wei tales, I did submit *Other Places, Other Times* to Regal House, who, after a few months of silence, said they were no longer publishing collections of short fiction, which sold badly. And so, I tried Pelekinesis once more and was lucky once again—lucky that Mark likes my work and is apparently unconcerned by poor sales.

LC: Among the many varied stories is the engaging "Three Noons" from a 2009 issue of *SN Review*. What stirred you to take a shot at writing a Western?

RW: Thank you for noticing this old story. Once again, you've posed the right question. I wrote "Three Noons" because I wanted to take a shot at a Western. I'll try anything, any genre, but I also like to find unexpected ways of telling stories, and I seem to lean toward triptychs, as in the petites suites. I expect "Three Noons" has its origins in a childhood watching old B Westerns and, of course, classic films like *High Noon* itself. Writing variations on the theme reflects the same impulse to incorporate music into narrative that is behind the petites suites.

LC: Having been moved by the tuneful and lyrical brilliance of your collection *Petites Suites*—a hybrid of fiction and music—it's interesting to see the entertaining "Petite Suite Littéraire" (from an issue of *BlazeVox*) included in *Other Places, Other Times*. Using this piece as an example, how do you start assembling a suite? Does it begin with the music, the title, or the germ of a story? How do you decide on the instruments and the tone? What motivated you to write an additional twenty-third suite, and might you attempt more in the future?

RW: I wrote a lot of these suites in a relatively short period of time. They usually began with failures; that is, with ideas for longer stories that didn't develop but worked as short pieces, like those in the French suites that were the musical model

I followed. I would look for a loose common theme and, in the spirit of Eric Satie, assign them whimsical titles and instrumentation that was fitting but no less quirky. This was all playfulness, fun. Serious pieces would be in minor keys, lighter ones in major. Instruments would mimic the voices in the stories. In recent years, the fever of suite-writing let up, as did writing posthumous Sidney Fein essays. But in both cases, it's been the same as with Hsi-wei tales and poems. I return to these forms, about which I feel a little proprietary, intermittently, always with gratitude and pleasure.

LC: Together with the previous volume, *Hsi-wei Tales*, forty-one of the celebrated poet's adventures are now in print. Are there published or unpublished ones you didn't include in either book? Do you intend to continue to write more of these "posthumous" tales?

RW: All my Hsi-wei tales have been published, all but the last now collected in books. I wrote one more after the new book was complete when I discovered that the beautiful and innovative Anji Bridge was constructed during the Sui Dynasty. So, I arranged for Hsi-wei meet the architect and wrote a story about it along with the customary poem. It was recently published in a literary journal.

LC: You once mentioned that the books *Petites Suites*, *Hsi-wei Tales*, and *The Posthumous Papers of Sidney Fein* all began in the 1990s as one-off experiments. "Hsi-wei's Skull," from the Fall 1997 issue of *Sou'wester*, was the first Hsi-wei story to emerge, and apparently, you drew inspiration from a footnote in an essay by Italian chemist and writer Primo Levi. Exactly how challenging was it imagining the Sui period and depicting (vividly so) this benevolent but crusading character? What persuaded you to make him a poet?

RW: It's true that, like the first petite suite and the initial Sidney Fein essay, the original Hsi-wei tale was to be a one-off. It's also true that it was inspired by a footnote to one of Primo Levi's essays. It told of a Chinese general sending a secret message inscribed on the scalp of an illiterate courier. It was only later that I discovered that scalp-inscribing is called steganography and read up on it. I liked the idea of a peasant boy with fast-growing hair being recruited for the perilous mission, surviving, rejecting material rewards, asking instead to be educated. I liked the idea that this intelligent but illiterate boy would want to have language inside as well as on the top of his head. That he would become a poet was part of the plan all along, but he required some schooling first. I read up, superficially, on the Sui Dynasty, gathering just enough to seed my imagination. Sixth Century China is far away and long enough ago that I didn't feel excessively constrained either by facts or my ignorance of them, nor did it seem likely anybody would charge me with cultural appropriation. Later on, I read more deeply into Chinese history, also mining the internet and other sources for details of the period, out of which I could fashion stories.

LC: Given his fame and the influential power of his verses, were you initially hesitant to include an example of his work?

RW: Not at all. I always felt a little cheated by stories with poets as characters that didn't include any of their poems. The first Hsi-wei tale actually begins with a poem which the narrative then explains. Subsequently, I switched the order so that the narratives precede the poems for which they account.

LC: Chinese history and customs aside, how would you describe your research on the poetry of this era? Were there particular poets or poems that were monumental in helping shape the way you constructed your verses?

RW: There is little poetry from the Sui Dynasty. The greatest and most famous of Chinese poets came in the following dynasty, the Tang. This was a disappointment, but it allowed me free rein for Hsi-wei's verses. He wasn't tied to specific forms or conventions besides which, as the only peasant/poet in China, everything he wrote would be unusual, original, and maybe uncouth as well. My sources cite only one outstanding poet from the era, and that was a shock. This was the second and last Sui emperor, Yangdi, generally considered China's worst. He is someone Hsi-wei deeply despises and whom he believes had murdered his father. Hsi-wei's verses are nothing like Emperor Yang's.

LC: As the verses are often intrinsic to the tale, the construction of the stories becomes more intriguing. Do you compose the poem first, or is it always a case of creating verses from the finished story?

RW: As I mentioned, I based many of the stories on facts I discovered about the Sui Dynasty: the wars in what is now North Korea and Vietnam, the building of the Grand Canal, the repairs to and expansion of the Great wall, the Sui currency and land reforms, funeral customs, the examination system, the duties of magistrates, folk beliefs about witches and ghosts. Just as often, I simply imagined Hsi-wei in some situation and how his keen moral sense, along with the sensibilities and resentments of an educated peasant, would cause him to respond. Then there were little details I turned up about Chinese court or peasant life. One story was inspired by what may be the sole surviving Sui-period painting.

But you've asked the very best question about the tales: the chicken-or-egg one. There are a few cases where the poem came before the story. For instance, last spring, I found myself writing a poem about Hsi-wei conversing with a court official in the gardens of the Duke of Shun. It was weeks later that the story preceding the poem took shape. But that is exceptional. It's more usual for the narrative to come before the poem. It was also useful to invent a Tang minister who is a Hsi-wei fan, have him take time off from his duties to visit the poet in his retirement and keep a journal of their conversations about his poems.

I'm pleased that you find the poems well integrated with the tales. Neither would exist without the other.

LC: Your many works comprise eight fiction collections, three books of verse, two books of essays, two novellas, and a novel. Roughly how many pieces of prose and poetry would you say you've published? Is there a particular work you prize above others?

RW: With the two books out this month, there are now ten fiction collections. I once read that men tend to count things, that there are few authors or academics who can't state with precision the total of their publications. Me, too. By my count, there have been 754. This is astonishing to me as I feel I'm not so productive at all. All the same, I sometimes think of the last page of Kafka's "A Hunger Artist" and joke that my supply wildly outstrips demand. I feel differently about the various publications. Many, even most, I entirely forget. The novel, *Zublinka Among Women*, took the most sustained effort, and so I feel for it the affection one might have for a difficult child who successfully navigates childhood and adolescence and makes it into respectable adulthood. The fiction collections merge in my memory so that I no longer can say which one contains which stories. I feel more affection for the long-term projects that all began as single experiments, the ones I called proprietary: *Petites Suites*, *Hsi-wei Tales*, and *The Posthumous Papers of Sidney Fein*. About the three books of poems, I feel some ambivalence because I don't think of myself as a poet, just as someone who occasionally writes verses, and mostly because I can't help it.

LC: And what are your long and short-term writing goals? Will you remain focused on short fiction, essays, and occasional poems, or do you have ambitions to someday write another novel?

RW: I don't think long-term, never have. I'm just grateful for any idea that gains sufficient traction to be made into a finished essay, poem, or story. I've become a simple creature. If I'm teaching and not writing, I'm okay. If I'm writing and not teaching, still better. But if I'm doing neither, I'm good for nothing. I will confess that I do sometimes wonder if I could produce another novel. I'd like that.

Something Different
Laurel DiGangi

After almost a year, we pined to burst free from our pandemic cocoons without ending up on ventilators. Then an email arrived inviting us to a pop-up drive-in movie: *The Greatest Showman*. Four years ago, when the film was released, we thought the concept of a P. T. Barnum musical biopic was hokey. But now we were counting the days until we'd park in the wilderness under the stars and watch the circus come to town.

In preparation for our first real date in almost a year, I spent a half-hour applying makeup and shaved my legs for the first time since Christmas. My husband had trimmed his Rip Van Winkle beard and dyed it a lovely shade of fawn brown.

"You look terrific!" I said.

"So do you," he said, "I like that glitter around your eyes."

"And I like that shirt. You look good in buttons. Where'd you get that shirt?"

"You bought it for me. Back in June-vember."

The event was sponsored by our local credit union. I thought they only loved us for our mortgage payments, but apparently, they cared about our emotional well-being by offering us this break from pandemic boredom at only thirty dollars a car. We could have stayed home and streamed that same movie for four bucks, but this was something different. And admission included a free goody bag.

I've always been passionate about mystery packages: Office party grab bags, secret Santas, boxes left on my doorstep by Amazon Prime. I hoped the goody bag would recreate my fond teenage memories of drive-in movies. Perhaps I'd find corn dogs, Good Humor ice cream bars, mosquito repellent, and a condom.

"I doubt that," said my husband. "The corn dog would melt the ice cream."

"You're right."

"And they told us to bring our own food."

He was right again.

As we drove along an unfamiliar, winding mountain road, the aroma of junk-food chicken wafting from its carry-out bag, I was stoked. I'd packed all necessities in the back seat: A blanket, flashlight, toilet paper, hand sanitizer wipes, and an AM/FM radio freshly ordered from Amazon Prime.

We finally reached a glowing pop-up marquee. We turned right and were greeted by a cheerful, masked middle-aged woman who scanned our ticket and gave us our goody bag. As we drove up the hill, I felt an electric surge of anticipation. In a moment, that big-ass screen would be looming over us! But when we reached the lot, all we saw was a tiny, distant white rectangle: the Tom Thumb of movie screens, only one-eighth the size of a fully grown screen.

A teenage boy with a gleaming red lightsaber was directing cars. He must have seen the disappointment on our faces because he said, "Go ahead and drive to the front row," which per the laws of perspective would have rendered the screen slightly larger, but then a group of boys stopped us, waving their lightsabers ferociously, and directed us to park in the last row behind a humongous SUV. We sucked it up and followed their instructions. After all, we were in a pandemic and liked to think of ourselves as good citizens and not Norse mask-hole war gods.

There was only one problem: Ninety percent of the screen had disappeared from our view. All that remained was a narrow strip of white peeking above the SUV's roof. I yearned for the drive-in movies of my youth, where screens loomed over us like Godzillas. So, when the lightsaber boys were distracted by other vehicles, we quickly backed up our little Scion toaster and repositioned it several feet to the left of the SUV. Now we could at least see the screen in the aisle between cars.

By the way, one of the first movies I saw at the drive-in was *Pollyanna*, in which young Haley Mills finds the bright side in any negative situation. I thought, It's good the screen is small and distant. It fits so snugly in the aisle between cars. It's also good that it's soft and inflated, providing an abstract pre-show to reduce our boredom. When the wind rippled across its surface, it was a sail. When a gust hit it from the front, I imagined a pillow where a weary ghost rested its head. And if a stronger gust picked it up and crashed it into several cars, it would make an even better story, or perhaps a lawsuit.

"You know, if we don't like the movie, we can always leave," my husband said.

"Maybe not. Look behind you," I said as a lightsaber boy led a Jeep Gladiator pickup to park directly behind us, practically kissing our bumper.

"Fuck, now we're trapped like circus animals," said my husband.

The wind finally died down, and the screen was starting to look like a fluffy white marshmallow, making me hungry. "It's starting to get dark. We better eat," I said.

We groped through our fast food bags in the last vestiges of magic hour. My husband fished out his sandwich and fries. I located my chicken strips, mashed potatoes, and coleslaw but could not find anything that felt like a plastic fork. I was hoping to be poked by prongs, but no luck.

"Aren't they supposed to give you forks?" I said.

"That doesn't mean they do."

I dug around the glove compartment and found two straws, hoping to use them as chopsticks, but I kept dropping coleslaw down my shirt. Then I tried shoveling the slaw in my mouth with one straw, but that was even worse. So, I gave up and grabbed a glob of slaw with my fingers.

Meanwhile, my husband was happily and gracefully munching away at his sandwich and fries. "Excuse me for asking," he said politely, "but are you eating that coleslaw with your fingers?"

"Shut up and find me a napkin," I said.

Fortunately, my emergency chopstick trick worked better with the mashed potatoes. It was now time for my traditional, ritualistic, pre-movie preemptive pee. Even though I didn't have to go, I wanted to make sure I wouldn't have to get up later.

"It's pee time!" I announced.

Outside, the air was brisk. Thick clouds obscured all the stars I hoped to see on this remote plateau. I meandered through the jumbled array of cars toward several portable toilets, carrying my flashlight and wad of toilet paper, expecting the worst. I pinched the facemask over my nose and held my breath.

But when I opened the door, I was hit by a blinding flash of heavenly light. Suddenly, I was stepping inside the cleanest, sweetest-smelling porta-potty I had seen in my six decades on planet earth. A real flushing system rather than a horrifying poop-infested pit, a sink with running water, jasmine-scented soap, hand towels, and ten-ply organic toilet paper. It seemed oddly larger inside than it had appeared from the outside, and at that moment, when my cheeks hit the stainless steel seat, it seemed as if the pandemic had never happened and that all the problems of the first, second, and third worlds had disappeared. I would've sat on this five-star toilet longer, but the movie was about to begin.

Once outside the porta-potty, I saw an image projected on the tiny pillow screen. An expanse of cobalt blue sky interspersed with, what were those? Drones? Alien Spaceships prepared to wage war with planet earth? Nope, even worse. We were watching out-of-focus icons, files, and folders. It looked like a trailer for *Laptop Screen: The Movie*. A cartoon or ad for concession treats would have been more appropriate, but at least this was a sign that the show was about to begin. And the glowing screen helped lead me through the maze of jumbled cars and back to our Scion toaster.

We sat in the car and waited. Soon it was 7:40. The film was supposed to start ten minutes ago. The desktop had changed several times to various troubleshooting documents, some with large red Xs and lots of drop-down menus.

"At least, at home, our computer screens are in focus," my husband said.

"Maybe they should try rebooting," I said.

And as if on cue, the screen went dark. Then, a few seconds later, back on again. But still terribly, head-achingly, out of focus.

Soon it was 7:50. Behind us, several children in pajamas lay in the pickup's flatbed, heads propped up on pillows, eagerly waiting for the show to begin. I hoped it would, for everyone's sake.

"How much did we pay for this again?" my husband asked.

"Thirty bucks."

"Ah yes!" said my husband, pausing for effect. "There's a sucker born every minute."

Suckers, eh? I could go for a lollipop right now. Then I remembered. The goody bag! I'd forgotten all about it. Now we had something to occupy ourselves while waiting for the movie magic to begin. Daring fate and the wrath of our fellow theater-goers, we turned on our dome lights and peered inside: Two bottled waters! A mini-flashlight! Two half-ounce bags of a puffed corn snack called Pirate's Booty. And finally, a keychain and lapel pin with our credit union's avatar so we could display brand loyalty to our mortgage holder.

It was now 8 pm. In the distance, a group of lightsaber boys hovered en masse over a laptop, none with the intestinal fortitude to yell out, "Is there an IT person in the house?"

Panicked, we turned on our new AM/FM radio to the required frequency, expecting an announcement, something like, "Sorry folks, we'll have this fixed in just a few minutes," but all we heard was static. I began to hyperventilate. How long would we be here, staring at an out-of-focus laptop, in this dark parking lot where we could only, per stern instructions in the email, leave our cars to visit the porta-potties? How long could two bottled waters and two half-ounce bags of Pirate's Booty sustain us?

I squeezed my husband's thigh and said, "I feel more trapped now than I ever did, at any time, throughout this entire pandemic."

"Don't worry, hon. It'll be over soon," he said.

"And what makes you so sure?"

"Because nobody knows what the fuck they're doing."

He was right. A few minutes later, the lightsaber boys were circulating through the parking lot, knocking on windows. A couple of engines began to fire. I heard a woman say, "You'll all get your money refunded." A chorus of other engines joined in. The sweet scent of exhaust swept into our open windows. And when the adults in the Jeep behind us roused their kids from slumber and packed them back inside the car, I knew that in a few minutes, we'd be free.

Once back home, we stood outside and gazed at the stars. The cloud cover had lifted, and they sparkled more intensely than ever. And when we walked inside our home again, I thought, what a big, big house. What a big, big TV screen. Thank you, oh great credit union, for lending us the money to live where we have all the space, food, drink, cutlery, and entertainment we need. And, of course, for reversing that thirty-dollar charge on our Mastercard.

Although, I have to say, in comparison, our bathroom seemed quite tacky.

Family Circus
Jeff Alphin

We once made a commercial for a lottery game called "El Gordo," the "Fat One." It was based on the annual La Loteria in Spain, and someone at the Maryland Lottery thought it would be a good idea to play off the concept in the U.S.

The commercial was a spaghetti western send-up, part Leone's Man With No Name, part Alex Karras as Mongo from *Blazing Saddles*. Baltimore Orioles big man and lord of the long ball Boog Powell starred as El Gordo, a mystery man who shows up out of the desert bestowing money bags upon the humble and nonplussed townsfolk.

We traveled to Old Tucson for the shoot, a replica of 1860s Tucson that doubles as a movie studio and Western theme park tourist attraction. Can-can girls in the saloon, stuntmen shootouts at high noon, panning for gold. Stuff like that.

Half the Westerns you've ever seen were filmed there. *3:10 to Yuma, Rio Bravo, Gunfight at the OK Corral*, and *The Trial of Billy Jack*. *The Outlaw Josey Wales*, and a personal favorite about the time the calvary tried using camels, called *Hawmps!*. Director legends from Howard Hawks to Kurosawa, John Sturges to John Landis with a cavalcade of leading men. Glenn Ford, Burt Lancaster, Paul Newman, Walter Brennan, Dean Martin, Charles Bronson, Kirk Douglas, Randolph Scott, and Lee Marvin walked the lamp-lit boardwalks along Main Street to the off-key tinkling of a player piano drifting through the swinging doors of the saloon.

Since it was close to Halloween, Old Tucson was trying to sell itself as a haunted attraction at night, lighting open fires and torches along a horror desert trail of scare skits featuring zombie gunslingers, skeletal sheriffs, calcified cowpokes, witchy women of the night, and mad doctors with rusty sawbones.

The whole week was pretty surreal.

We spent three days working with character actors, extras whose leather faces were oddly familiar, probably because they'd signed up for the posse, ridden on the cattle drive, or played cards in the saloon in just about every western you've seen for the last 20 years, the rough and tumble of the old West dripping off their mustaches like sarsaparilla.

The wardrobe guy on the shoot had been Clint Eastwood's main man for years. He told us that Clint was such a skinflint he wore the same pair of shoes for every *Dirty Harry* movie.

After the final wrap, we all went to dinner and ate Caesar salads with buffalo jerky instead of anchovies. Boog told a story about how he and Roy Clark used to pop greenies, shut all the windows at Roy's place in Florida, jack the air conditioning way up, then build a roaring fire in the fireplace and bat baseballs around the house.

The next day, the agency people got on a plane and went back to Baltimore. Jane and I decided to stay an extra day and experience a desert Halloween.

So, at twilight on October 30th, we stopped by the hotel bar for happy hour. The place was dead. Just the bartender and us. We scrounged a local paper for some action, debating the scare quality of a Jaycees Haunted House advertised on the local event listings.

The bar was a few steps down from street level, half-sunk into the hotel parking lot. It had long rectangular windows up high, giving you a prairie-dog's-eye view of landscape shrubbery, grass, and clouds, split diagonally by a wheelchair ramp. Nursing a happy-hour vodka drink and a beer, we stared up past the shrubs at the purple-orange of the parking lot sky.

There was movement on the wheelchair ramp. Enormous red clown shoes flopped down the incline and disappeared from view.

At least someone around here had plans.

Minutes later, a second pair of clown shoes came down the ramp. Hobo-style clown shoes with striped socks and a hole where the big toe would be. Five minutes later, another pair, this time elongated clown saddle shoes. And another pair after that, rainbow-colored clown brogans. And then another, flopping like swim fins. The clown shoes kept coming. None of them took the stairs. Clown shoes and stairs are not made for each other.

And then, just like in the joke, a clown walked into the bar.

A Bozo the Clown clown. White pancake makeup, flaming red wig, pom-pom buttons on a sack suit with blue piping.

His demeanor was quiet and matter-of-fact as he sat at the opposite end of the bar and ordered a drink. A sad clown.

A second clown walked into the bar, an unkempt one, blue wig askew, crooked hand-drawn eyebrows, and large plastic-frame eyeglasses. Bozo jumped up to greet him with a handshake. His drink was ordered, and the clowns clinked pints.

The next two clowns were a Ronald McDonald knockoff and a Red Skelton Freddie the Freeloader. Jane and I stared over the lips of our drinks as all four exchanged hugs.

For the next hour, clowns continued to enter in small groups. There were no other patrons, just 25 sloppy-kissing, beer-guzzling, guffawing clowns. From what we could tell under the wigs, noses, and makeup, they ranged in age from twenty-something to middle-aged to card-carrying AARP.

They all seemed to belong to different circuses. The classic style of Ringling Brothers' Emmett Kelly. The horror grin of a Killer Klown from Outer Space. Hastily smudged on Anna Nicole Smith clowns. Rubber masks, foam noses, flashy rentals, and homemade disasters. Clustered together as if in a Clowns Only section, they raised glasses, did shots, slapped backs, and hooted—a Dutch Masters painting for a box of exploding cigars.

My finger danced on the shutter release of my camera until I could resist no longer. I approached and asked.

There was an overwhelming *Hell, yes*. Within seconds my viewfinder contained the team photo for the Squirting Flower All-Stars. I snapped away as clowns draped themselves over one another, squeezing everybody into the shot, adjusting noses, and sloshing shot glasses.

One of the clowns bellowed, "Get in here and take one with us!" The bartender came out from behind the bar, and I handed him my camera.

The ice broken, I asked the burning question. "So…what's the story?"

I've never killed a party faster, before or since. The clowns fell quiet, looking amongst themselves for someone to address the issue.

A clown, whom I guessed was in her early 40s, soberly explained that they were all family—brothers, sisters, cousins, aunts, uncles, nieces, and nephews—originally from somewhere in the Midwest. Over a decade ago, her older brother moved to Arizona and cut off communication. No matter how they tried to reestablish contact or convince him to come to a Thanksgiving or Christmas or milestone birthday party, he wouldn't respond. Wouldn't even return the call.

A Greek chorus of clowns nodded in affirmation.

They decided to take action. They would come from all over the country to meet in Tucson on his birthday, the night before Halloween, and go out to his house in the desert to surprise him. Dressed as clowns.

Trick or treat.

As the odds of horrific backfire dawned on me, I noticed several looks of uncertainty be- hind clown greasepaint. I wasn't the only one who thought this might be a bad idea.

Nonetheless, this family was sticking together. I suspected now that these weren't party shots they were drinking. This was liquid courage.

Another round was ordered, and the clowns went back to acting like clowns. Jane and I moved closer. A couple of them asked where we were from. "Baltimore," we said. A place that seemed uncharacteristically normal at the moment.

The clock struck 7:00, and the clowns settled their tab.

We were saying goodbyes when two clowns I took for soccer moms asked about our plans for the night. Upon confessing we didn't have any, someone blurted, "You should come with us!" A concurring roar from the others.

Jane and I fumbled for appropriate regrets—this is a family thing; he's going to be so happy to see you; we would be intruding.

Nonsense, they replied. You're one of us now. You have to come.

As I have said, these clowns had been drinking. When 25 boozy clowns get in your face hell-bent on an invitation, you can fight it all you want, but you will eventually say yes.

They gave us directions and told us to be there by 9:00 so as not to spoil the surprise. The Halloween night of our dreams, slash nightmare, had been dropped in our laps. Heaven or hell.

How would the coin land?

It didn't seem right to show up without costumes. But not as clowns. That was reserved for family. We'd have to move fast. The Halloween aisle at the drugstore near the hotel had been picked down to the bones, lonely tubes of fake blood, and rubber teeth left dangling on the pegboard. With the clock ticking, we rummaged the floor bins and scored two rubber devil skull caps with horns, red and black makeup, some beard hair, and two red kiddie capes.

We bedeviled ourselves, leaving the hotel room bathroom

mirror looking like a murder scene. With our miniature capes flipping behind us, we hopped into the rental car, consulted our directions, and drove out into the desert.

Way out.

The lights of the city fell behind us.

Jane's black goatee fluttered in the cracked driver-side window wind. Despite our misgivings, my grin spread wide from one pointy red ear to the other.

I couldn't remember the last time Halloween felt so Halloween. The thrill of ringing an unfamiliar doorbell. The giddy butterflies of the unknown. An invitation to a haunted house.

We drove farther into the desert, the sky darkening to deep purple and blue with a canopy of bright diamonds, the campfire aroma of burning mesquite, the towering saguaros shapeshifting into monstrous sentries in the distance.

We had a CD mix with a live version of John Prine's "The Missing Years," about the unaccounted-for time in the life of Jesus. The possibility of cutting all connections and disappearing into the desert got me thinking. What had this guy done, or wanted to do, that made him decide to vanish?

The ranch house was far from its neighbors in a sparse development against a backdrop of intense starlight. The circular drive was lined with desert flora, cacti, and a couple jack-o-lanterns. Eerie gorgeous.

There were no cars out front other than a baby-blue VW Beetle. It was five minutes to nine. Unless the Beetle was a bona fide clown car that had transported the lot of them, there were no signs of a party.

Remembering standard surprise-party protocol, we drove past until we came to a line of cars in front of someone else's house. We parked and doubled back on foot. Reality set in. We were doing this, the night's most apprehensive trick-or-treaters. We began to second-guess our choice of costumes with the sick dread of having accepted a proposition to which one's better judgment fires a warning flare. We rang the bell.

After a gut-checking 30 seconds, a clown we didn't recognize opened the door, looking at us as if we were mentally stunted adults trick-or-treating a day early. We introduced ourselves and stumbled through how we'd come to be invited. As the door clown ushered us through the house, I looked around for clues about this man's personality. Nothing more than the standard Western furnishings and bric-a-brac. Painted steer skull, a Navajo blanket, a cowhide throw rug, and earthenware pottery. We were led into the kitchen, where the family of clowns who had embraced us two hours ago now looked at us as if we were some weirdo party crashers. The devil costumes made us impossible to recognize.

I pondered the mechanics of the night. How'd they get into the house? What was the ruse for getting the guy out of the house? Was there a decoy/escort clown?

But there was no time for Q&A. The guest of honor was due to arrive any minute, and the house was bustling with jittery clowns putting out the dip, setting up the bar, reconnecting in socially awkward clusters, and emitting nervous laughter. Everybody seemed out of sync.

We never did get a grip on their intended plan. They didn't even get the chance to hide and yell, "Surprise."

Without fanfare or announcement, the long-lost relative walked into the den filled with family he hadn't seen for ten years, dressed like an insane clown posse.

Then things got weird.

The guy, who at a glance looked like a pretty normal guy—slightly shaggy hair, sun-baked jeans, and a T-shirt—seemed to just quietly freak out. Wearing a vacant smile, his eyes jumped from red nose to red nose, receiving tentative hugs from tentative clowns. It was hard to tell if he recognized anyone.

I kept my distance, apprehensive of getting sucked into a drama I had no business in. Jane somehow got swept up in the encroaching tide of clowns, closer to the action. She told me the guy looked like he'd been through some shit. Drawn cheeks, nose collapsed like someone with tertiary syphilis. She hypothesized a vet returning home from the war, like Sam Stone, with a hole in his arm where all the money goes. I didn't get that impression, but like I said, I never got a good close-up look.

So as the guy was getting smothered by clowns, I backed into the kitchen and found my- self with another set of clowns I hadn't met yet who couldn't figure out why there was a devil by the guacamole. My explanation only seemed to create more confusion.

The trip was starting to go bad.

The unexpecting host only stayed in the den for about ten minutes before disappearing into the recesses of the house.

An uncomfortable silence fell over the scene. The clowns broke ranks, peripheral players retreating to the sanctuary of the kitchen, while those whom I assumed were closer, more immediate, or influential family members went off in pursuit of their quarry, presumably for some back-room powwow.

It dawned on Jane and me that this was no surprise party. This was some kind of intervention.

Instincts told us to beat it, but it was tricky. It felt rude to just disappear, and whom do you thank? As we tried to orchestrate a graceful escape, people started drawing us into a conversation, a distraction to get through this stomach-turner of an evening.

For the next hour, we holed up around the kitchen island, snacking nervously and making small talk. The scene was periodically interrupted by the emergence of a clown from the inner sanctum, exchanged whispers, and the next round of reinforcements selected for a private audience.

The rest of us ate cheese curls.

Reality was setting in for the clowns. Their misguided efforts, this heartbreakingly desperate, well-intended master plan, was a familial train wreck.

Noses were removed and faces scrubbed, revealing weary concern. Wigs accumulated like a pileup of psychedelic lapdogs at one end of the counter. Exposed patches of genuine bald pate shined under the kitchen fluorescents. Florid bulbous noses looked almost as red as the rubber ones. The room took on the air of a clown locker room after the last show in the last town on the circuit.

Reluctant to give up the protective cover of our costumes, Jane and I became comic relief, the story of the devils by now having circulated throughout. "So, you're that couple from the bar." No one could believe we had actually shown up.

The guest of honor never returned to the party, and fatigue set in. It was time to leave. We tried to spin positive, thanking everyone within earshot for the most unforgettable Halloween we never saw coming. Even though we hadn't really connected with anyone in particular, the parting round of hugs was surprisingly heartfelt. Like they needed to hug someone who would hug back without ten years of incommunicado baggage getting in the way.

Back in the rent-a-car, we exhaled. Who, what, how, and why the fuck was that? What will the family do now? Is that guy okay? Were we okay?

If I conjure a scenario where my extended family descends on me to confront a personal problem I have or a decision I've made, each with their own lifestyle, politics, prejudices, and hang-ups, dressed as clowns, well, let's just say I don't sleep too well.

For all we knew, the clowns were the villains, while their ambushed relative was just an alright guy trying to live his life. And for all they knew, the party-crashing devils could have been Natural Born Killers and left the place looking like *In Cold Blood*.

We'd just spent a week filming a commercial starring a retired first baseman dressed up as an oversized Pancho Villa in a Saturday-morning cowboy-serial town filled with stuntmen, good guys in sheriff badges shooting blanks at bad'uns in black mustaches. Makes it hard to tell who's who. It seemed like the guy who supposedly had something to hide was the only one not wearing a mask.

On the way back to the hotel, we pulled into the Jaycees Haunted House to calm our nerves.

Contributors

Jeff Alphin lives and writes with his wife, Jane, in Baltimore, MD. His work is included in *The Best of Fiction on the Web*, *Silk + Smoke*, and *Tiny Spoon*.

J.L. Austin is a Hapa (of mixed Asian descent) writer based out of California. She teaches English at a small college in California; her courses feature themes ranging from cyborgs to death in cartoons. She has a weakness for video games and cats.

Roger Camp lives in Seal Beach, CA, where he muses over his orchids, walks the pier, plays blues piano and spends afternoons reading under an Angel's Trumpet with a charm of hummingbirds. When he's not at home, he's photographing in the Old World. His work has appeared in *Spillway*, *Slant*, *North American Review*, *Pank*, *Southern Poetry Review*, and *Nimrod*.

Lorraine Caputo is a wandering troubadour whose works appear in over 300 journals on six continents and 20 collections of poetry—including *Notes from the Patagonia* (dancing girl press, 2017), *On Galápagos Shores* (dancing girl press, 2019), and *Caribbean Interludes* (Origami Poems Project, 2022). She also authors travel narratives, articles, and guidebooks. Her writing has been honored by the Parliamentary Poet Laureate of Canada (2011) and nominated for Best of the Net. Caputo has done literary readings from Alaska to Patagonia. She journeys through Latin America with her faithful knapsack Rocinante, listening to the voices of the *pueblos* and Earth. Follow her adventures at www.facebook.com/lorrainecaputo. wanderer or https://latinamericawanderer.wordpress.com.

Laurel DiGangi has had fiction and creative nonfiction published in *The Chicago Reader*, *Denver Quarterly*, *Fourth Genre*, *SLAB*, *Asylum*, *Atlanta Quarterly*, *Cottonwood*, *Two Hawks Quarterly*, and *Under the Gum Tree*, among others. A former graphic designer, illustrator, entertainment journalist, and film critic, she now teaches all sorts of writing at Woodbury University in Burbank, California. Fun fact: She once retrieved Johnny Depp's cigarette butt from an ashtray after an interview and sold it on eBay for $200.

Mary Donaldson-Evans' creative work has been published by the *Lowestoft Chronicle*, *Boomer Lit Magazine*, *The Literary Hatchet*, *The Metaworker Literary Magazine*, and *Spank the Carp*, among others. Her book, *Behind the Lines: A Soldier, his Family and the 10th Mountain Division*, was published by Austin-Macauley Publishers, London. She can be reached at marydonevans@gmail.com.

William Doreski lives in Peterborough, New Hampshire. He has taught at several colleges and universities. His most recent book of poetry is *Dogs Don't Care* (2022). His essays, poetry, fiction, and reviews have appeared in various journals.

Andrew Edwards is a recovering techie living in New York's Hudson Valley. In 2015 and 2018, Rowman & Littlefield published his non-fiction book *Digital is Destroying Everything*. His play "Squashed Like a Bug" was produced in New York's East Village. Andrew has written dozens of articles about digital marketing for ClickZ. He is a WTC 9-11 survivor, having lived one block from the towers. Today he is working on stories about cross-dimensional travelers and the cryptids who populate a Near Vibratory Present.

William Fleeson is a writer and former business journalist. A native and current inhabitant of Washington, DC, his writing has appeared in *National Geographic, Newsweek, The Washington Independent Review of Books*, and some really obscure journals. In longform narrative, he was a finalist for the New Millennium Writing Award 2020. www.willfleeson.com

David Hagerty is the author of the Duncan Cochrane mystery series, about a politician intent on avenging his daughter's murder. He has also published more than a dozen short stories online and in print. He is currently polishing a novel based upon the same character in this story, a did-he-do-it set amid the red rock of the Navajo reservation that spans the first half of the twentieth century. Read more about his work at http://davidhagerty.net.

Ann Howells edited *Illya's Honey* for eighteen years. Her most recent books are: *So Long As We Speak Their Names* (Kelsay Books, 2019) and *Painting the Pinwheel Sky* (Assure Press, 2020). Chapbooks include *Black Crow in Flight*, as Editor's Choice in *Main Street Rag*'s 2007 competition and *Softly Beating Wings*, 2017 William D. Barney Chapbook Competition winner (Blackbead Books). Her work appears in many small press and university publications, including *Plainsongs, I-70 Review*, and *San Pedro River Review*.

Mark Jacobs has published more than 175 stories in magazines, including *The Atlantic, Playboy, The Hudson Review*, and *The Iowa Review*. A complete list of his publications, including books, can be found at markjacobsauthor.com.

Ben von Jagow is a writer and poet from Ottawa, Canada, who lives in Stockholm. His work has appeared in literary journals such as *Amsterdam Quarterly, Marathon Literary Review, The Stockholm Review of Literature, Jersey Devil Press, Gordon Square*

Review, and the *Literary Review of Canada*. For more of Ben's work, visit benvj.com.

David Shawn Klein's first novel, *The Money*, won the 2021 Book of the Year Award from Best Thrillers. His children's book, *Sherlock Mendelson and the Missing Afikomen*, was published in June 2022 by Black Rose Writing. Two chapters from *The Money* were published as short stories in *The Hudson Review*.

Nicholas Litchfield is the author of the suspense novel *Swampjack Virus* and editor of eleven literary anthologies. His stories, essays, and book reviews appear in *BULL*, *Colorado Review*, *Daily Press*, *Shotgun Honey*, and *The Virginian-Pilot* and elsewhere. He has contributed introductions to numerous books, including eighteen Stark House Press reprints of long-forgotten mystery novels. Formerly a book critic for the *Lancashire Post*, syndicated to twenty-five newspapers across the U.K., he now writes for *Publishers Weekly*. Reach him at nicholaslitchfield.com.

Joan Mazza worked as a medical microbiologist and psychotherapist and taught workshops on understanding dreams and nightmares. She is the author of six self-help psychology books, including *Dreaming Your Real Self* (Penguin/Putnam). Her work has appeared in *Crab Orchard Review*, *Poet Lore*, *Slant*, *Prairie Schooner*, and *The Nation*. She lives in rural central Virginia.

Warren Merkel is an Associate Professor of Foreign Language and ESL Education at the Norwegian University of Science and Technology in Trondheim, Norway. His creative non-fiction has been published in *Hippocampus*, *Two Hawks Quarterly*, and *The Raven's Perch*.

Robin Michel's writing has appeared in *The Blue Mountain*

Review, The Comstock Review, Northampton Poetry Review, San Pedro River Review, South 85 Journal, and elsewhere. She lives and teaches high school English in San Francisco and is editor of *How to Begin: Poems, Prompts, Tips, and Writing Exercises from the Fresh Ink Poetry Collective--to improve your poetry practice or start a group of your own* (Raven & Wren Press, 2020).

Award-winning writer/filmmaker **Michael Robinson Morris**, a graduate of NYU, won the Grand Prize at the Eyelands Book Awards, was a shortlist nominee at the Adelaide Literary Awards, and has been published in *Adelaide Literary Magazine, Pure Slush, Down in the Dirt, Sammiches and Psych Meds, Lowestoft Chronicle,* and other journals.

James B. Nicola is the author of six collections of poetry: *Manhattan Plaza, Stage to Page, Wind in the Cave, Out of Nothing: Poems of Art and Artists, Quickening: Poems from Before and Beyond* (2019), and *Fires of Heaven: Poems of Faith and Sense* (2021). His theater career culminated in the nonfiction book *Playing the Audience: The Practical Guide to Live Performance,* which won a Choice award.

Don Noel is retired from four decades of prizewinning print and broadcast journalism in Hartford, CT. He took his MFA in Creative Writing from Fairfield University in 2013 and has since published more than five dozen short stories and narrative non-fiction pieces, including four in *Lowestoft Chronicle* (#33, #37, #43, and #50).

Jennifer Swallow writes technical manuals by day and contemporary fiction by night. She finds inspiration in everything from multivitamins to traffic jams. She and her Finnish Lapphund call Boulder home, for now.

Louise Turan's fiction and nonfiction have appeared in *Superstition Review, Forge, Diverse Voices Quarterly, the dap project,* and *Existere*. Her story "Obsessions" won the 2014 *Southeast Review* Spring Writing Regimen Contest. The daughter of a Turkish-born U.S. Army physician, Louise Turan spent most of her childhood overseas. A former singer/songwriter, prep cook, and nonprofit executive, she now writes full-time in Philadelphia and Maine. Read more of her work at www/louiseturan.com.

Ken Wetherington lives in Durham, North Carolina. His stories have appeared in *Ginosko Literary Journal, The Fable Online, Borrowed Solace: A Journal of Literary Ramblings, The Remington Review, Waymark Literary Magazine,* and others. His first collection, *Santa Abella and Other Stories* was awarded the B.R.A.G. Medallion from the Book Readers Appreciation Group in the literary fiction category. When not writing, he is an avid film buff and has taught film courses for the OLLI program at Duke University. He can be reached at https:// kenwetherington.com or on Twitter: @KenWetherington

Robert Wexelblatt is a professor of humanities at Boston University's College of General Studies. He has published eight collections of short stories; two books of essays; two short novels; two books of poems; stories, essays, and poems in a variety of journals, and a novel awarded the Indie Book Awards first prize for fiction.

Melissent Zumwalt is an artist, advocate, and administrator who lives in Portland, Oregon. Her written work has appeared in the *Whisk(e)y Tit Journal, Full Grown People,* Oregon Humanities' *Beyond the Margins, Pithead Chapel, Sisyphus,* and elsewhere. She learned the art of storytelling from her mother, a woman who has an uncanny ability to recount the most ridiculous and tragic moments of life with beauty and humor.

Copyright Notes

Bon Voyage!

Other titles in the acclaimed anthology series!

Lowestoft Chronicle 2011 Anthology

"This is a fine anthology that I found both provocative and enjoyable.
Highest praise: it made me want to write short stories again."
—LUKE RHINEHART, author of the cult classic *The Dice Man*

"All things considered, it might just be a very good thing if the Lowestoft
Chronicle were to achieve their goal of world domination."
—CHERYL LAGUARDIA, eViews *Library Journal*

Far-flung and Foreign

"Hot off the press [is] this terrific anthology culled from *Lowestoft Chronicle*.
The writing here is fresh, surprising, and alive. Not to be missed is the
bittersweet interview with the author Augustine Funnell. (Please write
more!) The book looks and feels great."
—NICHOLAS ROMBES, author of *The Absolution of Robert Acestes Laing*

"A tip of the hat (sombrero, fez) to *Lowestoft Chronicle* for fueling our urge
to turn off Jersey Shore, toss our cell phones into a lake, and go embrace this
amazing planet of ours. Bon Voyage!"
—FRANZ WISNER, NYT bestselling author of *Honeymoon with My brother*
and *How the World Makes Love*

Somewhere, Sometime...

"The latest collection of prose and poetry from the Lowestoft Chronicle
is a genuine pleasure. Nicholas Litchfield has put together something very
special, something to celebrate, enjoy, savor."
—JAY PARINI, bestselling author of *The Last Station*
and *Why Poetry Matters*

"What a lovely book. Well designed, thoughtfully laid out, and with a
grand assortment of content."
—MATTHEW P. MAYO, Spur Award-winning author of *Stranded*
and *Tucker's Reckoning*

To order, visit www.lowestoftchronicle.com

Other Places

Edited by Nicholas Litchfield

Foreword by Robert Garner Mcbrearty

"In the age of tweets and sound bites, it's heartening to read *Other Places*, a publication celebrating the power and beauty of a story well told."
—Sheldon Russell, author of the Hook Runyon Mystery series

"*Other Places*, a mouth-watering feast of short stories, poems, narrative non-fiction, and in-depth interviews, is the latest anthology from the much-admired *Lowestoft Chronicle*, an eclectic and innovative online journal. Packed into the pages are stories to entice, enthral, and entertain. Litchfield also serves up a tasty blend of pleasing and deftly prepared poems. And if you still aren't sated by this literary banquet, tuck into Litchfield's incisive and enlightening interviews with three critically acclaimed, multitalented writers."
—Pam Norfolk, *Wigan Evening Post*

"I really loved the latest anthology from Lowestoft, *Other Places*. It's a brilliant, savory, sharp, amusing and varied taste of my favorite magazine, *Lowestoft Chronicle*. I'm delighted that a place exists for this kind of travel writing—if that's a term for it. And it's not a good one. This is just great writing about place, ranging from the spirit of place to the human spirit."
—Jay Parini, internationally bestselling author of *The Passages of H.M.*

"*Other Places* is the usual delightful mix of stories, poems, author interviews, and non-fiction gleaned from the pages of the *Lowestoft Chronicle*, the only literary magazine I read on a regular basis. Always entertaining and insightful, *Other Places* is well worth your time, whether you're a veteran traveler or a hermit like me!" —James Reasoner, *Rough Edges*

"Armchair travelers, rejoice! Editor Nicholas Litchfield has released *Lowestoft Chronicle*'s anthology for summer 2015, *Other Places*. Filled with fiction, nonfiction and poetry about travel and destinations, the book brings the far corners of the world to the reader's armchair. The stories and poems vary in tone from dead serious to delightful whimsy, offering something for every taste. Humor, adventure and mystery share the pages with intriguing result." —Mary Beth Magee, Examiner.com

"Sick of fly-by journalism and travel dilettantes? The antidote is *Lowestoft Chronicle*'s most recent anthology, *Other Places*—a collection of essays, stories, and poetry devoted to the in-depth experience of culture. Whether humorous, touching, or revelatory, these expertly curated pieces throw you in contact with the real."
—Scott Dominic Carpenter, author of *Theory of Remainders*

To order, visit www.lowestoftchronicle.com

The Vicarious Traveler

Edited by NICHOLAS LITCHFIELD
Foreword by Michael C. Keith

"*The Vicarious Traveler* beckons you to escape, and I savored every locale. From the richly drawn desolation of the Texas panhandle in Sharon Frame Gay's "Song of the Highway" to the lush, bird-teeming lawns of "The Buzzing" by Philip Barbara; from the American nostalgia of "Mr. O'Brien's Last Soliloquy" by Robert Garner McBrearty to the Turkish apple orchard of Dave Gregory, this collection abounds with amazing language, arresting insight, and sharply drawn landscapes."
—LINDA BOROFF, screenwriter of *Murder in Fashion*

"Charm, a love of travel, often sly humor, and a clear reverence of story make up the backbone of *Lowestoft Chronicle*."
—KEITH ROSSON, acclaimed author of *Fever House* and *Smoke City*

"*The Vicarious Traveler* is a welcome travel-themed anthology that has something for everyone—adventure, crime, and humor all served up in sparkling prose and poetry."
—TIMOTHY J. LOCKHART, acclaimed author of *Smith*

An Adventurous Spirit

Edited by NICHOLAS LITCHFIELD
Foreword by James B. Nicola

"An amusing anthology of writing about travel from the online journal the *Lowestoft Chronicle*. Among the many standout works is Tim Frank's "Three Strikes," whose premise—about a London Underground driver actively seeking his third kill so he'll be eligible for indefinite leave—is inventively and uncomfortably dark, and readers will savor its devilish twist. Meanwhile, poems such as "Woman With the Red Carry-On" are drolly perceptive."
—KIRKUS REVIEWS

"The collected works in An Adventurous Spirit invite the reader to come away on a journey, and what a journey it is! This anthology is a wide-ranging showcase of Lowestoft Chronicle's writers, and the reader cannot help but be changed by this collective force."
—CAT DIXON, *The Good Life Review* Poetry Editor

"Across continents and even states of consciousness, *An Adventurous Spirit* moves deftly, displays a remarkable range, and reminds us why we crave travel literature. Read and enjoy!"
—CHARLES HOLDEFER, author of *The Contractor*

Grand Departures

Edited by NICHOLAS LITCHFIELD

Foreword by Robert Garner McBrearty

"The stories, poems, and essays in Nicholas Litchfield's latest anthology, Grand Departures, are haunting, idiosyncratic, and unexpected, like the true delights of travel."
—IVY GOODMAN, award-winning author of *Heart Failure*

"A must-have collection of travelers' delights and demons."
—NANCY CARONIA, contributor to *Somewhere, Sometime* and co-editor of *Personal Effects*

"An impressive collection of travel works that sweeps the reader across the globe." —DORENE O'BRIEN, award-winning author of *Voices of the Lost and Found*

"It is fun, edgy at times, international in its scope. It surprises. The work is a blend of the serious and the comical, dark shades, light shades, and as I said, ever surprising." —ROBERT GARNER MCBREARTY, acclaimed author of *The Western Lonesome Society*

Invigorating Passages

Edited by NICHOLAS LITCHFIELD

Foreword by Matthew P. Mayo

"A powerful literary passport—this adventurous anthology is all stamped up with exciting travel-themed writing. With humor, darkness, and charm, its lively prose and poetry will drop you into memorable physical and psychological landscapes. Pack your bags!"
—JOSEPH SCAPELLATO, acclaimed author of *Big Lonesome*

"A wonderful collection from a fine literary journal. Fine writing that stirs the imagination, often amuses and always entertains."
—DIETRICH KALTEIS, award-winning author of *Ride the Lightning*

"Invigorating Passages delivers on all counts, hits on all cylinders too. The writing is skilled, the choices rich, the passages manifold, and the invigoration unfailing."
—ROBERT WEXELBLATT, award-winning author of *Zublinka Among Women*

"Invigorating Passages is a rare and dynamic literary collection which grabs readers firmly and sweeps them away to strange and exhilarating places, presenting intriguing situations, colourful characters, and making us yearn to strap on the backpack and go exploring."
—PAM NORFOLK, *Lancashire Post*

www.ingramcontent.com/pod-product-compliance
Lightning Source LLC
Chambersburg PA
CBHW031308280626
47169CB00017B/908